www.skulduggerypleasant.co.uk

Also by Derek Landy:

Skulduggery Pleasant
THE FACELESS ONES

HarperCollins *Children's Books*

First published in hardback in Great Britain by HarperCollins *Children's Books* 2009
First published in paperback in Great Britain by HarperCollins *Children's Books* 2009
HarperCollins *Children's Books* is a division of HarperCollins*Publishers* Ltd
77-85 Fulham Palace Road, Hammersmith, London W6 8JB

The HarperCollins *Children's Books* website is
www.harpercollinschildrensbooks.co.uk

Skulduggery Pleasant rests his weary bones on the web at
www.skulduggerypleasant.co.uk

And has a bebo page at
www.bebo.com/Profile.jsp?MemberId=3605555366

Or join the Skulduggery Pleasant Appreciation Society on Facebook at
www.facebook.com/group.php?gid=4195977322

1

Copyright © Derek Landy 2009

Derek Landy asserts the moral right to be identified
as the author of this work

Illuminated letters © Tom Percival, 2009
Skulduggery Pleasant™ Derek Landy
SP logo™ HarperCollins*Publishers*

ISBN 978-0-00-730216-1

Printed and bound in England by
Clays Ltd, St Ives plc

Conditions of Sale
This book is sold subject to the condition that it shall not, by way of trade
or otherwise, be lent, re-sold, hired out or otherwise circulated without
the publisher's prior written consent in any form of binding or cover other
than that in which it is published and without a similar condition including
this condition being imposed on the subsequent purchaser.

Mixed Sources
Product group from well-managed
forests and other controlled sources
www.fsc.org Cert no. SW-COC-1806
© 1996 Forest Stewardship Council

FSC is a non-profit international organisation established to promote the
responsible management of the world's forests. Products carrying the FSC
label are independently certified to assure consumers that they come
from forests that are managed to meet the social, economic and
ecological needs of present and future generations.

Find out more about HarperCollins and the environment at
www.harpercollins.co.uk/green

This book is dedicated to my agent, Michelle Kass.

I'm not going to be sappy here, OK? I'm not going to talk about how much you've done for me (which is a lot), or the impact you've had on my life (which is immense), and I'm not even going to talk about the advice, encouragement, and counsel you've given me since we met. And I'm not going to mention conversations on tractors either, or iPods at dinner tables, or the amount of Yiddish words you've taught me that I've promptly forgotten.

All of which, surprisingly, leaves me with nothing much to say.

Sorry about that.

1

THE SCENE OF THE CRIME

he dead man was in the living room, face down on the floor beside the coffee table. His name had been Cameron Light, but that was back when his heart had a beat and his lungs had breath. His blood had dried into the carpet in a large stain that spread outwards from where he lay. He'd been stabbed, once, in the small of the back. He was fully clothed, his hands were empty and there was no other sign of disturbance in the room.

Valkyrie moved through the room as she had been taught, scanning the floor and surfaces, but managing to avoid looking at the body. She felt no compulsion to see any more of the victim than she absolutely had to. Her dark eyes drifted to the window. The park across the street was empty, the slides glistening with the rain and the swings creaking in the chill, early morning breeze.

Footsteps in the room and she turned to watch Skulduggery Pleasant take a small bag of powder from his jacket. He was wearing a pinstriped suit that successfully filled out his skeletal frame, and his hat was low over his eye sockets. He dipped a gloved finger into the bag and started to stir, breaking up the smaller lumps.

"Thoughts?" he said.

"He was taken by surprise," answered Valkyrie. "The lack of any defensive marks means he didn't have time to put up a fight. Just like the others."

"So the killer was either completely silent..."

"Or his victims trusted him." There was something odd about the room, something that didn't quite fit. Valkyrie looked around. "Are you sure he lived here? There are no books on magic, no talismans, no charms on the walls, nothing."

Skulduggery shrugged. "Some mages enjoy living on both sides. The magical community is secretive, but there *are* exceptions – those who work and socialise in the so-called 'mortal' world. Mr Light here obviously had a few friends who didn't know he was a sorcerer."

There were framed photographs on a shelf, of Light himself and other people. Friends. Loved ones. From the photos alone it seemed like he'd had a good life, a life filled with companionship. Now it was over of course. There *was* no Cameron Light any more, just an empty shell on the carpet.

Crime scenes, Valkyrie reflected, were rather depressing places.

She looked over at Skulduggery as he sprinkled the powder into the air. It was called rainbow dust because of the way any residual traces of magic in an area would change its colour. This time, however, the powder remained the same colour as it drifted all the way down to the floor.

"Not one trace," he muttered.

Although the couch was obscuring her view of the body, Valkyrie could still see one foot. Cameron Light had been wearing black shoes and grey socks with worn elastic. He had a very white ankle. Valkyrie stepped to the side so the foot was out of view.

A bald man with broad shoulders and piercing blue eyes joined them in the room. "Detective Crux is nearby," Mr Bliss said. "If you are caught at a crime scene..." He didn't finish. He didn't have to.

"We're going," Skulduggery said. He pulled on his coat and wrapped his scarf around the lower half of his skull. "We appreciate you calling us in on this by the way."

"Detective Crux is unsuited to an investigation of this nature," Bliss responded. "Which is why the Sanctuary needs you and Miss Cain to return to our employ."

There was a slight hint of amusement in Skulduggery's voice. "I think Thurid Guild might disagree with you there."

"Nevertheless, I have asked the Grand Mage to meet with you this afternoon, and he has promised me he will."

Valkyrie raised an eyebrow, but said nothing. Bliss was one of the most powerful men alive, but he also happened to be one of the scariest. He still creeped her out.

"Guild said he'd talk to us?" Skulduggery asked. "It's not like him to change his mind about something like that."

"Desperate times," was all Bliss said.

Skulduggery nodded and Valkyrie followed him outside. Despite the grey skies, he slipped a pair of sunglasses into place above his scarf, hiding his eye sockets from passers-by. If there *were* any passers-by. The weather, it seemed, was keeping most sensible people indoors.

"Four victims," Skulduggery said. "All Teleporters. Why?"

Valkyrie buttoned her coat, struggling a little. Her black clothes had saved her life more times than she wanted to count, but every move she made reminded her that she had grown since Ghastly Bespoke made them for her, and she wasn't twelve any more. She'd had to throw away her boots because they'd gotten too small, and buy a regular pair in an ordinary, average shop. She needed Ghastly to change from a statue back to a man and make her a new outfit. Valkyrie allowed herself a moment to feel guilty about being so selfish then got back to business.

"Maybe Cameron Light, along with the other Teleporters, did something to the killer and this is his – or her – revenge."

"That's Theory One. Anything else?"

"Maybe the killer needed something from them."

"Like what?"

"I don't know. Teleporter stuff."

"So why kill them?"

"Maybe it's one of those items where you have to kill the owner to use it, like the Sceptre of the Ancients."

"And so we have Theory Two."

"Or maybe the killer wanted something that one of them had, so he was just working his way through the Teleporters until he found whoever had it."

"Now that's a possibility, and so becomes Theory Two, Variation B."

"I'm glad you're not making this needlessly complicated or anything," Valkyrie muttered.

A black van pulled up beside them. The driver got out, looked up and down the street to make sure no one was watching, and slid open the side door. Two Cleavers stepped out and stood silently, dressed in grey, faces hidden behind visored helmets. They each held a very long scythe. The last occupant of the van emerged and stood between the Cleavers. Wearing slacks and a matching blazer, with a high forehead and a goatee beard pointing down in an effort to give himself a chin, Remus Crux observed Skulduggery and Valkyrie with a disdainful expression.

"Oh," he said, "it's you." He had a curious voice, like a spoiled cat whining for its dinner.

Skulduggery nodded to the Cleavers on either side of him. "I see you're going incognito today."

Immediately, Crux bristled. "I am the Sanctuary's lead detective, Mr Pleasant. I have enemies and, as such, I need bodyguards."

"Do you really need them to stand in the middle of the

street?" Valkyrie asked. "They look a little conspicuous."

Crux sneered. "That's an awfully big word for a thirteen-year-old."

Valkyrie resisted the urge to hit him. "Actually, it's not," she replied. "It's fairly standard. Also, I'm fourteen. Also, your beard's stupid."

"Isn't this fun?" Skulduggery said brightly. "The three of us getting along so well."

Crux glared at Valkyrie, then looked at Skulduggery. "What are you doing here?"

"We were passing, we heard there'd been another murder and we thought we could get a peek at the crime scene. We just arrived actually. Is there any chance...?"

"I'm sorry, Mr Pleasant," Crux said stiffly. "Because of the international nature of these crimes and the attention they're getting, the Grand Mage expects me to conduct myself with the utmost professionalism, and he has given me strict instructions as regards you and Miss Cain. He doesn't want either of you anywhere *near* Sanctuary business."

"But this isn't Sanctuary business," Valkyrie pointed out. "It's just a murder. Cameron Light didn't even *work* for the Sanctuary."

"It is an official Sanctuary investigation, which makes it

official Sanctuary business."

Skulduggery's tone was friendly. "So how's the investigation going? You're probably under a lot of pressure to get results, right?"

"It's under control."

"Oh, I'm sure it is. And I'm sure the international community is offering help and pooling resources – this isn't just an Irish problem after all. But if you need any *unofficial* help, we'll be glad to—"

"*You* may break the rules," Crux interrupted, "but *I* don't. You no longer have any authority here. You gave that away when you accused the Grand Mage of treason, remember?"

"Vaguely..."

"You want my advice, Pleasant?"

"Not especially."

"Find a nice hole in the ground somewhere and lie in it. You're finished as a detective. You're done."

Wearing what he probably thought was a triumphant sneer, Crux and the two Cleavers entered the building.

"I don't like him," Valkyrie decided.

2

KILLER ON THE LOOSE

The Bentley parked in the rear of the closed-down Waxworks Museum and Valkyrie followed Skulduggery inside. A thick layer of dust had collected on the few remaining wax figures who stood in the darkness. Valkyrie waited while Skulduggery searched the wall for the panel that opened the hidden door.

Idly, Valkyrie examined the wax figure of Phil Lynott, the lead singer from Thin Lizzy. It stood nearby, holding a guitar, and was actually a pretty good likeness. Her dad had been a big Thin Lizzy fan back in the 1970s, and whenever 'Whiskey in the

Jar' came on the radio, he'd still sing along, albeit tunelessly.

"The panel is gone," Skulduggery announced. "The moment we left, they must have changed the locks on us. I don't know whether to feel flattered or insulted."

"I get the feeling you're going to decide on flattered."

He shrugged. "It's a fuzzier feeling."

"So how do we get in?"

Someone tapped Valkyrie on the shoulder and she yelped and leaped away.

"I am sorry," the wax figure of Phil Lynott said. "I did not mean to startle you."

She stared at it.

"I am the lock," it continued. "I open the door from this side of the wall. Do you have an appointment?"

"We're here to see the Grand Mage," Skulduggery said. "I am Skulduggery Pleasant and this is my associate, Valkyrie Cain."

Phil Lynott's wax head nodded. "You are expected, but you will need an official Sanctuary representative to accompany you through the door. I have alerted the Administrator. She should be arriving shortly."

"Thank you."

"You are welcome."

Valkyrie stared at it for a few more seconds. "Can you sing?" she asked.

"I open the door," it said. "That is my only purpose."

"But can you sing?"

It considered the question. "I do not know," it decided. "I have never tried."

The wall rumbled behind them, and a door shifted and slid open. A woman in a sombre skirt and white blouse stood there, smiling politely.

"Mr Pleasant," the Administrator said, "Miss Cain, welcome. The Grand Mage is expecting you. Please follow me."

The figure of Phil Lynott didn't say goodbye as the Administrator led them down a spiral staircase, their way lit by burning torches in brackets. They reached the bottom and passed into the Foyer. It felt weird, walking into a place that had once been so familiar, and now seemed so alien. The irrational part of Valkyrie's brain was certain that the Cleaver guards were glaring at them from behind their visors, even though she knew they were far too disciplined and professional to display such petty behaviour.

The Sanctuary, she had only recently realised, was shaped like a massive triangle that had toppled over, and was now lying flat beneath the surface of Dublin City. The Foyer marked the dead centre of the triangle's base, with long corridors stretching out to either side and a central corridor running straight. The side corridors turned in at a 45-degree angle, and eventually met the central corridor at the triangle's point. Smaller corridors bisected these in a seemingly random pattern.

The rooms along the main corridors were mostly used for the day-to-day running of the Sanctuary and the Council of Elders' business. But down some of those narrower corridors lay rooms that were a lot more interesting – the Gaol, holding cells, the Repository, the Armoury and dozens more that Valkyrie had never even seen.

The Administrator chatted amicably with Skulduggery as they walked. She was a nice lady, brought in as a replacement for the Administrator who had died during Nefarian Serpine's raid on the Sanctuary two years before. Valkyrie closed her mind to the memory of the carnage. She had lived through it once – she saw no reason to do so again.

The Administrator showed them into a large room with no furniture. "The Grand Mage will be with you in a moment."

"Thank you," Skulduggery said, nodding politely, and the Administrator left.

"Do you think we'll be waiting long?" Valkyrie asked, keeping her voice low.

"The last time we were in this building, we accused the Grand Mage of being a traitor," Skulduggery said. "Yes, I think we'll be waiting long."

Almost two hours later, the doors opened again and a grey-haired man strode in, his face lined and serious and his eyes cold. He stopped when he saw Valkyrie, who was sitting on the floor.

"You will stand when I enter the room," he said, barely managing to keep the snarl out of his voice.

Valkyrie had *been* getting up before he had spoken, but as she got to her feet, she kept her mouth shut. This meeting was too important to risk ruining because of something stupid.

"Thank you for agreeing to see us," Skulduggery said. "We understand you must be very busy."

"If it were up to me, I wouldn't allow you to waste another moment of my time," Guild said. "But Mr Bliss continues to vouch for you. It is out of respect for my fellow Elder that you are even here."

"And on that positive note," Skulduggery began, but Guild shook his head.

"None of your jokes, Mr Pleasant. Say what you came here

to say and leave the sarcastic comments to one side."

Skulduggery's head tilted slightly. "Very well. Six months ago, while preparing to bring down Baron Vengeous, you fired us over a disagreement. Later that same day, we defeated both Vengeous and the Grotesquery, and the threat they posed was averted. And yet our role in that operation was overlooked."

"You're looking for a reward? I have to say, I'd be disappointed if I didn't already think so little of you. I didn't think money interested someone like you. Or perhaps you'd like a medal?"

"This isn't about a reward."

"Then what *is* it about?"

"Four Teleporters have been murdered in the past month and you still have no idea who is responsible. You *know* we should be in on this."

"I'm afraid I can't discuss an ongoing investigation with civilians. I assure you, Detective Crux has matters well in hand."

"Remus Crux is a second-rate detective."

"On the contrary, there is no doubt in my mind that Crux is the best man for the job. I know him and I trust him."

"And how many more people have to die before you realise your mistake?"

Guild's eyes narrowed. "You can't help yourself, can you? You come here, begging for your old job back, and even now you can't help but be insolent. Apparently, the only lesson you've learned since you were last here is how to shut that girl up."

"Bite me," Valkyrie snapped.

"And even at that you fail," Guild sighed.

Valkyrie's anger swirled inside her and she felt herself go red. At the sight of her flushed face, Guild smiled a smug little smile.

"This is a waste of time," Skulduggery said. "You were never going to even *consider* reinstating us, were you?"

"Of course not. You say you were fired over a *disagreement*. How simple that sounds. How innocent. How innocuous. What a very polite way of saying that you accused me of being a *traitor*."

"Vengeous had a spy in the Sanctuary, Thurid, and we know it was you."

"This is how you're spending your retirement, is it? Making up fantastic stories to fill in the gaps of whatever you call your life? Tell me, Skulduggery – since we're on a first-name basis – have you discovered what your purpose in life actually is? You've already killed the man who murdered your family, so it can't be revenge. You've done that one. So what is it, do you think? Redemption, for all the terrible things you've done? Maybe you're here to heal all those wounds you've inflicted, or bring back all those people you've killed. What is your purpose, Skulduggery?"

Before Skulduggery could respond, Guild gestured to Valkyrie.

"Is it to teach this girl? Is it to train her to be just like you? Is that what gets you up in the morning? But here's a question you maybe haven't asked yourself – do you really *want* her to be like you? Do you want her to live like you – devoid of warmth, and companionship, and love?

"If you suspect me of being this traitor, then you must think that I'm a monster, yes? A cold-hearted monster. And yet I have a wife I adore, and children I worry about, and a responsibility in my work that weighs on my shoulders every moment of every day. So if a cold-hearted monster like me could have all this, and you have *none* of it, then what does that make *you*?"

They left the Sanctuary, passed the wax figure of Phil Lynott in silence, and walked back to the car. Valkyrie didn't like it when Skulduggery went quiet. It usually meant bad things.

A man was standing by their car. He had tight brown hair and a few days' worth of beard growth. Valkyrie frowned, trying to remember if he'd been there a second ago.

"Skulduggery," the man said. "I thought I'd find you here."

Skulduggery nodded to him. "Emmett Peregrine, it's been a while. Allow me to introduce Valkyrie Cain. Valkyrie, Peregrine here is a Teleporter."

Peregrine was also a man who apparently didn't indulge in small talk. "Who's behind it? Who's killing the Teleporters?"

"We don't know."

"Well, why don't you know?" he snapped. "You're supposed to be the big detective, aren't you? Isn't that what they say?"

"I don't work for the Sanctuary," Skulduggery replied. "I don't have official sanction."

"Then who does? Because I'm telling you right now, I am not going to that idiot Crux. I'm not putting my life in the hands of someone like that. Listen, we may not like each other, and I know we have never warmed to each other's company, but I need your help or I'm next."

Skulduggery motioned to the wall and all three of them stepped over to it. From here they could talk without being seen.

"Do you have any idea who could be behind the murders?" he asked.

Peregrine made a visible effort to calm down. "None. I've been trying to think of what anyone could have to gain by killing us all and I've come up with nothing. I don't even have any random paranoid conspiracy theories to fall back on."

"Have you noticed anyone watching you, following you...?"

"No and I've been looking. Skulduggery, I'm exhausted. Every few hours I teleport somewhere else. I haven't slept in *days*."

"We can protect you."

Peregrine's laugh was brittle. "No offence, but you can't. If you can guard me, the killer can get to me. I'm better off on my own, but I can't run forever." He hesitated. "I heard about Cameron."

"Yes."

"He was a good man. The best of us."

"There is a way to draw the killer out."

"Let me guess – you want me to act as bait? You want me to sit still and let him come to me, and then you'll pounce and save the day? Sorry, I'm not in the habit of waiting to be killed."

"It's our best shot."

"It's not going to happen."

"Then you need to help us. Even when they knew their lives were in danger, Cameron Light and the others still let down their guard. They knew the killer, Emmett, and you probably do too."

"What are you saying? That I can't trust my friends?"

"I'm saying you can't trust anyone but Valkyrie and myself."

"And why should I trust you?"

Skulduggery sighed. "Because you literally have no other choice."

"Is there one person that all the Teleporters would know?" Valkyrie asked. "One person who you'd think you'd be safe with?"

Peregrine thought for a moment. "Sanctuary officials," he said, "a handful of sorcerers probably, but nobody that stands out. Teleporters don't tend to be well liked, maybe you've heard. Our social circles really aren't that wide."

"Have you made any new friends?" Skulduggery asked. "Any new acquaintances?"

"No, none. Well, apart from the kid."

Skulduggery's head tilted. "The kid?"

"The other Teleporter."

"I thought you were the *last* Teleporter."

"No, there's a seventeen-year-old English kid, turned up a while back. Renn his name is. Fletcher Renn. No training, no discipline, no clue to what he's doing – a right pain in the neck. Wait, you think he's the killer?"

"I don't know," Skulduggery murmured. "He's either the killer or the killer's next victim. Where is he?"

"He could be anywhere. Cameron and myself went to talk to him a few months ago, to offer to teach him. Cocky little sod laughed in our faces. He's one of those rare sorcerers, natural-born, magic at his fingertips. He has power, but like I said, no training. I doubt he could teleport a few miles at a time."

"He doesn't sound like a killer. But that means he's out there alone, with no idea what's going on."

"I think he's still in Ireland," Peregrine said. "He grunted something about planning to stay here for a while, and how we should leave him alone. He doesn't need anybody apparently. Typical teenager." Peregrine glanced at Valkyrie. "No offence."

"Valkyrie's not a typical anything," Skulduggery said before she could respond. "We'll track him down, but if you see him first, send him to us."

"I doubt he'll listen to me, but OK."

"How will we contact you if we need you?"

"You won't, but I'll check back every few days for an update. This would all be over a lot quicker if you'd take over the investigation. I don't trust Crux and I don't trust Thurid Guild. You're in close with Bliss, aren't you? Maybe you could get a message to him. Just tell him that there are a lot of us out here who would back *him* as the new Grand Mage, if he were interested. All he has to do is say the word."

"You're not talking about a coup, are you?"

"If a revolution is what it takes to get the Sanctuary back on track, Skulduggery, then that's what we'll do."

"A little drastic, one would think. But I'll relay the message."

"Thank you."

"There's nothing else? Nothing you can think of to help us? No matter how small or insignificant?"

"There is nothing, Skulduggery. I don't know why the other Teleporters were killed, and I don't know how. We are exceptionally hard to kill. The instant we think something's wrong, we're gone. Until last month, the only time I can remember a Teleporter being murdered was fifty years ago."

"Oh?" said Skulduggery, suddenly interested. "And who was that?"

"Trope Kessel. I barely knew the man."

"Who murdered him?" Valkyrie asked.

"No one knows. He told a colleague he was going to Glendalough, and he was never seen again. They found his blood by the shore of the Upper Lake, but his body was never recovered."

"Could Kessel's murder have anything to do with what's going on now?"

Peregrine frowned. "I don't see why it should. If someone

wanted the Teleporters dead, why wait fifty years between the first murder and the rest?"

"Still," Skulduggery said, "it might be somewhere to start."

"You're the detectives," Peregrine said with a shrug, "not me."

"You know Tanith, don't you?"

"Tanith Low? Yes. Why?"

"If you're in London and need someone to watch your back, you can trust her. It might be your only chance to catch some sleep."

"I'll think about it. Any other advice for me?"

"Stay alive," Skulduggery said and Peregrine vanished.

3

THAT FIRST KISS

By the time they got to Haggard, the lights turning the streets of the small town a hazy shade of orange, it was almost ten. There was nobody walking in the rain, so Valkyrie didn't have to slump down in her seat. That was the only problem with the Bentley – it wasn't the type of car that went unnoticed.

Still, at least it wasn't yellow.

They approached the pier. Six months earlier, Valkyrie had leaped from it, followed by a pack of the Infected – humans on the verge of becoming vampires. She'd led them to their doom, since salt water, if ingested, was fatal to their kind. Their screams of pain and anguish, mixed with rage and then torn from ruined throats, were as fresh in her memory as if it had all happened yesterday.

The Bentley stopped and Valkyrie got out. It was cold, so she didn't linger. She hurried to the side of her house and let her hands drift through the air. She found the fault lines between the spaces with ease and pushed down sharply. The air rushed around her and she was rising. There was a better way to do it – to use the air to *carry*, rather than merely *propel*, but her lessons with Skulduggery hadn't reached that level yet.

She caught the windowsill and hauled herself up, then opened the window and dropped into her room.

Her reflection looked up from the desk, where it was doing Valkyrie's homework. "Hello," it said.

"Anything to report?" Valkyrie asked as she slipped off her coat and began changing out of her black clothes into her regular wear.

"We had a late dinner," the reflection said. "In school, the French test was postponed because half the class were hiding in the locker area. We got the maths results back – you got a B. Alan and Cathy broke up."

"Tragic."

Footsteps approached the door and the reflection dropped to the ground and crawled under the bed.

"Steph?" Valkyrie's mother called, knocking on the door and stepping in at the same time. She held a basket of laundry under her arm. "That's funny. I could have sworn that I heard voices."

"I was kind of talking to myself," Valkyrie said, smiling with what she hoped was an appropriate level of self-conscious embarrassment.

Her mother put a pile of fresh clothes on the bed. "First sign of madness, you know."

"Dad talks to himself all the time."

"Well, that's only because no one else will listen."

Her mother left the room. Valkyrie stuck her feet into a pair of battered runners and, leaving the reflection under the bed for the moment, clumped down the stairs to the kitchen. She poured cornflakes into a bowl and opened the fridge, sighing when she realised that the milk carton was empty. Her tummy rumbled as she dumped the carton in the recycle bag.

"Mum," she called, "we're out of milk."

"Damn lazy cows," her mother muttered as she walked in. "Have you finished your homework?"

Valkyrie remembered the schoolbooks on the desk and her

shoulders sagged. "No," she said grumpily. "But I'm too hungry to do maths. Do we have anything to eat?"

Her mother looked at her. "You had a huge dinner."

The *reflection* had had a huge dinner. The only things Valkyrie had eaten all day were some bourbon creams.

"I'm still hungry," Valkyrie said quietly.

"I think you're just trying to delay the maths."

"Do we have any leftovers?"

"Ah, now I *know* you're joking. Leftovers, with your father in the house? I have yet to see the day. If you need any help with your homework, just let me know."

Her mother walked out again and Valkyrie went back to staring at her bowl of cornflakes.

Her father walked in, checked that they weren't going to be overheard, and crept over. "Steph, I need your help."

"We have no milk."

"Damn those lazy cows. Anyway, it's our wedding anniversary on Saturday, and yes, I should have done all this weeks ago, but I've got tomorrow and Friday to get your mother something thoughtful and nice. What should I get?"

"Honestly? I think she'd really appreciate some milk."

"The milkman always seems to bring her milk," her dad

said bitterly. "How can I compete with that? He drives a milk truck, for God's sake. *A milk truck.* So no, I need to buy her something else. What?"

"How about, I don't know, jewellery? Like, a necklace or something? Or earrings?"

"A necklace is good," he murmured. "And she *does* have ears. But I got her jewellery last year. And the year before."

"Well, what did you get her the year before that?"

He hesitated. "A... a certain type of clothing... I forget. Anyway, clothes are bad because I always get the wrong size, and she gets either insulted or depressed. I could get her a hat, I suppose. She has a normal-sized head, wouldn't you say? Maybe a nice scarf. Or some gloves."

Valkyrie nodded. "Nothing says 'happy anniversary' more than a good pair of mittens."

Her dad looked at her. "That was a grumpy joke. You're grumpy."

"I'm hungry."

"You've just eaten. How was school, by the way? Anything interesting happen?"

"Alan and Cathy broke up."

"Are either of them anyone I should care about?"

"Not really."

"Well, OK then." He narrowed his eyes. "How about you? Do you have any... *romances* I should know about?"

"Nope. Not a one."

"Well, good. Excellent. There'll be plenty of time for boys when you leave college and become a nun."

She smiled. "I'm glad you have such ambitious dreams for me."

"Well, I *am* the father figure. So, anniversary present?"

"How about a weekend away? Spend your anniversary in Paris or somewhere? You can book it tomorrow, head off on Saturday."

"Oh, *that's* a good idea. That's a *really* good idea. You'd have to stay with Beryl though. Are you all right with that?"

The lie came easily. "Sure."

He kissed her forehead. "You're the best daughter in the world."

"Dad?"

"Yes, sweetie?"

"You know the way I love you so much?"

"I do."

"Will you go out and get some more milk?"

"No."

"But I love you."

"And I love *you*. But not enough to get you milk. Have some toast."

He walked out of the kitchen and Valkyrie sighed in exasperation. She went to put on some toast, but they were out of bread, so she took some hamburger buns and slid them into the toaster. When they popped up, she covered them with freshly microwaved beans and took the plate up to her room, closing the door behind her.

"OK," she said, putting the plate on her desk, "you can go back in the mirror."

The reflection slid out from beneath the bed and stood. "There are a few homework questions still to do," it said.

"I can do them. Are they hard? Never mind. I can do them. Anything else happen today?"

"Gary Price kissed me."

Valkyrie stared. "What?"

"Gary Price kissed me."

"What do you mean? Like, *kissed you* kissed you?"

"Yes."

Her anger made her want to shout, but Valkyrie kept her voice low. "Why did he do that?"

"He likes you."

"But I don't like him!"

"Yes, you do."

"You shouldn't have kissed him! You shouldn't be doing anything *like* that! The only reason you exist is to go to school and hang around here and pretend to be me!"

"I *was* pretending to be you."

"You shouldn't have kissed him!"

"Why?"

"*Because I'm supposed to!*"

The reflection looked at her blankly. "You're upset. Is it because you weren't around for your first kiss?"

"*No,*" Valkyrie shot back.

The reflection sighed and Valkyrie looked at it sharply. "What was that?"

"What was what?"

"You *sighed*, like you were *annoyed*."

"Did I?"

"You *did*. You're not supposed to *get* annoyed. You don't have any feelings. You're not a real person."

"I don't remember sighing. I'm sorry if I did."

Valkyrie opened the wardrobe to show the reflection the mirror.

"I'm ready to resume my life," she said, and the reflection

nodded and stepped through. It stood there in the reflected room, waiting patiently.

Valkyrie glared at it for a moment, and then touched the mirror and the memories came at her, flooding her mind, settling alongside her own memories, getting comfortable in her head.

She had been at the lockers, in school, and she'd been talking to... No, the *reflection* had been talking to... No, it had been *her*, it had been *Valkyrie*. She'd been talking to a few of the girls, and Gary had walked up, said something that everyone laughed at, and the girls had walked off, chatting. Valkyrie remembered standing there, alone with Gary, and the way he smiled, and she remembered smiling back, and when he leaned in to kiss her, she had let him.

But that was it. There was the memory of the thing, of the act, but there was no memory of the feeling. There were no butterflies in her stomach, or nerves, or happiness, and she couldn't remember liking any of it because there was no emotion to accompany it. The reflection was incapable of emotion.

Valkyrie narrowed her eyes. Her first kiss and she hadn't even been there when it happened.

She left the beans on toasted buns on the desk, her hunger

fading, and sorted through the rest of the memories, sifting through to the most recent. She remembered watching herself climb through the window, then she remembered sliding beneath the bed, waiting under there, and then crawling out when she was told.

She remembered telling herself that Gary Price had kissed her, and the argument they'd just had, and then she remembered saying, "You're upset. Is it because you weren't around for your first kiss?", and the sharp "*No*" that followed. And then a moment, like the lights had dimmed, and then she was saying, "I don't remember sighing. I'm sorry if I did."

Valkyrie frowned. Another gap. They were rare, and they never lasted for more than a couple of seconds, but they were definitely there.

It had started when the reflection had been killed in Valkyrie's place, months earlier. Maybe it had been damaged in a way they hadn't anticipated. She didn't want to get rid of it and she didn't want to replace it. It was more convincing than ever these days. If all Valkyrie had to worry about was a faulty memory, she figured that wasn't too high a price to pay.

4

THE SEA HAG

he narrow roads twisted like snakes, and on either side rose the tallest trees Valkyrie had ever seen. Now and then there was a break in the treeline and she could see how far up they were. The mountains were beautiful and the air was crisp. Clear.

They arrived in Glendalough a little before ten. They were here to talk to someone who may have witnessed the murder of the Teleporter fifty years ago. Valkyrie had been complaining about the cold and Skulduggery told her she didn't have to come along, but there was no way she was going to pass up this opportunity. After all, she'd never even *seen* a Sea Hag before.

Skulduggery parked the Bentley and they walked the rest of the way. He was wearing a dark blue suit, with a coat he left open and a hat pulled low over his brow. His sunglasses were in place and his scarf was wrapped around the lower half of his skull, obscuring his skeletal features from the hikers and tourists they passed.

Valkyrie, for her part, was once again dressed in the all too snug black clothes that Ghastly had made for her.

They got to the Upper Lake. It was like someone had reached down and scooped out a huge handful of forest, and then the rain had come and filled it with liquid crystal. The lake was massive, stretching back to the far shore, where the mountains rose again.

They walked along the edge, between the water and the trees, until they came to a moss-covered stump. Skulduggery hunkered down and dipped his gloved hand through the hollow at its base, while Valkyrie looked around, making sure they weren't being watched. But there was no one around. They were safe.

From the tree stump, the skeleton detective withdrew a tiny silver bell, the length of his thumb, then straightened up and rang it.

Valkyrie arched an eyebrow. "Think she heard that?"

"I'm sure she did," he nodded as he removed the sunglasses and scarf.

"It's not exactly *loud* though, is it? *I* barely heard it and I'm standing right next to you. You'd think the bell to summon a Sea Hag would be big. You'd think it would be the kind of bell that *tolls*. That was more of a *tinkle* than a *toll*."

"It *was* rather unimpressive."

Valkyrie looked at the lake. "No sign of her. She's probably embarrassed because her bell is so rubbish. What kind of a Sea Hag lives in a lake anyway?"

"I think we're about to find out," Skulduggery murmured as the waters churned and a wizened old woman rose from the surface. She was dressed in rags, and had long skinny arms and hair that was indistinguishable from the seaweed that coiled through it. Her nose was hooked and her eyes were hollow, and instead of legs she had what appeared to be a fish's tail that stayed beneath the water.

She looked, in Valkyrie's opinion, like a really old, really ugly mermaid.

"Who disturbs me?" the Sea Hag asked in a voice that sounded like someone drowning.

"I do," Skulduggery said. "My name is Skulduggery Pleasant."

"That is *not* your name," the Sea Hag said.

"It's the name I've taken," Skulduggery replied. "As my colleague beside me has taken the name Valkyrie Cain."

The Sea Hag shook her head, almost sadly. "You give power to names," she said. "Too much of your strength lies in your names. Long ago, I surrendered my name to the Deep. Cast your eyes upon me now and answer truthfully – have you ever seen such happiness as this?"

Valkyrie looked at her, all seaweed, wrinkled skin and dour expression, and decided it best to contribute nothing to this conversation.

When it became clear that no one was going to answer, the Sea Hag spoke again.

"Why have you disturbed me?"

"We seek answers," Skulduggery said.

"Nothing you do matters," the Sea Hag told them. "In the end, all things drown and drift away."

"We're looking for answers that are a tad more specific. Yesterday, a sorcerer named Cameron Light was killed."

"On dry land?"

"Yes."

"That does not interest me."

"We think the case may be connected to a murder, fifty years ago, that happened *right here*, by this lake. If the victim told you anything as he died, if you know anything about him or the one who killed him, we need to hear it."

"You want to know another's secrets?"

"We need to."

"The girl has not spoken a word since I appeared," the Sea Hag said, turning her attention to Valkyrie, "yet she spoke, with scarcely a pause, before that. Have you nothing to say now, girl?"

"Hello," said Valkyrie.

"Words travel far beneath the waves. Your words about my bell travelled far. You do not like it?"

"Um," said Valkyrie. "It's fine. It's a fine bell."

"It is as old as I am, and I am far too old for beauty to reach. I was beautiful once. My bell, the sound it makes, is beautiful still."

"It makes a pretty sound," Valkyrie agreed. "Even if it is a bit small."

The Sea Hag swayed on her giant fish tail, or whatever it was, and leaned down until she was an arm's breadth away from Valkyrie. She smelled of rotting fish.

"Would you like to drown?" she inquired.

"No," Valkyrie said. "No, thank you."

The Sea Hag scowled. "What is it you want?"

Skulduggery stepped between them. "The man, fifty years ago?"

The Sea Hag returned to her original position and resumed her swaying. Valkyrie wondered how big the fish part of her actually was. It was more like the body of a snake than a fish. Or a serpent.

"Your questions do not interest me," the Hag said. "Your search for answers is of no importance. If you seek the knowledge of the dead man, you can ask him yourself."

The Hag waved her hand, and the remains of a man broke the surface of the lake beside her. This man of rot and bone, his clothes congealed into what was left of his skin and stained the same mud-brown colour, rose so that his feet were the only part of him still hidden beneath the small, choppy waves. His arms dangled loosely by his sides, and his eyes opened and water trickled from his mouth.

"Help me," he said.

The Sea Hag looked annoyed. "They cannot help you, corpse. They are here to ask you questions."

"Why do you need our help?" Skulduggery asked.

"I want to go home," the corpse told him.

"You *are* home," the Hag interjected.

The remains of the man shook his head. "I want to be

buried. I want to be surrounded by earth. I want to be dry."

"Tough," said the Sea Hag.

"If you help us," Skulduggery told the remains, "we'll see what we can do. Fair enough?"

The corpse nodded. "I will answer your questions."

"Are you Trope Kessel, the Teleporter?"

"I am."

"We are here because four Teleporters have been killed in the past month. There is a possibility, however faint, that those murders are somehow linked to yours. How were you killed?"

"With a knife, in my back."

Valkyrie raised an eyebrow. The other Teleporters had been killed in exactly the same way. Maybe there *was* a link after all.

"Who killed you?" she asked.

"He said his name was Batu."

"*Why* did he kill you?" Skulduggery pressed.

"I was, I suppose, a scholar," the dead man said. "Eons ago, the Faceless Ones were driven from this reality, and even though I had no wish to see them return, the mechanics behind their exile, the magic, the theory... It was a puzzle and I became obsessed trying to solve it. I died because of my curiosity and my blind trust. I believed people were, by nature, good and decent and worthy. Batu, it transpired, was none of those things. He killed me because I knew how to find the thing he desired, and once I had told him, he had to protect his secret."

"What did he desire?"

"The gate," the corpse said. "The gate that will open and allow the Faceless Ones to return."

There was a moment where nothing was said. Valkyrie realised she had taken a breath and had yet to release it. She made herself breathe again.

"Such a gate exists?" Skulduggery asked. He spoke slowly, cautiously, as if the answers were a dog he didn't want to disturb. He actually sounded worried.

"It does, but I merely worked out *how* to find it – I never had the chance to put that theory into practice. The wall between our realities has weakened over time. Their darkness and their evil have bled through. A powerful enough Sensitive should be able to trace the lines of energy in our world to their weakest point. It is here that the gate will open."

"So why haven't the Faceless Ones come through already?" Valkyrie asked.

"Two things are needed," the corpse told them. "The first is an Isthmus Anchor, an object bound by an invisible thread travelling from this reality into the next. This thread is what keeps the gate from closing forever. But the Anchor is useless without someone to force the gate open, and only a Teleporter can do this."

Valkyrie frowned. "But all the Teleporters are being killed."

Skulduggery looked at her. "So what does that suggest?"

"I don't know. It doesn't make sense. Unless... I don't know, unless the killer *doesn't* want the Faceless Ones to return, so he's killing all the Teleporters to make sure they *never* open the gate."

"Which would mean?"

"It'd mean that maybe he's not a bad guy at all – maybe he's just a really twisted good guy."

Skulduggery was quiet and then nodded to the corpse. "Thank you. You have done the world a great service."

"And you will help me now?"

"Indeed we will."

The Sea Hag laughed. "You will never leave this lake, corpse."

Skulduggery looked at her. "What do you want in exchange for him?"

The Hag curled a lip. "I want nothing. He belongs to me. This lake is the place of his death. Its waters have already claimed him."

"There must be something you want, something we can give you in exchange."

"I want nothing you can offer. I am a Maiden of the Water. I am above temptation."

"You're not a Maiden of the Water," Valkyrie said. "You're a Sea Hag."

The Hag's eyes narrowed. "When I was younger, I was a Maiden of the—"

"Don't care," Valkyrie interrupted. "You may have been beautiful once, but now you're an ugly old fish-woman."

"Do not raise my ire, girl."

"I have no intention of even *touching* your ire, but we're not leaving without the dead man. So hand him over or things are going to go bad for you."

"It seems you *do* want to drown after all," the Hag snarled, and lunged, and in an eye blink her bony hands were gripping Valkyrie's shoulders. She reared back and Valkyrie was lifted off the ground, high into the air and tossed, like a rag doll. She hit the water hard and went under. She twisted and through the bubbles, she saw the Sea Hag's long serpent-like body tapering off into a tail. And then the body coiled and the Hag was beside her, eyes wide and triumphant, grabbing her again and holding her under.

Valkyrie tried to punch, but her fist moved way too slowly underwater. The Hag laughed, the lake filling her mouth, running down her throat, and for the first time Valkyrie saw the lines of gills on either side of her neck.

Valkyrie's lungs were already burning. She hadn't had time to take a breath. She went for the Hag's eyes, tried to jab at them, but those bony fingers closed over her wrists. The Hag was too strong for her.

And then something moved towards them, and Valkyrie saw Skulduggery, shooting through the water like a torpedo. He was right up beside them before the Hag even realised he was close.

The Hag tried clawing at him, but Skulduggery took hold of Valkyrie's wrist, the wrist that the Hag had released, and Valkyrie was yanked free.

She clutched Skulduggery tight, feeling the water part in front and boost them from behind. The Hag was after them, her body undulating as she gave chase, her face furious. She drew close and reached out, but Skulduggery veered, taking them into the murky depths of the lake, and then they rolled, changing course, heading back, passing right by the Hag, who screamed her rage in escaping bubbles.

The lake bed was close as they passed over it and getting closer. Valkyrie could have reached out and touched the pebbles and the rocks and the silt and the sand.

And then Skulduggery kicked upwards and they burst free of

the water, rising high through the air and falling now, falling to the treeline. Then there was a screech, and the Sea Hag erupted from the churning waves behind them and grabbed Skulduggery, her thin arms encircling his waist, pulling him back under.

Valkyrie dropped, grabbing for a tree branch. She couldn't hold on. She hit the ground and grunted, barely aware that her hands were cut and bleeding, lacerated by splinters.

She groaned and moved her head slightly to look back at the water. She couldn't see Skulduggery or the Hag, and the ripples were already spreading out and dying, as if the lake was trying to hide what was going on beneath its surface. Valkyrie rolled over, her dark hair hanging in front of her face, and got up slowly, grimacing when she saw her hands.

The corpse was still standing in the water where they had left him, probably waiting for the Hag to come back and reclaim what she saw as hers. Valkyrie started moving. The corpse had helped them and they'd promised to return the favour.

She ran along the edge of the lake, slipping every now and then, coming too close to the water for her liking. Even so, the Hag didn't jump out at her, didn't snatch her as she passed. Skulduggery was probably kicking the hell out of her. At least, she *hoped* he was.

She got back to the corpse, breathing hard, holding her hands away from her body because they were starting to sting.

"Hey," she said. "Come on out of there."

He shook his head. "I can't move on my own. I've spent the last fifty years at the bottom of this lake. I don't think I can even remember *how* to move."

"In that case," Valkyrie said, "I'll come and get you."

"Thank you," said the corpse.

Valkyrie stepped into the lake. The waters here were calm. No sign of the Sea Hag – which meant that Skulduggery was either keeping her busy or she was lying in wait for Valkyrie to step within easy reach. Valkyrie walked in up to her knees, then her thighs, and when she was waist-deep, she thrust herself forward and swam.

So far, so good. So far, no hands grabbing her and pulling her under.

She reached the corpse and looked up at him. "How do I get you down?"

"I'm afraid I don't know," he replied.

She took a breath and plunged her head underwater. He wasn't standing on anything. It was as if the lake itself was keeping him upright.

She surfaced, reached out to try and pull him down, but the

moment she touched his skin the lake stopped holding him and he splashed down.

"Sorry," he said.

"It's OK," Valkyrie responded, hooking her hand under his chin. She fought the urge to shiver as her hand closed over his ice-cold, mottled flesh, and she swam back to land, taking him with her. Her feet touched the bottom. She held him under the arms and started dragging him out.

"Thank you for doing this," he said.

"We owe you."

"It was horrible, in that lake."

"We'll find you a nice dry grave, don't you worry."

His managed to twist his head and look back at her. "If the Faceless Ones return, the world will end. Please promise me you'll stop them."

She gave him a smile. "Stopping the bad guys is what we do."

The moment his feet left the water, his head lolled forward and he stopped talking. He was just a corpse once again.

Valkyrie kept dragging him until they were well clear of the lake and then, very carefully, she laid him down.

She was drenched, she was freezing, her hands were cut and stinging, she had muck and dead flesh under her fingernails and she needed to wash her hair as soon as humanly possible.

Something was happening in the middle of the lake. She looked closer, saw a ripple, moving fast, something breaking the surface. Skulduggery rose up out of the water until he was standing. He skimmed across the lake, hands in his pockets, like he was waiting for a bus.

He slowed as he neared and then stepped on to land.

"Well," he said, "that takes care of *that*." He waved a hand and the water lifted from his clothes, leaving him dry.

"You still haven't taught me how to do that," Valkyrie scowled.

Skulduggery picked his hat off the ground and brushed off the dirt. "You're the one insisting that lessons on fire and air manipulation are more important than lessons on water. You can't really blame me for how much you resemble a drowned rat, now can you?"

"I'm sure I could manage it," she said grumpily. "How's the Hag?"

He shrugged. "Regretting her life choices, I imagine. I see you've rescued the corpse."

"Yes. He's dead."

"Corpses usually are."

"I mean he's not talking any more."

"Then there is nothing left to do except honour his wishes.

We'll carry him to the car, trying very hard not to be seen by any passers-by, and take him with us back to Dublin."

She nodded. Bit her lip.

"What?" Skulduggery asked. "What's wrong?"

"Well, I don't mean to sound disrespectful or anything, but it might be weird, being in a car with the remains of a dead man..."

"You *do* realise that I'm the remains of a dead man too, don't you?"

"I know, yeah, but... you don't smell."

"You make an excellent point. Don't worry, we'll put him in the boot. Now then, do you want to take his arms or his legs?"

"Legs."

Skulduggery picked the corpse up, hands under the armpits. Valkyrie took a hold of the corpse's ankles and lifted, and the right leg fell off.

"You can carry that," said Skulduggery.

5

TRACKING
THE TELEPORTER

The Bentley parked near the tenement building where China Sorrows kept her library. Skulduggery had insisted, as part of her ongoing training, that Valkyrie dry herself, and although she had done her best to lift off the lake water, she hadn't quite managed to get all of it. Patches of her clothes were still slightly damp and her hair stank.

"I'm a mess," she grumbled as she got out of the car. "I hate seeing China when I'm a mess. She's always so immaculate. How does my hair look?"

Skulduggery activated the car alarm. "You have a twig in it."

Valkyrie yanked the twig out and scowled in pain. She glanced at the car boot as they walked. "Where are you going to bury the body?"

"I know a place."

"You *know a place*? Do you bury lots of bodies there?"

"A few."

"That's kind of creepy. What about the guy who killed him? Batu? Have you ever heard of him?"

"Never."

"Maybe the Teleporter murders have nothing to do with Trope Kessel's murder."

"And the fact that they've all been killed the same way?"

"Could be coincidence."

"So you're not worried then? You're not concerned about the threat of the Faceless Ones coming back?"

She pursed her lips.

"Valkyrie?"

She sighed. "I just wish you didn't have to be right all the time."

"It *is* a burden. But the question becomes, why was there a fifty-year gap between the first murder and the other four?

What has our Mr Batu been doing for those intervening years?"

"Maybe he was in prison."

"You're thinking more like a detective every day, do you know that? There are some people who owe me favours – I should be able to get a list of recently released felons."

She sighed. "This would be a lot easier if we were still with the Sanctuary."

As they were walking into the tenement building, they bumped into Savian Eck, a sorcerer Valkyrie had met only twice before. He was carrying a large book under his arm. It was bound in leather and looked old. He held it tightly against his side and nodded distractedly.

"Afternoon, Skulduggery. Valkyrie."

All three of them climbed the stairs.

"What's that you've got there?" Skulduggery asked.

"A book. A book for, for China. She wants it. She said she'd buy it off me."

"Is it expensive?"

Eck's laugh was as sudden as it was desperate. "Oh, yes. Oh... oh, yes. Quite rare, this one is. Priceless, I'd say."

"And what is the going price for a priceless book these days?"

"A lot," Eck said decisively. "I'm not going to be a pushover, you know? You see these other people and the moment they see her, they forget about money, or a fair deal, and all they want to do is make her happy. Well, not me. I'm a businessman, Skulduggery. This is business."

By the time they reached the third floor, Eck's teeth were chattering. Skulduggery knocked on the door marked *library*, and the thin man opened it and beckoned them inside. Eck's legs gave out a little, but he managed to stay upright, and they followed him through the labyrinth of bookcases until they came to the desk.

China Sorrows, hair as black as sin and eyes as blue as sky, saw them coming, rose from her chair and the most beautiful woman in the world smiled.

Savian Eck fell to his knees, held the book out before him, and whimpered, "I adore you."

Skulduggery shook his head and left Valkyrie's side to peruse the bookshelves.

"Savian," China said, "you're so sweet." The thin man took the leatherbound book from Eck's trembling hands and placed it on the desk.

"Now, about payment..."

Eck nodded quickly. "Yes. Payment, yes."

"How are you, by the way? You're looking well. Have you been exercising?"

He smiled weakly. "I like to jog."

"It definitely shows," China said, eyes narrowing appreciatively.

Eck whimpered again.

"I'm sorry," China said, giving a light laugh and appearing flustered. "You have a tendency to distract me. Back to business, if I can keep my mind on the job for more than three seconds. We were talking about payment."

"You can have it," Eck said in a strangled voice.

"I'm sorry?"

Eck rose off his knees. "I give it to you, China. It's my gift. There's no payment necessary."

"Savian, I couldn't *possibly*—"

"*Please*, China. Accept it. Accept it as a token of my, of my..."

Valkyrie was impressed by how large and hopeful China could make her eyes.

"Yes, Savian?"

"...my *love*, China."

China pressed a delicate finger to her lips, like she was struggling to hold back a torrent of passion. "Thank you, Savian."

Eck bowed, swayed slightly and turned. Judging by his smile, he was outrageously, deliriously pleased, and he hurried back the way they'd come. The thin man followed along behind to make sure he didn't stumble into anything.

"*That*," Valkyrie said, "was disgraceful."

China shrugged, resumed her seat and opened the book. "I do what I must to get the things that I want." She used a magnifying glass to examine the pages more closely. "You look like you've been swimming, Valkyrie," she said, without raising her head. "And what happened to your hands? All those little cuts look sore."

"I, uh, I hit a tree."

"Well, I'm sure it had it coming."

Desperate to steer the conversation away from her appearance, Valkyrie asked, "What's the book?"

"It's a spell book, written by the Mad Sorcerer, over a thousand years ago."

"Why was he called the Mad Sorcerer?"

"Because he was mad."

"Oh."

China straightened up and pursed her lips. "This book's a forgery. I'd say it's at least 500 years old, but it's still a forgery."

Valkyrie shrugged. "Good thing you didn't pay for it then, or you'd have to get your money back."

China closed the book and examined the cover. "I'm not sure I'd want to. The Mad Sorcerer, as well as being quite mad, was also a second-rate sorcerer. The majority of the spells in his spell book did absolutely nothing at all. But this forger, whoever he was, corrected every mistake as he went along. I dare say this is the most important academic discovery of the last fifteen years."

"Wow."

"And it's mine," China said with a contented smile.

Skulduggery came back, carefully turning the pages of a book that had seen better days. "We need your help," he said.

China made a face. "Small talk's over *already*? Well *that's* no fun. We didn't even get to trade barbs. Oh, how I miss the old days. Don't you, Valkyrie?"

"They had their moments."

"They did, didn't they? It was all 'Sanctuary business' this, 'saving the world' that, but now what is it? Now you're on the outside, looking in at a few measly murders. Is this really a case that is worthy of the magnificent Skulduggery Pleasant?"

"Murder's murder," Skulduggery said, not looking up from the book.

"Oh, I suppose you're right. So tell me, how is Guild's man handling the Irish end of the investigation?"

"You mean you don't know?" Valkyrie asked, genuinely puzzled. She'd learned by now that every good detective makes full use of information brokers, and China was by far the best in her field.

China smiled. "Do you really think that Remus Crux would associate with *me*, a person of *my* dubious history? Remember, dear Valkyrie, I once consorted with the enemy. I once *was* the enemy. Crux is a limited man of limited imagination. He has his rules, as set down by Thurid Guild, and he follows them. People who follow rules do not come to *me*. Which explains why I speak to both of you with such regularity."

"We rogues have to stick together," Skulduggery said absently.

"That kind of defeats the purpose of *being* a rogue though, doesn't it?"

"Isthmus Anchor," Skulduggery said, reading aloud from the book. "An object belonging to one reality, residing in another. Animate or inanimate. Magical or otherwise. Casts an Isthmus Stream, linking realities through dimensional portals." He closed the book and his head tilted thoughtfully.

"So?" Valkyrie asked.

"So we have to figure out what form this Anchor takes, and find it before the enemy does. Let me muse on it awhile. China, we need to find someone. An English boy – Fletcher Renn."

"I've never heard of him. Is he a mage?"

"Natural-born Teleporter."

She arched an eyebrow. "I see. In that case, I may have heard of him after all. Three reports of a 'ghost boy' in three different nightclubs in County Meath. The nightclub staff either refused him entry or refused to serve him, and he grew petulant, stormed off and vanished into, as they say, thin air. Because his vanishings were only witnessed by the intoxicated, the inebriated, and the stupid, the authorities aren't exactly taking it seriously."

"Where in Meath?" Skulduggery asked.

China motioned to the thin man, who was standing so still that Valkyrie had forgotten all about him. The thin man disappeared for a moment, then came back with a map and spread it over China's desk.

"Here, here and here," China said, her manicured fingernail tapping lightly on the map.

Skulduggery took a pencil from the desk and drew a circle around the three points. "If what Peregrine says is true, and Mr Renn can only teleport a few miles at a time, then that would put him somewhere in this area."

"That's a lot of buildings to search," China noted.

Skulduggery tapped the pencil against his skull. It made a pleasing hollow sound. "A seventeen-year-old boy with the power to appear anywhere. If he needs money, he appears in a bank vault. If he needs clothes, a clothes shop. Food, a supermarket. He's not going to be just anywhere. He's starting to see himself as better than everybody else. He'll only stay in the best places. The best hotels." The pencil made an X on the map, within the circle.

"The Grandeur Hotel," China commented. "Very likely the only hotel in the area with a games console in every room."

"That's where he is," Skulduggery said, wrapping his scarf around his jaw. "That's where we'll find him."

6

FLETCHER RENN

The hotel lobby was wide, with a small row of plants against one wall and a delicate waterfall feature against the other. Two huge marble pillars rose from floor to ceiling, and Skulduggery used one of these pillars to shield himself from the smiling receptionist. He had only his hat and the scarf wrapped around his jaw as a disguise. He casually strolled to the elevators, Valkyrie behind him. She kept her hands, which she had bandaged, in her pockets, and returned the receptionist's smile until they were both out of sight.

The elevator doors slid open and an elderly couple stepped out. The woman looked curiously at Skulduggery as they passed. Valkyrie joined him in the elevator and pressed the button for the top floor, Fletcher Renn's most likely location. As they started to rise, Skulduggery checked his gun.

From the elevator they walked down a long corridor. They turned a corner and almost bumped into the man coming the other way. He had blond hair and was wearing sunglasses. There was a moment of stunned silence.

"Oh," Billy-Ray Sanguine said, "hell."

He stepped back as his hand darted for his pocket, but Skulduggery slammed into him and the straight razor flew from Sanguine's grasp.

Skulduggery's elbow cracked against his jaw and Sanguine stumbled, hand reaching for the wall. Upon contact, the wall started to crumble and Sanguine began passing through, but Skulduggery grabbed him and hauled him out again.

Valkyrie heard a door open and turned to see a good-looking boy who loved his hair staring at them from the doorway of his room.

She lunged at him, pushing him into the room, and slammed the door behind them. The room was luxurious, with a couch and armchairs, a huge TV and a gigantic bed, none of which mattered in the slightest right now.

"You're Fletcher Renn," she said. "You're in great danger."

Fletcher Renn looked at her. "What?"

"There are some people who want to kill you. We're here to help you."

"What are you talking about?"

He had an English accent, not too dissimilar to Tanith Low's. He was better-looking than she'd imagined and China had been right about his hair. It was spiky and carefully, meticulously untamed.

"My name's Valkyrie Cain."

"Valerie?"

"*Valkyrie*. I know all about you and what you can do, and you're going to need to teleport right now."

His eyes flickered to something behind her. She turned to see a million little cracks appear in the plaster on the wall. Sanguine passed through into the room, his lip bleeding and his sunglasses missing.

Fletcher saw the black holes where Sanguine's eyes used to be and swore under his breath.

Valkyrie ripped the bandage off her right hand and clicked her fingers, felt the spark generated by the friction and fed it her magic. The spark ignited into flame and grew, swirling in her palm. She hurled the fireball and Sanguine threw himself to one side, barely avoiding it.

The blade of his straight razor gleamed wickedly. Valkyrie took one step forward and extended her arm, hand open. She sank into the stance, knees bending slightly, as she snapped her palm against the air and the space in front of her rippled. Sanguine dived to one side and the displaced air hit the couch where he had just been standing and sent it crashing against the wall.

Sanguine threw a lamp at Valkyrie and the base struck her cheek. She stumbled and he moved straight towards her. Even as she was ducking the swipe of the razor, she knew it had been a feint, and he grabbed her and hauled her back as the hotel room door was kicked open and Skulduggery stormed in. His hat and scarf were gone, and Fletcher gaped as he caught his first real glimpse of the skeleton detective.

"Let her go," Skulduggery said, the revolver in his hand, ready to fire.

"But then you might shoot me," Sanguine said. "An' getting' shot *hurts*. Drop the gun, gimme the kid with the freaky hair-do or I kill the girl."

"No."

"Then I reckon we got ourselves a good old-fashioned stand-off."

The blade of the straight razor pressed deeper into Valkyrie's throat and she didn't even dare swallow. Her cheek throbbed with pain and she felt a trickle of blood run down her face where the lamp had struck her.

Nobody moved, or said anything, for the next few moments.

"Old-fashioned stand-offs are mighty borin'," Sanguine muttered.

Fletcher was staring at Skulduggery. "You're a skeleton."

"Get behind me," Skulduggery said.

"What's going on? There's a guy with no eyes and a razor versus a skeleton in a suit with a gun. Who's the good guy here?"

Valkyrie clicked her fingers, but had to do it softly or else Sanguine would hear. She tried again, but still couldn't summon a spark.

"Fletcher," Sanguine said, "unlike these two, I came here to make you an offer. My employers are very generous people and they'd like to pay you a lot of money to do one little job for them."

"Don't listen to him," Skulduggery warned.

"Why would I need money?" Fletcher asked. "I teleport wherever I want to go and I take whatever I need. I don't have to pay for anything."

"There are other rewards," Sanguine tried. "We can work something out."

Fletcher shook his head. "I'm sorry, I don't know what any of you want, or why guns and knives are being waved around, and why the girl has just been taken hostage, but everyone seems to be acting like having a *talking skeleton* in the room is perfectly normal. And you, where are your eyes? How can you see? How come the only people with eyes in this room are me and her?"

"Very good questions," Sanguine nodded. "If you come with me right now, I'll give you all the answers you want."

"This man's a killer," said Skulduggery. "You can't trust anything he says."

"I'm not planning on it," Fletcher replied, and he picked up his jacket and put it on. "I don't care why you or your bosses want me to work for you," he said to Sanguine. "The fact is, nobody tells me what to do any more. I'm going to go ahead and say no."

"That's a mistake, boy."

"Come with us," Skulduggery said. "We can protect you."

"Don't need protection," Fletcher shrugged. "Don't need anything from anyone. I've got this really cool power and I intend to use it to do whatever I want."

"You're in danger," Skulduggery insisted. "Most of the other Teleporters in the world are dead."

Fletcher frowned. "So I'm one of the last?" He took a moment to absorb this information, and when he shrugged, it was with the beginnings of a smile. "Then that just makes me even cooler."

He vanished with a soft pop, as the air around him rushed in to fill the sudden vacuum.

"Damn it all to hell," Sanguine muttered.

Valkyrie clicked her fingers and summoned a single flame into her palm, then pressed it into Sanguine's leg. He yelped and his hold loosened. She grabbed his right wrist and held the straight razor away from her as Skulduggery moved in. Sanguine cursed and pushed Valkyrie into Skulduggery's path.

"I really hate you guys," he said, sinking down into the ground.

They waited for a few moments, making sure he wasn't going to jump out at them from somewhere.

"Are you all right?" Skulduggery asked as he crossed to Valkyrie and tilted her chin to one side. "Did he cut you?"

"Not with his razor," Valkyrie said, reclaiming her chin. She knew she'd been lucky. Scars left from that blade never healed. "We lost Fletcher. He's probably miles away by now.

After this, how are we ever going to find him again?"

There was a sound from the bathroom and they both looked at the closed door. Skulduggery walked over and knocked. A few seconds later it opened, and Fletcher Renn looked out at them sheepishly.

"Oh," Valkyrie said. "Well, that was easy."

Valkyrie sat opposite Fletcher, neither of them saying anything. He had adopted an air of complete boredom on the drive over, and this obvious attempt at nonchalance was starting to bug her. She dabbed a wadded clump of napkins to her cut cheek, making sure the bleeding had stopped. Her hands still stung from the dozen splinters that had lacerated them.

The diner they'd come to was a tacky attempt at 1950s America – blue and pink, miniature jukebox on every table and a neon Elvis jerking his hips from left to right on the wall. It was a little past three on a Thursday afternoon and there were more than a few curious glances at the tall, thin man with the scarf, sunglasses and hat, who joined them at the table. Skulduggery waved away the waiter even before he approached.

"The man with the razor was Billy-Ray Sanguine," he said.

"We believe that he is either working *with* or working *for* a man named Batu. Have you ever heard this name?"

Fletcher shook his head lazily.

"In the last month, there have been four murders – all Teleporters like you. Now there are only two of you left."

"But that guy wasn't after me to kill me. He said he wanted my help."

"And I can assure you that if you *did* help him, you'd be dead soon after."

"He'd *try* to kill me," Fletcher said with another one of his shrugs, "but I'd just teleport a hundred miles away."

"If that were true," Skulduggery said, "then why did you only teleport as far as the bathroom?"

Fletcher hesitated. "Sometimes, like, I have to be calm to teleport more than a few metres..." He brushed his hand through his hair, like he was checking that it was still ridiculous. Valkyrie could have saved him the effort. "Anyway, you're wasting my time here, all right? So let's get this over with."

Skulduggery tilted his head. "Excuse me?"

"You want to give me the talk, don't you? Just like those old guys?"

"What old guys?"

"Two old guys came up to me a few months back, and they

were all, 'you're one of us, you have power and blah, you can now join this magical community and something else about wonder and awe,' I don't know, I wasn't really listening. They were trying to recruit me into this little world within a world that you guys have and they were none too happy when I told them I wasn't interested. And I'm *still* not interested."

"Did they tell you their names?"

"One of them was, I think, Light something."

"Cameron Light."

"That was it, yeah. He dead too?"

"Yes, he is."

"That's a shame. I'm sure somebody, somewhere, cares."

"Did they say anything else?"

"They said that without the proper training I could be dangerous. Said I could attract the wrong kind of attention."

"We usually try not to attract *any* kind of attention," Valkyrie said, trying to keep the annoyance out of her voice.

Fletcher looked at her. "Is that what we try?"

"Fletcher," Skulduggery said, and once again Fletcher's eyes flickered to him. "I'm sure that the idea that known killers are after you is one that, at the very least, is causing you some worry."

"Do I look worried?"

"No, but neither do you look intelligent, so I'm giving you the benefit of the doubt."

Fletcher glared at him, and sat back and said nothing.

"If Batu is behind these murders," Skulduggery continued, "then he wants to use your powers to open a gateway that will enable the Faceless Ones to return. Do you know about the Faceless Ones?"

For a moment, Valkyrie thought Fletcher might be too sullen to respond, but eventually he nodded. "The old guys told me about them. But that's just a story, right? None of that stuff's real."

"I used to think the same way," Skulduggery said. "But my mind has been changed."

"So if these Faceless Ones come back, the world ends?"

"It probably won't end *immediately*. They'll come back, inhabit indestructible human bodies, tear down the cities and the towns, burn the countryside, kill billions, enslave billions more, work them until they die, and *then* the world will end. Are you OK, Fletcher? You're suddenly looking very pale."

"I'm fine," Fletcher mumbled.

Skulduggery went quiet for a moment, thinking it all through. "But if Batu needs a Teleporter to make this all happen, why didn't he go for someone with experience? You don't even have any formal training. You may be a natural, as I've heard, but compared to Cameron Light, your powers are practically nothing."

"If Cameron Light's so bloody good," Fletcher said with a sneer on his lips, "how come he's so bloody dead?"

There was nothing Valkyrie wanted more in the world than to reach across that table and smack Fletcher Renn. Skulduggery, for his part, remained as impassive as ever.

"Even though this will go against your instincts," he said, "for your own safety I think you should be put in protective custody."

Fletcher's grin was back. "Ground me, you mean? Not a chance, skeleton-man."

Valkyrie scowled. "He has a name."

"Oh, yeah, Skulduggery, right? Skulduggery. That's an unusual one. Were you born a skeleton or were your folks just disturbingly hopeful?"

"Skulduggery is my taken name," Skulduggery said evenly.

"That's the advantage of being in this little 'world within a world' of ours," Valkyrie added. "You're told a few of the rules, a few tricks you'll need to survive."

Fletcher's shoulders made a slight movement, like they were too lazy to give another shrug so soon after the last one. "I'm doing OK."

"So far. But how do you feel about being someone's puppet? Because if you don't take on a name of your own, any sorcerer who can be bothered might decide he wants a new pet."

"Aha. So *Valkyrie* Cain isn't your real name, that right?"

"That's right. It's the name I took, the name that stops anyone from controlling me."

"Well I changed my name when I ran away from home, so I guess I'm safe too, right?"

He was enjoying this. That made her dislike him even more.

"Are we done?" he asked. "I've got places to go and people to see."

"They're not going to stop," Skulduggery said. "No matter where you go, they will find you. And if they find you, they will force you to help them."

"No one forces me to—"

"I've not finished talking yet," Skulduggery interrupted.

Fletcher sighed and raised an eyebrow expectantly.

"As I was saying, if they find you, they will force you to help them. And if you help them, Fletcher, then you're on their side."

Fletcher frowned. "Meaning what?"

"Meaning you won't have to worry about them. You'll have to worry about *us*."

Fletcher grew even paler than before. Skulduggery, Valkyrie reflected, could be a very scary person when he wanted to.

"You don't want me as an enemy, Fletcher. You want to be my friend. You want to do as I say, and for your own good, you want to enter into protective custody. Am I right?"

For a moment, Valkyrie thought Fletcher was going to defy him again, just for the sake of it, but then his eyes softened and he nodded. "Yeah, OK."

"Excellent news. And I have the perfect place for you to stay."

7

BATU

"Where's Gallow?" Billy-Ray Sanguine asked the empty room.

"Elsewhere," said the voice, distorted over the tinny old speaker that hung in the corner. "They are all elsewhere."

The walls were cold stone. There was one door, no window and a mirror. Sanguine was fairly certain there was a camera behind the mirror, watching him.

"So who are you?" he asked.

"I'm nobody," the voice said.

Sanguine smiled. "You're Batu, ain't you? You're the one they keep talkin' about."

"Am I?"

"Yeah, you are. You're the big boss. So how come you ain't here in person? I been workin' for you for over a year now. Ain't it time we met, face to face?"

"I value my privacy."

Sanguine shrugged. "I get that."

"You failed me, Mr Sanguine. I paid you to do a job and you failed me."

"You said nothin' about the skeleton detective and the girl gettin' involved. That's what we call extenuatin' circumstances. If I'd have known they'd be there, I could have prepared. Or at least charged double."

"You will have a chance to redeem yourself."

"Yippee," Sanguine said, without enthusiasm.

"I'm going to need you to steal something for me, as soon as Gruesome Krav returns. There is a very good chance you will encounter opposition."

"So you'll double my rate?"

"Naturally."

"Yippee," Sanguine said and this time he smiled.

8

THE CIVILISED MAN

The Hibernian Cinema was as quiet and dark as ever, the sound of laughter and applause long since faded. Skulduggery went first, down the aisle between the red-covered seats. Fletcher made comments as they walked, comments that neither Valkyrie nor Skulduggery responded to. As they approached the small stage, the heavy curtains parted and the screen lit up. Valkyrie allowed herself an inner smile when they moved to the projected image, an open doorway, and passed through, and Fletcher was finally impressed enough to shut up.

The darkness was replaced by the bright lights of the corridors that snaked between the laboratories, and the smell of disinfectant replaced the mustiness. Clarabelle, one of Professor Kenspeckle Grouse's new assistants, drifted by them dreamily, humming to herself. She wasn't, in Valkyrie's opinion, all there.

They walked into a circular room with a high ceiling. There were spotlights on the wall, casting a hazy glow on to a statue of a man on his knees, one hand touching the ground. His bald head was ridged with scars and the expression on his face was one of resignation.

Ghastly Bespoke had used the final Elemental power – the earth power – to save himself while he held off the White Cleaver. Valkyrie still had dreams about that moment, looking back in time to see the concrete of the floor latch on to Ghastly's body and spread, even as the White Cleaver swung his scythe. Tanith Low had thrown her into the back of the Bentley and they had escaped, but Ghastly had been left as a statue, and no one knew how long the effect would last.

Professor Kenspeckle Grouse stood behind the statue, hands glowing as he passed them over its surface. His eyes were closed, his white eyebrows furrowed in concentration. For two years now, Kenspeckle had worked to return Ghastly to a flesh and blood state. He had used all kinds of science-magic, brought in every sort of expert, tried everything he could think of and then went even further, with no success.

"Who's the old guy?" Fletcher asked loudly. Kenspeckle scowled and looked up.

Valkyrie smiled and waved. Kenspeckle left the statue and came over.

"Valkyrie. You're injured again."

"A few little cuts; nothing to worry about."

"I'm the medical genius, Valkyrie. I think I'll make up my own mind about that." He examined the cut on her face and then her hands. "Who's the annoying boy?"

"I'm not—" Fletcher began.

"This is Fletcher Renn," Skulduggery interrupted. "I was hoping he could stay here for a few days."

"And why would you imagine that I would agree to that?" Kenspeckle growled.

"He needs to be kept somewhere safe, with someone responsible."

"You want me to stay *here*?" Fletcher asked, clearly appalled.

"Shut up," Kenspeckle said, his eyes never leaving Valkyrie's cut. "Are you trying to bring trouble to my door, Detective?"

"No, I am not, Professor."

"Because the last time you brought trouble to my door, people died."

He looked at Skulduggery and Skulduggery looked at him.

"It's not safe for him out there. He's untrained, doesn't know what he's doing. He's basically an idiot. I need to know he's somewhere safe. I need him kept out of harm's way. You're the only one I can trust to do that."

"And this has to do with the Teleporter murders that everyone is talking about?"

"Yes."

Kenspeckle turned back to Valkyrie. "Come with me to the Infirmary."

He walked out without glancing at Skulduggery and she followed. When they got to the Infirmary, he told Valkyrie to hop up on the bed, then dabbed at her hands and cheek with a sweet-smelling cloth.

"It seems like every second day you come here," he said, "mortally wounded, bones broken, bleeding to death, hanging on by a thread, and you expect me to perform some amazingly astounding miracle cure."

"These are mortal wounds?" she asked sceptically.

"Don't be cheeky."

"Sorry."

He shrugged, then shuffled off to the small table beside the bed. The medical department in Kenspeckle's science-magic facility was small, but perfectly formed, and usually quiet – except for the times when one of Kenspeckle's experiments went impressively wrong, or when old gods awoke in the Morgue. But nothing like that had happened in months.

"Do you know the problem with people your age, Valkyrie?"

"We're too pretty?" she answered hopefully.

"You think you'll live forever. You rush into situations without considering the consequences. You're thirteen..."

"Just gone fourteen."

"...and how do you spend your days?"

He came back to the bedside and started dabbing ointment on the cuts on her hands.

"Well, usually we're on a case, so we're tracking down suspects, or we're doing research, or I'm training, or Skulduggery's teaching me magic, or, you know..."

"And how, pray tell, do other just gone fourteen-year-old girls spend their days?"

Valkyrie hesitated. "Pretty much the same as me?"

"Amazingly, no."

"Ah."

"Once you become an adult, you can endanger yourself as much as you want and I promise I will not admonish you, but I'd hate to see you miss out on all the things normal teenagers do. You're only young once, Valkyrie."

"Yeah, but it goes on for ages."

Kenspeckle shook his head and sighed again. He took a black needle and started to stitch the cut on her face. The needle went through her flesh without drawing blood, and instead of pain, she felt warmth.

"Has there been any progress?" she asked. "With Ghastly?"

"I'm afraid not," he sighed. "I have come to the conclusion that there is nothing I can do. He will emerge from his current state when he emerges, and there is nothing anyone can do to speed up the process."

"I miss him," said Valkyrie. "Skulduggery misses him too, although he'd never say it. I think Ghastly was his only friend."

"But now he has you, yes?"

She laughed. "I suppose so, yes."

"And apart from him, do *you* have friends of your own?"

"What? Of course I do."

"Name three."

"No problem. There's Tanith Low..."

"Who joins you on investigations, trains you in combat and is over eighty years old."

"Well, yeah, but she *looks*, like, twenty-two. And she *acts* like a four-year-old."

"That's one friend. Name two more."

Valkyrie opened her mouth, but no names came out. Kenspeckle finished the stitching.

"I can afford to have no friends," he told her. "I am old, and cranky, and I have long ago decided that people are an annoyance I can do without. But you? You need friends and you need normality."

"I like my life the way it is."

Kenspeckle shrugged. "I don't expect you to take my advice. Another problem with young people like you, Valkyrie, is that you think you know everything. Whereas I am the only one who can make a claim like that without fear of ridicule." He stood back. "There. That should keep your face from falling off. The splinters should be out now too."

She looked at her hands, just in time to see the last splinter rise from her skin into the clear ointment. She didn't even feel it happen.

"Wash your hands in the basin, there's a good girl."

She got up, went to the basin and put her hands under the tap. "Will you help us out?" she asked. "Can Fletcher stay here?"

Kenspeckle sighed. "There is nowhere else to keep him?"

"No."

"And he truly is in danger?"

"Yes."

"Very well. But only because you asked so nicely."

She smiled. "Thanks, Kenspeckle. Really."

"You'll probably be back to see me again before the day is out," he said as he walked to the door. "You'll no doubt want me to sew your head back on or something."

"And you'll be able to do it, right?"

"Naturally. I'm just going to fetch you a bandage, then you can go."

He left and Clarabelle breezed in.

"Hello," she said brightly. "You got into another fight. Did it hurt much?"

Valkyrie smiled faintly. "Not really."

"The Professor is always going on about how you'd be dead if it wasn't for him. Do you think that's true? I think it's probably true. The Professor's always right about things like that. He said one of these days he's not going to be able to save you. He's probably right about that too. Do *you* think you'll die one of these days?"

Valkyrie frowned. "I hope not."

Clarabelle laughed like she'd just heard the funniest thing ever. "Of course you *hope* you won't die, Valkyrie! Who would *hope* to die? That's just *silly*! But you probably *will* die, that's what I'm saying. Don't you think so?"

Valkyrie dried her hands. "I'm not going to die any time soon, Clarabelle."

"I like your coat by the way."

"Thanks."

"It's a little small for you though."

"Yeah."

"Can I have it when you're dead?"

Valkyrie paused, trying to think of an appropriate response, but Clarabelle had already flitted out of the room. A few moments later, Kenspeckle returned.

"Clarabelle's odd," Valkyrie said.

"She is at that," Kenspeckle agreed. He fixed a small bandage over the stitches. "Give it an hour or so. The stitches will dissolve. It's not going to scar."

They walked out of the Infirmary.

"I heard Cameron Light was killed yesterday," he said. "I've never liked Teleporters, but even so, it's a terrible world we live in."

"Why does everyone dislike Teleporters?" Valkyrie had to ask. "Practically no one I've met has a good word to say about them."

"Teleporters are a sneaky lot. Sagacious Tome was a Teleporter, in case you've forgotten, and he turned out to be a traitor. I just don't trust anyone who would choose it as their magical discipline. How are the rest of us supposed to feel safe if there are people out there who can appear anywhere at any moment? When I was a younger man, I had a stifling fear that someone would appear beside me as I was using the toilet – and I had an anxious bladder at the *best* of times."

"Oh my God," Valkyrie breathed. "I didn't need to know that."

Skulduggery was waiting for them at the next corner, and immediately Kenspeckle's face soured. "Are you going to be dragging her into more danger, Detective?"

"She can handle it," Skulduggery said. "Fletcher, on the other hand, cannot. Can he stay here?"

"As long as he doesn't annoy me too much," Kenspeckle replied grumpily.

"I can't promise that."

"Then do me a favour, Detective, and solve this particular case as fast as you possibly can."

"Maybe you could help with that. If you could examine the body of the last victim..."

Kenspeckle shook his head. "Unlikely. The Sanctuary has its own supposed *experts*, as you well know, and they wouldn't appreciate my... input. From what I have heard, however, the killer has left no traces and no clues. He is, distastefulness aside, quite admirable."

"I'll be sure to pass on the compliment when I'm hitting his face," Skulduggery assured him.

Kenspeckle shook his head. "Do you really think Valkyrie needs a role model that meets every obstacle with his fists? She is at a very impressionable age."

"I am not," she said defensively.

"Valkyrie is doing important work," Skulduggery said. "She needs to be able to handle herself."

"That's right," Valkyrie agreed. "And you're not my role model."

"The war is over," Kenspeckle countered. "Those days of death and mayhem are gone."

"Not for some of us."

Kenspeckle looked at Skulduggery, and there was something in his eyes Valkyrie had never seen before.

"Perhaps," the old man conceded. "For those of you who need it."

Skulduggery was quiet for a moment. "Professor," he said at last, "I hope you're not implying that I *like* the death and the mayhem."

"Without it, where would you be? Or, more to the point, *who* would you be? We are defined by the things that we do, Detective. And you tend to hurt people."

Skulduggery's chin tilted slightly. "The world is a dangerous place. In order for people like you to live in relative safety, there need to be people like me."

"Killers, you mean."

The simple viciousness of the words stunned Valkyrie, but Skulduggery's body language showed no signs of anger, or even annoyance. "You are an interesting man, Professor."

"Why is that, Skulduggery? Because I'm not scared of you? Even during the war, with the reputation you and your friends enjoyed, I spoke out against your methods. I wasn't afraid of you then and I'm certainly not afraid of you now."

There was a pause, then Skulduggery said, "We should probably go."

"That's probably a good idea," Kenspeckle agreed. "Valkyrie, it was lovely seeing you again."

"Right," she murmured, unsure.

She walked with Skulduggery to the double doors. Just as they reached them, Kenspeckle spoke again.

"Detective, have you ever considered the fact that violence is the recourse of the uncivilised man?"

Skulduggery looked back. "I'm sophisticated, charming, suave and debonair, Professor. But I have never claimed to be civilised."

They walked out and the doors swung shut behind them.

9

THE ENEMY

anith Low didn't much like protection detail. It was often dull and deathly boring, and being in the same confined space as the person you're protecting meant a lot of cross words and general crankiness. She just wasn't cut out to be a bodyguard.

But Skulduggery had called her, told her she'd be doing him a favour if she helped out Emmett Peregrine, and she'd said OK. Peregrine wasn't bad anyway, and all he really needed was for her to look out for him while he grabbed a few hours' sleep. By the looks of him, he needed it.

Tanith didn't agree with Peregrine's choice of safehouse though. They were in an apartment he owned in London, and he insisted nobody knew about it. She'd tried to persuade him to go somewhere else, anywhere else, but he had that Teleporter arrogance she'd seen before. For hundreds of years, he had been a man who could not be captured, or cornered, or hunted, and that arrogance was still with him, even now.

Together, they'd drawn enough protective symbols on the walls of the bedroom so that if anyone entered while he was sleeping, the entire building would know about it. They weren't taking any chances, not when the enemy had someone like Billy-Ray Sanguine in their employ.

Tanith spent the first few hours on a chair in the hall, looking at the door. She took a bathroom break, then went to the kitchen to look for something to eat. She was trying to figure out how the microwave worked when her phone rang.

She answered and a man with a deep African accent said, "It does my heart good to hear your voice."

She smiled. "Hi, Frightening."

Frightening Jones was an old friend. They'd dated briefly back in the 1970s, before he took up a position within the English Sanctuary. Her natural distrust of authority meant that the relationship couldn't continue, but they'd remained close, and any time he heard something that involved her, he would call and let her know.

"What have I done wrong now?" she asked.

She could hear the TV on in Peregrine's bedroom.

"You've broken no laws lately," Frightening replied, "or at least if you have, you have broken them very, very quietly. No, this is just a routine report that had your name on it. One of my agents has seen you with Emmett Peregrine."

Tanith's smile vanished. "What?"

"You are at his apartment, yes?"

"Frightening, who else knows about this?"

"The agent who saw you, and Elder Strom, whom I report to, and myself. Is anything wrong? You can trust my agent, and Elder Strom is a good man. No one is going to hear about this that doesn't have to, I assure you. And of course, Elder Strom has informed the Irish Sanctuary."

Tanith unsheathed her sword. "Why?"

"The Irish are spearheading the Teleporter investigation. It was common courtesy that... Tanith, what is the matter?"

"There's a spy in the Irish Sanctuary," she said, whispering. "If *they* know, the Diablerie knows."

She hung up. That wasn't the TV she had heard – it had been Peregrine, talking to someone. And he hadn't been in his bedroom either. He had been at the apartment door.

Tanith lunged out of the kitchen in time to see the shadow of Peregrine's killer in the corridor outside the apartment.

In an instant, she was at Peregrine's side. He was already dead. His warm blood was soaking through the back of his shirt.

She ran to the open door, managing to catch a glimpse of the killer on the stairs, heading up. She gave chase, fearing that she was already too late. She reached the stairs and jumped, running up the wall, closing the gap between them. A door slammed shut overhead.

Tanith grabbed the stairwell railing and vaulted over. Her boot met the door and it sprang open, and she ran out on to the roof of the building. A fist hit her like a wrecking ball. She went down and rolled, dimly aware that the sword was no longer in her grip. She got to her feet and fought the dizziness, backing away from the huge man with silver hair tied in a ponytail.

His fist came at her again and she ducked, responding with a punch of her own that got him in the ribs, but it was like hitting a brick wall. It was like hitting Mr Bliss. Tanith dodged back. He wasn't the one who had killed Peregrine. He was much too big. Which meant that there was someone else on the roof.

She tried to turn, but it was no use. A black boot came at her and she went spinning. She fell to one knee and a dark-haired woman grabbed her and hauled her backwards. Tanith saw a pretty face contorted with savagery and ruby-red lips that twisted in a sneer. She struck out with her elbow and the woman grunted, but when she tried to follow it up with another strike, she was flipped over the woman's hip.

This woman wasn't the killer either. Tanith cursed. She was being distracted, while her quarry got away. She somersaulted backwards and got up. The big man wore trousers with old-fashioned braces, and his shirtsleeves were rolled up on his muscular forearms. The red-lipped woman's outfit was made up of an assortment of black straps that wrapped tightly around her body. Most of those straps held knives of varying sizes.

Tanith waited for them to say something, to boast or threaten or tell her how they were going to take over the world, but neither of them spoke.

Her sword was behind them. There was no way she could get to it, and she didn't fancy the idea of taking them on unarmed, not without knowing who they were or what they could do. They moved with a violent confidence she found unsettling.

She backed up to the edge of the building and they followed her. There was a man standing by the door she had come through. He must have been there all along and she hadn't noticed him. He was slender, with dark hair, and he watched her with indifference.

A thought came into her head and she didn't like it. She was outclassed. Whoever these people were, she didn't stand a chance against them.

"This isn't over," she said and blew them a kiss.

The woman moved like nothing Tanith had ever seen. There was a flash of steel and suddenly a knife was sticking through the hand she had used to blow the kiss. She roared in pain and stepped back into nothing, then she was falling down the side of the building.

Her hair whipping in her face, she reached out and felt brickwork. The friction peeled the skin from her fingertips. Her good hand snagged a window ledge and her body swung in and smashed against the wall and she was falling again. She tried getting her feet against the bricks, to use her skills and shift her centre of gravity, but her own momentum was working against her and still she fell.

She stuck both arms out and grabbed a window ledge. Her knees slammed against the wall and she screamed as the knife shifted in her hand. But she didn't let go.

Muscles straining, sweat coating her entire body, Tanith hauled herself up and through the window, into an empty apartment. She had failed her assignment, lost her sword and her hand was bleeding profusely, but she didn't have time to feel sorry for herself. They'd be after her.

Her face burning with anger, Tanith ran.

10

FINBAR'S LITTLE TRIP

It was raining again by the time they got to Temple Bar, and dark. People hurried through the narrow pedestrian streets, collars turned up. Valkyrie nearly had her eye taken out by a spoke from a wayward umbrella, and she glared, but the woman was already moving on.

"Skul-man!" Finbar Wrong said when he opened the door to greet them. His face, adorned as it was by piercings, split into a slow and happy grin. He was wearing a Stiff Little Fingers T-shirt that showed off the tattoos on his skinny arms. "Valkyrie!" he exclaimed with equal delight when he saw her. "C'mon in, the pair of you!"

They stepped into his tattoo parlour, the walls of which were layered with designs and pictures and photographs. The *whir* of the needle drifted down from upstairs. Music was playing somewhere.

"How's it going?" Finbar asked, nodding his head as if they had already answered.

"We're on a case," Skulduggery said. "We're hoping you might be able to help us."

"That's awesome, man, yeah. Hey, Skul-man, did you hear? Sharon's pregnant! I'm gonna be a dad!"

"That's... great news, Finbar."

"It is, isn't it? I know, I mean, I know it's a lot of responsibility and all, and I know I haven't been, like, the most responsible of cats. I know what you're thinking – you're thinking, *now that's an understatement*, isn't that right?"

Finbar laughed and Skulduggery shook his head.

"Not really."

"You know me too well, man! You remember how I used to be? Remember all the crazy stuff I used to get up to?"

"No."

"Man, those were the days, huh? But hey, I've calmed down. Sharon's been, like, this beacon of light, yeah? I have mended my ways, I can tell you that much. I'm ready for a kid. I'm ready for that responsibility."

"That's wonderful to hear," Skulduggery said.

"Hey, you know, I was thinking... Skul-man, would you do us the honour of being godfather to our child?"

"No," Skulduggery said immediately.

Finbar shrugged. "That's cool, that's cool. Sharon might be disappointed though."

"Sharon doesn't know me."

"And hopefully that'll ease the blow, but... I'm sorry, man, you wanted my help with something?"

Skulduggery explained that they needed him to go into a trance and find the location of the gateway and Finbar nodded, eyes half closed. Once or twice, Valkyrie was sure he was already *in* the trance, but when Skulduggery had finished explaining, he nodded again.

"No problemo, el Skulduggo," he said. "I'm gonna need absolute peace and quiet though. Being a Sensitive isn't like any other kind of magic. I need total and utter seclusion, you know? Most Sensitives are hermits, like, living in caves and monasteries, somewhere in the mountains..." He looked around, eyes settling on the small kitchen at the back of the shop. "I'll do it in there."

They followed him in. He flicked on the light and Valkyrie closed the door while Skulduggery drew the tattered curtains across the window. Finbar took a map from a cupboard and laid it on the table.

He sat and closed his eyes, and began to mutter in a language Valkyrie didn't understand. Then he started to hum. At first, she thought he was humming an ancient chant, something to elevate his consciousness to the higher plane. Then she recognised the first few bars of 'Eat The Rich', by Aerosmith, and she stopped trying to guess what he was doing.

"OK," he said in a dreamy voice, "I'm floating, man. I'm up here. Floating up through the ceiling... into the open... floating through the sky... Dublin looks so pretty, even when it's raining..."

"Finbar," Skulduggery said. "Can you hear me?"

Finbar murmured happily.

"Can you hear me, Finbar?" Skulduggery said louder.

"Skul-man," Finbar smiled, "hey, how are you? Coming in loud and clear..."

"Do you remember what you're looking for?"

Finbar nodded, his eyes still shut. "Oh yeah. The gate. For the Faceless Ones. Creepy critters, man."

"Yes, they are."

Valkyrie watched Finbar frown slightly.

"I think," he said slowly, "I think I can *feel* them, man..."

Skulduggery tilted his head. "Stay away, Finbar. Stay away from them."

"That's a... that's a good idea..."

"You're looking for the lines of magic, remember?"

"Yep... I remember..." His hands drifted across the map. "I'm flying now. Ooh, this is nice. I can feel the clouds between my fingers. I can see the lines all around me. They're glowing, like gold, like glitter. So pretty..."

His smile faded a little. "Wait. These... these lines aren't glowing. They're dull. Getting duller."

"Where are you?"

"Hold on, man, just going a bit closer..."

"Keep your distance, Finbar."

"I'll be OK..."

Valkyrie glanced at Skulduggery. They waited a few moments.

"It's rotten," Finbar said. Something in his voice had changed. He was no longer dreamy. "The lines, they've turned black. They're rotting away."

"Where are you?"

"I can hear them. I can... I can hear their whispers..."

"Who can you hear?"

"The Faceless Ones."

"Don't. Can you hear me? Stay away from them."

"Oh God."

"Finbar, stay away—"

"Oh God, they know where we are. *They know where we are.* They've found us and they're waiting to be let in. *They're at the gate and they're waiting to be let in!*"

"Finbar," Skulduggery said urgently. "Where are you? Tell us where you are right *now*."

Finbar extended his arm towards the sink, and Valkyrie jerked her head back to avoid the knife that flew into his hand. He stabbed downwards into the map, and then his arms dropped by his sides and his head dipped.

"Finbar?" Skulduggery said softly. "Finbar, can you hear me?"

A low chuckle escaped his lips. He flew into the air, knocking both Valkyrie and Skulduggery off their feet. The table collapsed and Finbar turned to face them. His limbs were twitching and his eyes were still closed.

He opened his mouth and a voice that was not his, a voice that was a hundred thousand *other* voices, said, "*Cannot stop us.*"

Skulduggery scrambled up, and something hit him and sent him crashing back against the wall.

"*World will fall*," the voices said. "*World will crumble. We are coming.*"

Finbar fell to the floor, crumpling like a puppet with its strings cut. Valkyrie stood. Behind her, Skulduggery groaned and got up.

Finbar raised his head and looked around drowsily.

"Whoa," he said.

Valkyrie helped him into the only upright chair in the kitchen.

"I hate being possessed," he said. "Happens all the time when you're a Sensitive. Usually, it's pretty easy to spot, because you've got red eyes or a deep voice or you're hovering in mid-air or something, but sometimes it isn't. I was possessed by the spirit of Napoleon for a week before Sharon noticed anything strange about me. I think it was the accent."

"Can you tell us anything about whatever that was?" Skulduggery asked.

"I'm sorry," Finbar said and Valkyrie noticed how pale he was. "That was freaky, man. That was some powerful mojo. Like, insanely powerful, y'know? My mind just got touched by a god's mucky fingers and it didn't feel too good."

Skulduggery lifted the map, examining the spot where the knife had plunged. "This is it, is it?"

Finbar shrugged. "If that's where I pointed to, that's where the walls of reality are at their weakest. That's where the gateway is."

"Batu probably already knows the location," Valkyrie said. "He's had fifty years to find it."

"But without the Isthmus Anchor and a Teleporter, that information has been useless to him." Skulduggery folded the map. "Do you mind if I take this, Finbar?"

"Not at all, Skul-man." Finbar stood on shaky legs. "Anything else I can help you with?"

"You've done more than enough."

"That's cool." Finbar looked at Valkyrie. "Want a tattoo?"

"Yes," Valkyrie said.

"No," Skulduggery said. "We're leaving now."

Valkyrie scowled as she followed him out into the rain. "I could have just got a small one."

"Your parents would kill me."

"Being around you puts my life in constant danger. I've fought monsters and vampires and I've almost died twice, and you think they'd choose to kill you over a *tattoo*?"

"Parents are funny that way."

Skulduggery's phone rang and the moment he realised who was calling him, his voice went frosty. He made no attempt to hide his distaste. He hung up as they got to the Bentley.

"We have a meeting," he said.

"Who with?"

"Solomon Wreath. He has some information he'd like to share."

"Who's Solomon Wreath?"

"The *who* is not important. It's the *what* you should be worried about."

"All right then – *what* is Solomon Wreath?"

"He's a Necromancer," Skulduggery said and got in the car.

11

WREATH

Skulduggery and Valkyrie drove in silence. Gradually, the streets became dirtier and the buildings smaller. The rain added to the grey effect of their surroundings as they swung into a large, run-down residential estate, the car drawing curious gazes from the few locals who were out tonight.

The house they stopped outside was abandoned. The walls were defaced with graffiti, none of it any good. Skulduggery wrapped his scarf around his jaw and pulled his hat down low. They left the car and walked through the open door.

The streetlight shone through the cracked and dirty

windows, enough to see by. The house had been stripped bare. There were remnants, here and there, of wallpaper. The floorboards were old, and they were damp. Valkyrie let Skulduggery go on ahead and wandered into the living room. There was no graffiti in here, as if the brave souls who had scrawled their slogans so inelegantly on the outside were not quite bold enough to venture indoors.

She turned to go and a figure stepped through the door, blocking her exit. Valkyrie looked at him. He didn't move. It had got even gloomier in the room, like the man had brought a cloud of shadows with him.

"I'm with Skulduggery Pleasant," she said, but got no response. Valkyrie took a step closer, as much to see his face as to indicate her desire to leave. His hair was dark, but his eyes were so bright they almost gleamed. He was dressed in black, a finely tailored suit that she couldn't appreciate in this light. He held a slender cane in his hand.

"Are you Solomon Wreath?" she asked, refusing to be intimidated by his silence.

"I am," he answered and gave a little bow of his head. "I've heard about you. You helped take down Nefarian Serpine and Baron Vengeous. You stopped the Grotesquery. Such talent. Such potential. Has he corrupted you yet?"

"I'm sorry?"

"He corrupts everyone he meets. Have you noticed that? Have you noticed how much you're changing, simply by being around him?"

"I'm not sure I know what you mean."

"You will," he promised.

He stepped into the room and she saw the shadows moving with him. She knew very little about Necromancers, but what she *did* know was that they preferred to place most of their power in objects or weapons. Lord Vile had placed his power in his armour. By the way the shadows were coiling, Solomon Wreath seemed to have placed *his* in his cane.

"This house has had a rather bland life," he said. "It was built and people lived here. They ate here and slept here. They grew old. Someone, an elderly man, passed away peacefully in the bedroom, a little over ten years ago. A very, *very* ordinary house.

"Until two years ago. You may remember this from the news actually. Four people were murdered – three were shot; one was stabbed. Two people died *here*, in this room. The third was killed in the kitchen. The fourth in the hall, within arm's reach of the front door."

Valkyrie looked at him, noticing the way his eyes glittered as he described the scene.

"Who killed them?" she asked, determined to keep her voice steady.

He laughed. "Ah, you think all this is a preamble to me announcing that *I'm* the killer? I'm afraid not. I'm fairly certain that the police caught him, whoever he was, and put him in jail. But violent death lingers in a place." He closed his eyes and breathed in slowly. "A murder can imprint itself on the walls. You can taste it, if you try. You can drink it in."

Valkyrie stepped away, her mind conjuring images of all that horrible dark energy swirling around him. She knew she shouldn't have been surprised. Necromancy was death magic, shadow magic – it was only natural that its practitioners would be drawn to places that reek of death.

And then, as if he was remembering he had company, Wreath stopped, opened his eyes and looked at her again.

"My apologies. For our first meeting, I should have chosen a more civilised spot."

"Don't feel too bad," Skulduggery said as he walked slowly in. "Valkyrie is my partner. You can treat her like you'd treat me."

"That's a shame," Wreath said. "I actually liked her."

"What do you want, Solomon? Our time is precious."

"All time is precious, but you'll want to hear what I have to say none the less. Or maybe you would rather I go to Remus Crux with this? I hear he's running all over town, desperate for something with which to impress the Grand Mage." Wreath shook his head. "His actions are deplorable. As one detective to another, Crux is a man who values a progress report over actual progress."

"If you're hoping we can bond because we share a distaste for the man, you will be disappointed."

"That's not all we share actually. We have a common enemy."

"Is that so?"

"Your investigation into the Teleporter murders, however unofficial it may be, coincides with an investigation I have been running for the past few years, into the Diablerie."

Skulduggery didn't say anything for a moment, then turned to Valkyrie. "The Diablerie was a group of the sickest fanatics Mevolent had at his disposal. A group that China founded and led."

"China?" Valkyrie echoed.

"She had a misspent youth," Wreath smiled.

Skulduggery ignored him. "When China left and became, to use her own word, *neutral*, Baron Vengeous took over, but it's been 120 years since they've been considered a real threat.

It's been over 80 years since they were actually *heard of*."

"All that's about to change," Wreath said. "Jaron Gallow, Murder Rose and Gruesome Krav reunited two years ago. I have found evidence that they have since hired Billy-Ray Sanguine, to add to their ranks. The Diablerie are back, Detective, and they are killing Teleporters."

"And Batu? What do you know of him?"

"I suspect Batu doesn't even *exist*," Wreath said. "It's a name taken to divert attention. The real leader is Jaron Gallow. He just *pretends* to answer to a mysterious master. He's been at it for years – it keeps everyone off balance."

"That still doesn't make any sense," Valkyrie said. "Batu, or whoever was using that name, killed Trope Kessel *after* he found out how to bring back the Faceless Ones. But since they need a Teleporter to open the gate, why kill them all?"

"They need a Teleporter?" Wreath asked. "How many?"

"Just one."

"And how many Teleporters are left?"

"Two," Skulduggery said. "Emmett Peregrine and one more. We're not going to be sharing either his name or location with you, so don't bother asking."

Wreath frowned. "You obviously haven't heard. Peregrine is dead. He was murdered an hour ago."

Valkyrie's mouth went dry. "What about Tanith?"

"Who?"

"The girl who was with him," Skulduggery said quickly.

"Ah, the English girl. I don't know all the details, but from what I have heard, she was attacked by Krav and Murder Rose, and escaped with her life. Which is an admirable feat in itself."

Valkyrie closed her eyes. *Thank God.*

"Now," Wreath continued, "if there *is* only one Teleporter left, and since all the Teleporters I know about are dead, then he must be new. Which makes sense."

"How does it make sense?" Valkyrie asked.

"None of the seasoned Teleporters would co-operate with the Diablerie," Skulduggery said. "They'd be too experienced, too powerful. The chances of escape would be much too high."

"But why kill them?"

"Because if the gate opens, they'd be able to close it. The Diablerie have taken out the biggest obstacles to their success before we even knew what was happening."

"Those in the Necromancer temples have taken an oath not to involve ourselves in the trivialities of your affairs," Wreath said. "But there are those who share my view, that the Diablerie's plans affect everyone, Necromancers included. You will have my help should you need it, Detective. Me and three others."

"I don't trust you, Wreath."

"Of course not, but like I said, we have a common enemy. I think we should put our differences aside, don't you? For old times' sake, if nothing else?"

Skulduggery hit him so hard and so fast that Valkyrie didn't even register the punch; she just saw Wreath slamming back against the wall.

Wreath wiped the blood from his lip. "You certainly hit as hard as you ever did, and that's no mistake."

When Skulduggery spoke, his voice was even and without anger. "Solomon, so glad to have you onboard. Welcome to the team."

"A delight, sir, as always."

Skulduggery nodded his farewell and walked from the house, out into the rain. Valkyrie followed.

"What was *that*?" she demanded as they approached the Bentley.

"History," Skulduggery replied.

"You never told me you had a history with the Necromancers."

"I'm over 400 years old," he said. "I haven't told you a lot of things."

12

IN THE OFFICE OF THE GRAND MAGE

emus Crux knocked and the Grand Mage bid him enter. The office was crammed full of books, and maps covered every centimetre of the far wall. Thurid Guild was not one to become complacent just because he had reached a certain level of power. Crux admired that and was determined to follow his example. Together, they would make the Sanctuary strong again.

"You idiot," the Grand Mage said and Crux lost his little smile.

"Sir?"

"Do you know how many calls I've been getting? Our people are terrified, Crux. They're looking at what is going on and they're thinking, *if someone can kill the Teleporters without leaving one single trace, then they can kill me too*. That's what they're thinking."

"Grand Mage, I assure you, I am doing everything in my power—"

"You *assure* me? I've assured *them*, Crux, that my best detective is on the case. And do you know what they say?"

Inwardly, Crux swelled a little at this compliment, but shook his head.

"They say, *oh, I didn't know you'd got Skulduggery Pleasant back*."

Crux felt the blood rush to his face.

"They are scared and they are looking for results. I brought you in to do the job, and you have yet to impress me."

"But, sir—"

"There's another Teleporter. Did you know that? The *last* Teleporter. A boy."

"Sir, yes, sir. His name is Renn, sir. He was last seen in a nightclub in County Meath. I have our agents combing the area. We'll find him."

"Do not let me down, Crux."

"I won't, sir."

"Leave me."

Crux bowed and hurried out, closing the door gently behind him.

13

THE HOUSE ON CEMETERY ROAD

Skulduggery had a home. When Valkyrie had first discovered this, her initial reaction had been surprise. Her second reaction, following hot on surprise's heels, had been logical acceptance. Of course he had a home; of course he had somewhere to live. Had she really thought that he just drove around all day in the Bentley? A part of her actually *had* thought that, but that was a silly part, and not very bright.

His house was the only residential building on Cemetery

Road. There wasn't an actual cemetery on Cemetery Road, but there *were* two competing funeral homes, situated directly opposite each other, and Skulduggery's house sat proudly at the top, like a parent overseeing squabbling siblings. He told her stories of the arguments the funeral directors would get into as they stood just inside their gates and hurled abuse at each other from a safe distance.

One of the first things Valkyrie noticed about the inside of the house was that every room seemed to be a living room.

"I don't need anything else," Skulduggery had explained. "I don't need a kitchen or a bathroom, and I don't need a bed so I don't need a bedroom."

"Don't you sleep?"

"I don't *have* to, but I've developed the skill and I quite like it. Though I suppose you'd call it meditation. The effect's still the same – I shut down completely, let my mind wander where it wants to wander, totally unhindered by conscious thought. It's good. It's relaxing."

He'd shown her the chair he liked to sit in while he 'slept'. It was an armchair, nothing particularly impressive about it. Valkyrie had looked at it, felt pretty bored and gone snooping.

There were a lot of books and a lot of files. The biggest room in the house had a large sofa, and whenever Valkyrie had to spend any time on Cemetery Road, this was where she'd usually end up.

The front door opened and Valkyrie walked in, dropped her coat on the floor and sprawled on the sofa. Skulduggery walked in after her, picked up her coat, folded it neatly, and put it on the table.

"Will you be OK there?" he asked. "Do you want anything to eat or drink?"

"You never have anything to eat or drink," Valkyrie said, her words muffled by the cushion her face had sunk into.

"I think I have some leftover pizza from last time you were here."

"That was two weeks ago."

"You think it's gone off?"

"I think it's *walked* off. Really, I'm fine. Have you figured out what the Isthmus Anchor is yet?"

"I'm... working on it."

"You might want to work faster. When are we going to look for the gate?"

"First thing in the morning."

Valkyrie sighed. "In that case, I need to get some sleep."

Friday came, with a morning that threatened rain, and they drove out of Dublin, took the motorway and turned off at Balbriggan. Half an hour later, they pulled up beside a sign that announced, in faded red letters, that this was Aranmore Farm and that it was private property. The land was vast, with hills and meadows that stretched deep into the woodland that bordered it.

"So this is where the world ends," Valkyrie said, putting the map away. "Certainly prettier than I'd imagined."

Skulduggery put the Bentley in gear and they started up the hill. Long grasses grew on either side of the track and the wheels rumbled heavily. A white farmhouse came into view, with a slate roof and large windows. Behind it, stone sheds of varying sizes surrounded a yard on which old farm machinery stood in neat lines.

They reached the house and Skulduggery turned off the engine. He made sure his disguise was in place and then they both got out.

They approached the front door and Valkyrie knocked. She knocked again and looked back at Skulduggery.

"Who do you think lives here?"

"At a guess? A farmer."

"You're amazing," she said dryly.

"A single farmer," Skulduggery continued, "living alone. Never married, by the looks of things. No children. I'd say he'd be in his early seventies, judging by the clothes on the line we passed."

"We passed a clothesline?"

"What have I told you about keeping your eye out for details?"

"You said I shouldn't worry about that because I have you to do it for me."

"Yes, I'm pretty sure that's the exact *opposite* of what I said."

"Maybe he's taking an afternoon nap or something." Valkyrie peered in through the window. "I don't think there's anybody around."

"That's lovely, that is," said a voice from behind them, and they turned to see an elderly man striding towards them. He had wiry grey hair, bald on top, and a large nose. He was dressed in a tattered shirt with black braces holding up his trousers, which were in turn tucked into mucky wellington boots. "Reach a certain age and suddenly you're a nobody, suddenly you're not even worth counting. You know the problem with people your age, young lady?"

Valkyrie remembered her talk with Kenspeckle. "We think we'll live forever?" she answered hopefully.

"You have no respect for your elders."

She scowled, wondering how she could ever get that one right if the answer kept changing.

"So what do you want?" the farmer continued. "Why have you come all the way down here? And you," he said, turning his attention to Skulduggery, "why are you all wrapped up like the Invisible Man? You got something wrong with your face?"

"Actually," Skulduggery said, "yes. My name is Skulduggery Pleasant. This is my associate, Valkyrie Cain."

"What, do they give out prizes for silly names now?"

"And you are...?"

"Hanratty," the old man said. "Patrick Hanratty."

"Mr Hanratty—" Valkyrie began, but he shook his head.

"Call me Paddy."

"OK, Paddy..."

"Wait, I've changed my mind. Call me Mr Hanratty."

Valkyrie smiled patiently. "Have you noticed any strange people in the area lately?"

"Strange how? Strange like you or just normal strange?"

"*Any* kind of strange."

Paddy folded his arms and pursed his lips. "Well now, let me see. There was that O'Leary lad, from the village; he comes by every Wednesday with my bag of shopping. I'd call *him* strange,

I suppose. He has a thing in his eyebrow. An iron bar. Haven't a clue what it does. Maybe it picks up radio."

"I think Valkyrie meant strange people that you haven't seen before," Skulduggery said.

"Apart from you two?"

"Apart from us two."

Paddy shook his head. "Sorry, you're the two strangest people I've never seen before that I've seen in a long time. Do you want to tell me what this is about, or do you want me to guess?"

"Mr Hanratty—" Valkyrie began.

"Call me Paddy."

"Are you sure?"

"Probably not."

Skulduggery took over. "We have reason to believe that a gang of criminals will be using your land as a rendezvous point."

Paddy looked into Skulduggery's sunglasses. "A gang of criminals, you say? Kidnappers? Jewel thieves?"

"Bank robbers."

"Bank robbers," Paddy repeated, nodding his head. "I see. Yes, that makes sense. I can see why they'd choose my land. The fact that the nearest bank is over half an hour's drive from here would mean that this gang of criminals, after pulling off their daring heist, would need to make their way back through thirty miles of narrow roads, pulling in occasionally to allow tractors and assorted farm vehicles to get by, then pass unnoticed through the local village where the neighbourhood watch scheme is enforced with exceptional vigour, then—"

"Fine," Skulduggery interrupted. "Your land is not going to be used by a gang of bank robbers."

Paddy nodded, smug in triumph. "Well, that's a relief to hear. I may as well save us all some time, all right? I have no interest in selling up. I've lived here for forty years and I'm not moving. Now, unless there is something vitally important you have to tell me, I'm going to have to ask you to leave. I have to get back to work."

Skulduggery didn't answer for a moment, and Valkyrie thought he was actually getting angry, but his head turned like he'd suddenly remembered he was in a conversation.

"Of course," he said quickly. "We are sorry we took up your time."

He hurried back to the Bentley, Valkyrie right behind him.

"What's wrong?" she asked.

"I've figured it out," he said as he walked. "It's the Grotesquery."

"What is?"

They reached the car and got in. Skulduggery turned the key and the engine roared to life.

"The Isthmus Anchor is something that keeps the gateway between realities from sealing over," he said. "It's something that is *here*, but belongs over *there*. That's why Batu had to wait fifty years between murders – he needed Baron Vengeous to bring the Grotesquery back. The *Grotesquery* is the Isthmus Anchor."

"But... Bliss cremated it. Right?"

Skulduggery's voice was hollow as they sped back to the road. "He burned what he could. He burned its limbs and most of its organs, everything about it that had been added from another creature. But the torso comes from an *actual* Faceless One, or at least the human vessel it was inhabiting, and they're a lot harder to destroy."

Valkyrie was almost afraid to ask her next question. "So, like, where did he put it? Who has it? Skulduggery, *who has the Grotesquery?*"

"It's being kept at the Sanctuary," Skulduggery said, something new in his voice. "Thurid Guild has the Isthmus Anchor."

14

THE DIABLERIE

Batu took the vial in his right hand and carefully let the liquid drip on to the inside of his left forearm.

The liquid burned like acid and carved its way through his skin, forming a symbol of blood and scorched flesh.

When the symbol was complete, he put down the vial and examined his arm. The pain was excruciating.

The Diablerie looked at him.

"This will protect you," he said. "When the Dark Gods come, this symbol will mark you out as a believer."

"And Sanguine?" asked Gruesome Krav. "Do we tell him about this mark?"

"Sanguine is a mercenary. He has no faith, and as such, deserves no special treatment."

"Good," Krav said. "I don't like him."

Batu left the room as they began tattooing the symbol into their own arms, and went to the adjacent building to check on his army.

He slid open the door and turned on the light. The rows of Hollow Men looked back at him, awaiting his orders.

"Soon," he promised.

15

BREAKING AND ENTERING

hey hurried up to the wax figure of Phil Lynott, standing there, holding its guitar with a frozen half-smile on its face.

"We're here to see Mr Bliss," Skulduggery said.

For a moment, nothing happened, and then the figure turned its head and looked at them. "Do you have an appointment?"

"We don't, but we need to see Bliss. It's urgent."

"I'm afraid I have strict instructions regarding you and your partner. You are not to be allowed into the Sanctuary without—"

"Call the Administrator," Skulduggery interrupted. "Let me speak with somebody human."

"As you wish." There was a pause. "The Administrator has been informed of your presence. Please wait here and she will be with you shortly."

They looked at the wall, waiting for it to open up. Skulduggery pressed the call button on his phone and listened for a few seconds, then shoved the phone back into his pocket without saying anything. He'd been trying to call Bliss for the last twenty minutes, but Bliss wasn't answering.

The wall rumbled and the hidden door opened. The Administrator stepped into the corridor.

She smiled politely. "I'm afraid the Grand Mage is too busy to speak with anyone at the moment, but if you'd state your business—"

"We're not here for Guild," Skulduggery said. "We're here for Bliss."

"I'm sorry, Mr Pleasant, Elder Bliss is away."

"Away? Where?"

"I'm afraid I can't divulge that information."

"We don't have time for this. The remains of the Grotesquery need to be moved *now*."

For the first time since Valkyrie had known her, the Administrator frowned. "How did you know about that? The removal of the Grotesquery is a classified operation, Mr Pleasant. Only two people in the Sanctuary are even *aware* of it."

"Those two people," Skulduggery said, "that's you and the Grand Mage? Why does he want to move it?"

"We move items around all the time, for matters of storage, space or suitability. It's nothing out of the ordinary."

"When is it being moved?"

"I'm not—"

"Where is it being moved *to*?"

The Administrator bristled slightly. "I don't know actually. The Grand Mage will instruct the transport team personally."

"How big a transport team?"

"I'm not going to—"

"Let me guess. Guild doesn't want to attract attention, so it will be low-key. Two or three Cleavers, is that it? In an armoured van?"

"The Grand Mage assures me it will be perfectly adequate."

"The van's going to be attacked," Valkyrie said.

The Administrator's eyes narrowed. "Why would you do that?"

"*We're* not going to attack the van," Skulduggery told her.

"But we *are* going to have to steal the Grotesquery."

There was a pause and then the Administrator turned to run. Skulduggery held up a hand. Valkyrie felt the faint ripples as a bubble formed around the Administrator's head, robbing her of oxygen. She gasped for a breath that wouldn't come and Skulduggery caught her as she staggered.

"I'm very sorry," he murmured.

Valkyrie clicked her fingers and whirled to the figure of Phil Lynott, holding a fireball close to his wax face.

"If you sound the alarm," she warned, "I'll melt you."

"No need," the wax figure said. "My communications link is to the Administrator only. They keep promising to extend my link to the entire Sanctuary, but they haven't. As long as I open and close this door, I think they're quite happy to forget about me."

Skulduggery laid the unconscious Administrator on the ground. "She'll wake up in a few minutes," he said. "Please apologise to her for me."

The wall rumbled behind them, but they darted through the doorway before it closed up.

"Nice try," Valkyrie called back.

The Phil Lynott figure shrugged, then looked down at the Administrator, and right before the door sealed, she heard it start to sing 'Killer on the Loose'. Another one of her dad's favourites.

Skulduggery led the way down the stone staircase.

"How are we going to get out again?" she asked. "The two of us walking around down here is going to look suspicious enough, but walking around while carrying the *Grotesquery*?"

"We're not coming back this way."

"But this is the only way in."

"But it's not the only way *out*."

They slowed as they reached the bottom of the stairs, then entered the Foyer. Skulduggery walked calmly while Valkyrie's knees shook. The Cleaver guards turned their heads, watching them as they walked through the nearest set of doors, but did not move to intercept.

They walked side by side through the corridor, like they had every right to be there. They drew surprised looks from sorcerers, but nobody questioned their presence. They left the main corridor and walked deeper through the narrower ones, their footsteps picking up pace.

They approached the Sanctuary Gaol, where some of the sickest criminals in the world were imprisoned. Skulduggery had told her about some of them. Serial killers, mass murderers, sociopaths and psychopaths of every description were kept in these cages. Valkyrie could almost feel the evil seeping out through the door like a cold damp, chilling her as she passed.

Ahead of them was the Repository, the giant room that housed mystical and magical artefacts, including the remains of the Grotesquery. But today, unlike every other time Valkyrie had been here, there were two Cleavers standing guard at the double doors. Skulduggery and Valkyrie stepped into an adjoining corridor and stopped, just out of the Cleavers' sight.

"OK," he said, "that's good."

"It's good? What's good? What's good about it?"

"If the Cleavers are still guarding the room, it means the Grotesquery is still in there. We have a little time. So what we need now is a distraction."

"Maybe we should release one of the criminals from the Gaol and have them chase after him."

"Do you *really* want to release a magical serial killer back into the world?"

"I was only joking," she muttered defensively.

He paused. "Actually, that's not a bad idea. But we don't need anyone from the Gaol. They're just too dangerous. Someone languishing in the holding cells, however, might be more suitable."

Valkyrie grinned. "See? Even my jokes are brilliant."

Skulduggery started walking and she struggled to keep up. "But won't the cells be guarded by Cleavers too?" she asked.

He shook his head. "After the events of the last two years – first Serpine's attack on the Sanctuary, then taking down the Grotesquery – Cleaver numbers have been decimated. These days, Cleavers are being treated like the precious commodities they are, and used only where absolutely necessary.

"For the minimum security holding cells, I doubt there'd be any Cleaver presence at all. We'll probably encounter a Sanctuary agent, and if things go our way, the agent will know us and might even allow us our pick of the prisoners."

"When do things *ever* go our way?"

"Think positive, that's the spirit."

They reached the holding area without encountering anyone who realised they shouldn't be there. The corridor became narrow, with steel doors on either side. A gangly young man with bright red hair stood up from behind his desk, eyes narrowed in suspicion.

"You're Skulduggery Pleasant," he said.

"Yes, I am. And this is my partner, Valkyrie Cain. And you are?"

"My name is Staven Weeper. You're not supposed to be here."

Skulduggery waved his hand airily. "We have full co-operation, don't worry about that."

"The Grand Mage has warned us about you."

"You're sure it was me he warned you about? Not someone else?"

"You are not allowed to be here without supervision," Weeper said, forcing some authority into his tone. "Who let you in?"

"The door was open."

"I'm calling my superior."

Weeper reached for the button on the desk, but Skulduggery grabbed his wrist and twisted. Weeper howled in pain. Skulduggery moved around and slammed him against the wall.

"Shackles," he said. Valkyrie opened one of the desk drawers. Inside were half a dozen clear plastic bags containing the personal effects of the prisoners. She opened another drawer and found a pair of shiny new shackles that she tossed to Skulduggery. He cuffed Weeper's hands behind his back and let him go.

Weeper stumbled away, eyes wide. "You attacked me!"

"We just want to borrow one of your prisoners," Valkyrie assured him.

"I can't allow that to happen," Weeper snarled, settling into a combat stance that Valkyrie had never seen before.

She watched, wondering what martial art he knew that was good enough to make up for the fact that he couldn't use his hands. She was expecting some jumping around, maybe a few flips and definitely a lot of kicking. What she witnessed was more along the lines of Weeper trying to butt his head into Skulduggery's chest. He charged, Skulduggery stepped out of the way and Weeper hit his knee against the desk and fell to the ground in pain.

"Keep an eye out," Skulduggery said, hauling Weeper up and dragging him to the cells. He left him curled up against the wall, and moved to the first of the steel doors, opened the small latch and peered in. He closed the latch again and moved to the next door.

Valkyrie stood at the corner, making sure they weren't going to be interrupted. She glanced back to see Skulduggery guiding Weeper into a cell and then beckoning the prisoner out. Her gaze returned to the corridor. At the junction a sorcerer strode by, but didn't look her way. She waited without breathing, but he didn't reappear.

The cell door closed and Valkyrie turned to see which prisoner Skulduggery had chosen. The prisoner, his hands shackled in front of him, glared at her defiantly. She knew him.

He saw himself as the Killer Supreme, the man to make murder into an art form, even though he had yet to successfully kill anyone. The first time they'd met, he had tried to throw her off a building. He was not a very smart man.

"We meet again," Vaurien Scapegrace snarled.

Valkyrie laughed.

His snarl vanished and his shoulders sagged. "I wish, just once, people would see me and not laugh."

"Quiet now," Skulduggery said, prodding him forward. Valkyrie did her best to stifle her grin as they headed back to the Repository.

"I was framed," Scapegrace said, walking slightly ahead of them. "I've been accused of a crime I didn't commit. I shouldn't even *be* here."

"That's right," Skulduggery said. "You should be in a proper prison for attempted murder."

"I broke out," said Scapegrace with a shrug.

"That's not strictly true though, is it? To break out implies something dynamic and adventurous. You were being transported to another facility and they simply forgot about you at the rest stop."

"I escaped."

"You were left behind."

"I was a free man. And then I was accused of a crime I didn't commit and got rearrested. I shouldn't even be here. You call that justice?"

"I call that amusing," Valkyrie murmured.

Scapegrace ignored her. "Where are you taking me? This isn't the way to the interrogation rooms. Why do you want me?"

"Because you're great company."

Scapegrace slowed and all the colour drained from his face. "You're going to execute me, aren't you?"

"We're not going to execute you," Skulduggery said.

"That's why this is all hush-hush. Oh, God, you're going to execute me."

"We're not, I promise."

"But why? Why am *I* going to be executed? You fear me, don't you?"

"That's not exactly what's happening here."

Scapegrace's legs gave out, and Skulduggery caught him and kept him walking.

"You fear my wrath," Scapegrace said weakly.

Skulduggery stopped him, undid the shackles and gave him a small push. "Run away now."

Scapegrace spun to face them. "Why? So you can have your bit of sport? That is *cruel*."

"We're not going to execute you," Valkyrie insisted.

Scapegrace fell to his knees. "Please don't kill me."

Skulduggery shook his head. "I should have picked someone else."

"We just want you to distract some people," Valkyrie told him. "We need you to divert their attention."

"I don't want to die," Scapegrace sobbed.

"Vaurien, seriously, get up. We're not going to hurt you."

"Once I turn my back—"

"We're not going to do anything. We need you to distract some people, but this isn't just about us. This is your chance to escape. Look at yourself. No shackles. No injuries. What's to stop you from just running out of here?"

"OK," said Scapegrace, getting back to his feet. "So I just run, right?"

"That's right."

"And what about if—"

Scapegrace bolted past them halfway through his question, hoping to take them by surprise.

"Wrong way," Valkyrie called.

Scapegrace staggered to a stop and turned.

"If you go that way, you'll just arrive back at the holding cells."

Scapegrace looked around, getting his bearings, then nodded and walked back.

"Just because I'm helping you," he warned, "does not mean we are allies."

"We know that," Skulduggery said.

"The next time I see you I will be trying to kill you."

"We know that too."

"How do I get out of here?"

"Go straight ahead and turn left. Follow your nose from there."

Scapegrace stopped beside them and snarled. "Until we meet again."

He jogged to the corner and glanced right, shrieked and sprinted left.

"We probably should have told him he'd be running from Cleavers," Skulduggery said, as they watched both Cleavers blur past the intersection.

They hurried to the Repository doors, and just before they slipped inside, Valkyrie looked back as the Cleavers pounced on Scapegrace and he squealed.

16

STEALING THE GROTESQUERY

kulduggery took a small spool of thread from his pocket and started wrapping it around the door handles.

"That'll hold?" Valkyrie asked sceptically.

"This is Resolute Thread. The more pressure applied, the stronger it gets. It's very rare. They say it was made from the stomach lining of an emperor dragon, over 2000 years ago."

"Was it?"

"No, it's just really strong thread."

The door handles tied together securely, they walked deeper into the room. The Repository was vast and dark, with rows of shelves and tables groaning under the weight of the magic artefacts it contained. In the centre, where once the Book of Names had stood on its pedestal, there was now a cage of black steel, about the size of a small truck. The remains of the Grotesquery, little more than a torso and head wrapped in soiled bandages, hung suspended off the ground by a dozen taut chains. There were symbols carved on each of the cage bars, and they started to glow as the two of them neared.

"Don't touch the cage," Skulduggery warned.

"How do we open it?"

"Very, very carefully, I'd imagine. I'm not as fluent in the language of these symbols as China is, but I know enough to recognise a death field when I see one. It'd kill anyone who even puts a hand inside those bars."

"Can we turn it off?"

"If we knew the right symbol to touch, yes. Unfortunately, if we touch the *wrong* symbol, the field will swell and kill everything in the room."

"Would it kill you?"

"Seeing as how I'm already dead?"

"Well, would it? Serpine used his red right hand on you and

it didn't have any effect. Maybe this would be the same."

"If I knew a little more about how I ended up as a living skeleton with impeccable dress sense, I could give it a try. But there is every chance that the death field would kill whatever's left of me."

"So how *are* we going to get the Grotesquery?"

Skulduggery walked in among the shelves. "There has to be something here that will help us," he said.

Valkyrie followed, browsing the artefacts on display, although she really had no idea what she was looking for, let alone how they could use any of it to open the cage.

She picked up a wooden sphere, about twice the size of a tennis ball. It had a thin groove running all the way around its circumference.

"And this is...?" she asked, holding it up for Skulduggery to see.

"Cloaking sphere," he said. "Not very many of those around actually."

"What does it do?"

"It makes magic people invisible."

"Cool."

Valkyrie replaced it and turned to follow him, but Skulduggery was gone.

She heard a sound from somewhere in the stacks and saw movement. There was a grunt and Skulduggery came flying over the shelves. He hit a table and smashed the vials that had been sitting there, then rolled off the edge, hit the ground and groaned. A big man with long silver hair strode out after him. Valkyrie recognised him from the description she'd been given. Gruesome Krav.

The Diablerie were here to steal the Grotesquery before them.

Valkyrie backed off, her heart suddenly slamming against her chest, and then there were footsteps behind her.

She turned to see Sanguine approach, smiling that wicked smile. She clicked the fingers of both her hands and flames filled her grip, but cracks spider-webbed at Sanguine's feet and he sank into the floor. Valkyrie turned, wary, ignoring the sounds of Skulduggery's fight, listening for the tell-tale crumbling that signified Sanguine's movements underground.

She heard it and knew he was rising up out of the ground directly behind her. She lashed out a back kick and felt it connect. She turned to see Sanguine sprawling, hands at his face, his sunglasses broken neatly in two and his nose pumping blood. His eyeless face contorting in pain and fury, he scrambled up and made a grab for her.

Valkyrie ducked under his right arm and kicked at his leg and he went down on one knee, and she followed through with an elbow to the back of his head. He dropped forward, on to his hands, and swung his leg back viciously, catching both of her ankles. She crashed to the ground and his hands were on her as he got to his feet. She tried to break his hold, but he was too strong and he hurled her into a row of shelves. The shelves toppled, artefacts smashing, and Valkyrie followed them to the floor.

She scrambled up and tried to push at the air, but Sanguine was too fast. He punched, and her head snapped around and white light exploded in her vision, and even as she was falling, she tasted the blood. Suddenly she was on the ground, her left hand covering her mouth, aware that one of her front teeth was missing. Her body was leaden, drained of its strength, and all she could think about was that her tooth had been knocked out and the hassle it would be to explain that to her mother.

A brown shoe appeared beside her face and Sanguine knelt, opening his straight razor, the blood from his nose flowing freely on to her coat.

"You deserve this," he snarled, bringing the blade to her throat.

There was a gunshot and he screamed and fell to one side,

clutching his leg. Behind him, Skulduggery switched targets, but Krav slapped the gun out of his hand.

Cursing in pain, Sanguine got up and, ignoring Valkyrie, lurched to the cage. He pressed his hand against a symbol and it flashed. Valkyrie rolled away, expecting the death field to envelop them all as Skulduggery had warned. But the symbol faded, as did all the others. The cage door opened and Sanguine dragged himself inside. He reached for the Grotesquery, and at his touch, the chains released their hold and the bandaged torso fell heavily.

"I have it!" he snapped.

Krav snarled at Skulduggery, cheated out of his kill, and strode for the cage, as the ground crumbled beneath them and Sanguine took Krav and the Grotesquery down and away.

Skulduggery snatched up his gun and hurried to Valkyrie. She became aware of the pounding on the double doors. The Resolute Thread was holding, but even as she watched, the blade of a scythe pierced the door and withdrew. The Cleavers were hacking their way in.

"Let me see," Skulduggery said, helping her to sit up. He took her face in his gloved hand and tilted her head back. Blood was running down her chin and she was doing her best not to swallow. "Open your mouth."

Valkyrie shook her head. She had tears in her eyes – partly from shock, partly from distress. Billy-Ray Sanguine had taken her smile with one vicious punch.

Skulduggery pulled her to her feet. A sliver of cold air hissed through her teeth and she moaned in pain. She kept her lips pressed tightly together.

The double doors fell apart and Thurid Guild stormed into the Repository, flanked by two Cleavers. He saw the empty cage.

"Get them!" he thundered.

Skulduggery grabbed Valkyrie's hand and dragged her into the maze of shelves. One of the Cleavers bounded from Guild's side and leaped high, landing in front of them, scythe swinging to block their way. Skulduggery thrust at the air, but the Cleaver moved through the ripples. The other Cleaver was coming in from behind, moving to trap them.

They couldn't afford to be arrested. The Diablerie had the Isthmus Anchor, which meant their next move would be to track down and snatch Fletcher Renn. They had to get out of here.

Skulduggery's gun was still in his right hand and he fired, point blank, into the first Cleaver's chest. The Cleaver staggered, his uniform protecting him, and Skulduggery added to his backward momentum with a kick. The Cleaver went down and they jumped over him.

They ran to the end of the row and Skulduggery grabbed the cloaking sphere, then rammed a shoulder into the shelf and the whole thing toppled over. Artefacts crashed to the ground, unnatural smoke billowed and there were cries, like a dozen trapped souls suddenly released. In the confusion, Valkyrie ducked low and followed Skulduggery on a course through the shelves, heading for the door. She could hear Guild barking orders as reinforcements arrived.

The smoke reached her and smelled foul, and by instinct she took a breath through her mouth, immediately stumbling with the pain. Clamping both hands over her bloody lips, she blinked the tears away and saw Skulduggery disappearing into another row of shelves. She hurried after him, but froze as a Cleaver stepped in front of her.

His visored helmet swept his surroundings. She stayed frozen. He'd see her in a matter of moments.

Gloved hands emerged from the gloom behind the Cleaver and yanked him back out of sight.

Valkyrie stayed where she was, waiting for the fight to erupt, but there was only stillness.

She peered through the shelves and saw Guild, standing there with a furious look on his face. There was movement behind him and Valkyrie realised that a Cleaver had been standing there only moments before.

She moved forward, staying low and quiet. She darted across the gap between shelves and followed another row which led her closer to the door. Another Cleaver ran in and Guild waved to him to stop.

"Stay there," he ordered. "Make sure they don't leave."

The Cleaver pulled out his scythe. He was the only thing between her and the door. The unnatural smoke trailed and sank and swept up, and it passed in front of her, obscuring her line of sight. When the smoke cleared, the Cleaver was gone.

Skulduggery moved out of the darkness and waited by the door. Valkyrie checked to make sure no one was looking. She crept to the end of the row and Skulduggery nodded to her, then she hurried by him and out into the corridor.

They ran.

A sorcerer Valkyrie vaguely recognised saw them and frowned, but Skulduggery pushed at the air and the sorcerer shot back off his feet. They took the corridor to their left, heading away from the busiest areas.

"There's another way out," Skulduggery said as they sprinted. "Eachan Meritorious told me about it once. For emergency use only. Guild doesn't know I know about it."

They burst into a large oval-shaped room with a single light source that kept the edges of the room in darkness. It was the room where Valkyrie had first met the Elders, two years before.

Valkyrie turned to swing the door shut, but Remus Crux charged through, sending her to the ground. His gun was in his hand and Skulduggery moved into him, trapping his gun hand against his ribs. Crux tried to protest, but Skulduggery caught him with a right hook. Crux's knees wobbled and Skulduggery disarmed him and flipped him to the floor.

Valkyrie heard footsteps in the corridor and clicked her fingers to get Skulduggery's attention. He took the cloaking sphere from his jacket and twisted both hemispheres in opposite directions. A bubble of haze erupted outwards, enveloping them and Crux.

Thurid Guild ran up to the door, followed by three Cleavers. Valkyrie tried to ignore the pain in her mouth and prepared to fight, but Skulduggery laid a hand on her shoulder.

"They can't see or hear us," he said. "Everything magical is now cloaked."

The sphere in his hand was gently ticking, as both hemispheres slowly worked their way back into alignment.

"Grand Mage," Crux called weakly. "Help me."

But Guild couldn't hear him. He turned to the Cleavers. "They must have doubled back. I want the exit sealed. Nobody in or out unless I say so. Go!"

The Cleavers sprinted off and Guild stalked back the way he had come. Crux moaned in misery and Skulduggery looked down at him.

"We didn't steal the Grotesquery, Remus. The Diablerie did. That's who is behind this. Jaron Gallow, maybe someone named Batu. Focus your investigation on them."

"I'm placing you under arrest," Crux whimpered.

"Guild is working with them. He told them which symbol deactivated the death field. You can't trust him. You can only trust Bliss."

The cloaking sphere clicked one last time and the bubble of haze withdrew. Skulduggery pocketed the sphere and led Valkyrie to the dark edges of the room. He clicked his fingers, summoning a bright flame.

"Timing is everything," he told her. "When we start running we cannot stop, are we clear?"

She murmured an affirmative, in too much pain from her missing tooth to open her mouth. Skulduggery leaned in and whispered so that Crux wouldn't hear.

"The moment we're out of here, we'll get Professor Grouse

to fix up your tooth, OK? You've got nothing to worry about."

She murmured again and his head tilted sympathetically for a moment. Then he nodded to the wall. "Touch the wall and be prepared to run."

Valkyrie reached out, her palm on the cold wall, and there was a rumble as the wall opened up, wide enough for the two of them to enter.

"Now," Skulduggery said and they bolted. The wall closed up behind them as the space immediately ahead opened. It was disconcerting to run full pelt at solid rock, but just as they were about to hit it, it parted, then resealed at their heels. They were sprinting in a bubble of space that was moving quickly through the ground, and the rumbling was huge and loud and reminded her of Billy-Ray Sanguine taking her to see Baron Vengeous. She hadn't liked it then and she didn't like it now.

They were running up an incline, Valkyrie could feel it in her legs. Skulduggery had doused the flame so it wouldn't burn up the oxygen, so now they were running in complete darkness. Valkyrie opened the side of her mouth to suck breath through, trying not to let the cold air hit her damaged tooth.

She was getting tired. They had been sprinting for far too long. She needed to slow down, just for a moment, but she knew this little bubble of space would carry on without them. She didn't much fancy being crushed to death, no matter how fast it would be.

"Didn't think it would be quite so far," Skulduggery said over the noise. The good thing about not having breath was that he would never be out of it, and the good thing about not having muscles is that they could never scream at him. She envied him right now.

Valkyrie's coat snapped her back – she realised immediately that the coat-tails had been caught in the crush – and she ripped her arms out of the sleeves, abandoning the coat to the darkness, and stumbled. She felt Skulduggery's gloved fingers close around her hand and he yanked her up alongside him, practically dragging her. She got her feet under her once more and was running on her own again, but she gripped his hand and didn't let go.

And then there was a blinding light and a rush of fresh air and they were outside. Valkyrie slipped on wet grass and landed on her back. The rumbling abruptly ceased. She lay there, both hands covering her mouth, breathing fast and squinting as her eyes adjusted.

Skulduggery was wrapping his scarf around his jaw. He dipped his hat low over his eye sockets. "The Garden of Remembrance," he said. "Not the most inconspicuous place for a secret tunnel to emerge, but I'm not complaining."

Valkyrie grunted a response, indicating that she wasn't about to complain either. He helped her up. Her arms were bare and prickling with goosebumps in the cold air. The only people she could see were an elderly couple, out for a quiet stroll. Nobody had seen their arrival. They walked to the gate.

"We have a problem," Skulduggery said. "Apart from all the obvious ones, I mean. The Bentley is back at the Sanctuary and we're not going to be able to get to it."

She moaned.

"The good news is, after it was damaged two years ago, I took the precaution of stashing a few replacements around town. There's one a few minutes' walk away."

Valkyrie looked at him and mumbled a question.

He laughed. "It's not yellow, no. I'm sure you'll like this one."

They walked to a small car park behind a crumbling building, with Valkyrie doing her best to hide the blood from the people they passed. The only car parked here was a Ford Fiesta. She glared at Skulduggery.

He nodded. "I suppose it *is* kind of small."

She mumbled something again and he shook his head.

"Actually, you'd be surprised at how nimble it is. It doesn't have the speed, the comfort or the sheer power of the Bentley, but, especially in city traffic, a Fiesta is a fine—"

She interrupted him with another angrier mumble, and he took a moment before nodding.

"I suppose you're right. It *is* sort of purple, yes."

She sagged. Skulduggery took the key from its hiding place in the tailpipe, opened the car and got in. Valkyrie slid in beside him, buckled up without enthusiasm and Skulduggery started the engine.

"Starts first time," he said happily.

They drove out of the car park and headed for the Hibernian Cinema. The Purple Menace wasn't as bad as the Canary Car, but it was close. At least it didn't make people stop and actually laugh as it passed. After a few minutes, Valkyrie even stopped thinking about it and instead started worrying about her tooth.

They got to the Hibernian and parked across the street. Skulduggery went first, making sure Guild hadn't sent a squad of Cleavers to arrest them, and then he beckoned Valkyrie over. It was starting to rain as they entered, and Valkyrie led the way through the screen and into the Medical Facility.

Fletcher swaggered up, started to say something cocky, but saw the dried blood on Valkyrie's face and hands, and his eyes widened. They passed each other in silence.

Kenspeckle was in one of the labs, drinking a cup of tea and eating a scone. He muttered when he saw them approaching, but his eyes narrowed when Valkyrie neared. Up until now, she had been pretty brave about it, but the look of concern on Kenspeckle's face brought tears to her eyes and she couldn't help it. She started crying.

Skulduggery stepped back like she had stung him, but Kenspeckle rushed forward.

"Oh, my dear," he said tenderly, "there's no need to cry, there's no need. What's happened to you, eh? Let me have a look. A broken tooth? Is that all? That's nothing, Valkyrie. That's a half-hour's work at the very most. You've nothing to worry about."

Normally, Valkyrie would have had something to say to show she wasn't rattled, but today she was without words.

Kenspeckle shot Skulduggery a glare. "You can wait elsewhere, Detective Pleasant. Maybe you can keep an eye on that annoying boy you stuck me with – try and make sure he doesn't break anything else. I'll have her back to you soon enough."

Skulduggery nodded and looked at Valkyrie, then walked away.

"We'll get that smile working again," Kenspeckle promised, giving her a wink. "Don't you worry."

17

THE DARK LITTLE SECRET

China was sitting at her desk, cataloguing new arrivals to her library, when Remus Crux came storming into the apartment. His entrance was so dramatic that she almost arched an eyebrow. If he had had a chin, it would probably be thrusting.

"Remus," she said. "What a lovely surprise."

"Your charms won't work on me," Crux sneered. "Unlike every other simpleton who falls in love with you, I have a will of iron. You won't be able to cloud my thoughts."

"I doubt I'd even be able to find them."

She smiled graciously and his face slackened for a moment, but then he closed his eyes and shook his head.

"Stop what you're doing or I will arrest you."

China stood up from the desk. She was wearing blue today. "Remus, despite what you've heard, I can't control what other people feel. I'm just standing here. Any emotion you're feeling is coming all by itself."

His hand moved into his jacket, and she didn't try to stop him as he pulled out his gun and aimed at her.

"Stop it," he snarled.

"I can't."

"You are influencing the mind of an agent of the Sanctuary. That is a criminal offence."

"It is?"

"You are impeding an investigation!"

"You came to see *me*, Remus, and you still haven't told me why. Would you like some tea?"

Without waiting for his response, she crossed to the sideboard. The symbols she had carved into the wood glowed with heat as she lifted the teapot to the delicate cup and poured.

Out of the corner of her eye, she saw him gripping the

gun so tightly that his knuckles turned white.

"Skulduggery Pleasant and Valkyrie Cain," he said. "They are fugitives from justice and you will deliver them to me."

"I don't know where they are."

"But you can find them. You can use your network of informants and spies to track them down."

She laughed. "*Informants and spies?* You make it all sound so glamorous."

Holding the saucer in her left hand, she raised the cup to her lips and took a delicate sip.

Realising that the gun was having no effect on her, Crux holstered it. "You will do what I say or I will make your life uncomfortable."

"I don't mean to upset you, Remus, but there is nothing about you that scares me in the slightest. When I look at you, all I see is an insecure little man trying to step out of the shadow of your predecessor. But Skulduggery casts a long shadow, doesn't he?"

"You think it's jealousy?" Crux smiled. "That's why I'm so keen to bring him in? It's not jealousy, Miss Sorrows. I know who he is. I've heard the stories about him. I've even heard a story that very few people have heard. I think you know it."

"I'm sure I do. Are you sure you won't have some tea?"

"You're not grasping the seriousness of the situation. I heard this one particular story from a dying man, who wanted to pass on his biggest secret before he left us. He was a Necromancer actually. I've never had much time for death magicians, but he was different. Do I have your attention yet?"

China sighed and took her tea over to the desk. "Say what you have to say, Remus. I have a business to attend to."

He leaned in. "I know how Skulduggery Pleasant came back from the dead, Miss Sorrows, and I know what happened after. And I know what you did."

She observed him with cold eyes and said nothing.

"I've known for the last two years," Crux continued. "I went looking for evidence to support this claim, but I had neither the resources nor the authority available to me. But since the Grand Mage brought me in, I've been working at it, behind the scenes, bit by bit, piecing it together."

"I genuinely don't know what you're talking about."

"Do you think he knows what you did? What am I talking about? Of course he doesn't. If he knew, you'd be dead, am I right?"

"You do not want to upset me," China said, pushing her cup to one side. "You wouldn't like me when I'm upset."

"Bring them to me," said Crux. "Arrange a meeting, spring

a trap. Pleasant and Cain. I want them gift-wrapped and handed over."

"No."

"If you don't, I go public with my suspicions, and you know what would happen then. He has a thing for revenge, doesn't he?"

China's blue eyes narrowed. "He's trying to save us."

"He's working with the Diablerie."

"Don't be *absurd*."

"He aided the enemy, Miss Sorrows. He will be arrested, tried and imprisoned. The only thing I care about, the only result I'm interested in, is that he is taken off the streets, and I can do that with, or without, your help. For your own well-being, I think you should co-operate."

"We need him."

"No," he said, "we don't. He's an unpredictable quantity. We need someone with rules, with ethics, with a moral sense of duty. Someone like me. Good day, Miss Sorrows. I will be expecting your call."

18

IN THE FLESH

Very lightly, Valkyrie ran her tongue over the cap on her broken tooth, scared she might dislodge it before it had time to set. Kenspeckle examined his handiwork and nodded.

"It'll be fine."

"It feels a little big," she admitted.

"That's because it is. In a few weeks you'll wear it down and have it level with the rest of your teeth, and you'll forget it's even there. Don't bite anything for a few hours – you might want to avoid eating anything particularly chewy or tough – and you really ought to stop getting punched in the face."

Valkyrie looked down at her boots. "Sorry," she muttered.

"You don't have to apologise to *me* – I'm not the one getting hit."

"Thanks for doing this, Kenspeckle."

He sighed. "I may have my issues with Mr Pleasant, and I may have a problem with what you're being taught and how you are treated, but never mistake any of that for a problem with *you*, my dear."

"But I'm treated well."

"You're treated like an adult," Kenspeckle said. "That's not being treated *well*. The fact is, no matter how much you act otherwise, you are a child and you should be treated like a child."

"*You* don't treat me like a child."

He smiled. "Of course I do, but you seem to have this ridiculous notion that being treated like a child means to be treated with any less respect than an adult."

"Not everyone sees things the way you do."

"And what have I always told you about other people?"

"They're idiots," she grinned.

"And your beautiful smile is back. You know, sometimes I think I'm better than even *I* think I am."

"Is that possible?"

"I wouldn't have thought so."

Valkyrie picked up her coat and heard Kenspeckle sigh irritably. Skulduggery stood in the doorway.

"We'd better go," Skulduggery said. "Sooner or later, Guild is going to send someone here to look for us."

"Oh, that's right," said Kenspeckle. "I'm harbouring fugitives now, aren't I? Would you look at that? You ask me to help you and then you turn me into a criminal."

"They won't know we've been here," Skulduggery promised.

"And what about the annoying boy? Are you taking him with you?"

"It might be safer if he comes with us."

Kenspeckle laughed. "Safer? *Safer?*"

"Thurid Guild can't be trusted. If he finds out who Fletcher is, he might turn him over to the Diablerie. He might *be* the Diablerie."

"Do you hear yourself? Do you? You're delusional! You're seeing enemies and conspiracies round every corner! You are endangering those around you with no thought to their well-being!"

"The threat posed by the Diablerie is real, Professor."

"Then let the Sanctuary handle it. They have the resources.

They have the Cleavers. You have a fourteen-year-old girl who puts her life on the line every time she's with you."

Skulduggery turned and started walking. Valkyrie gave a hesitant smile to Kenspeckle and followed. But Kenspeckle wasn't through. He stormed up to Skulduggery and grabbed his arm, swinging him around.

"Do you not feel one iota of responsibility? Valkyrie was in a fight with a grown man less than two hours ago. Don't you feel bad about what happened to her?"

"But I'm OK," Valkyrie said softly.

"She could have been killed," Kenspeckle continued. "Yet again, while out with you, she could have been killed. Would you have felt anything then?"

"Let go of my arm, Professor Grouse."

"Think back to when you were a man, Skulduggery, to when you were flesh and blood, and tell me – do you remember ever actually *having* a heart or were you *born* dead?"

Before Skulduggery could respond, Clarabelle ran into the corridor. "It's gone!" she shouted. "The statue of Ghastly is gone!"

Skulduggery ran, Valkyrie right behind him. They passed Clarabelle and sprinted for the chamber. Fletcher emerged from a room and had to jump to one side to avoid being knocked down.

They burst through the doors and Skulduggery ran to the spot where the statue had lain. Valkyrie hurried around the edge of the chamber, hand trailing along the walls. Kenspeckle and Clarabelle rushed in and Fletcher followed.

"Has anyone been in here?" Skulduggery demanded.

"No one," Clarabelle said. "What are you looking for?"

"Cracks," Valkyrie told her. She cast her eyes around for any sign that Sanguine had been in the room.

"They have him," Skulduggery said tightly. "The Diablerie. They got in here somehow and they took Ghastly. I don't know how, but they did."

Tanith ran in, and even though Valkyrie hadn't seen her in weeks, she was in no mood to smile. Tanith, on the other hand, seemed to be in a great mood.

"Hey!" she said brightly.

"Get your sword," Skulduggery said, taking out his gun. "They may still be in the area."

"I lost my sword," Tanith confessed. "And then I fell off a building. And I got stabbed through the hand." She held up her right hand, which had a thick bandage around it. "Who might still be in the area? What's going on?"

"Ghastly," was all Valkyrie could say.

"I know!" beamed Tanith. "Isn't it amazing?"

Skulduggery turned his head sharply. "Isn't what amazing?"

Tanith's smile faded and uncertainty clouded her eyes. "Um, Ghastly."

"What's amazing about Ghastly? He's missing."

Tanith frowned. "But I was just talking to him."

They stared at her, then heard footsteps, and they looked at the door and a man walked through. A man with a boxer's build and a tailor's clothes, with scars that covered his entire head and a smile that was weak but sincere.

"Ghastly!" Valkyrie shrieked, embarrassingly high, and launched herself at him. He grunted with the ferocity of her hug, then laughed.

"Out of the way," Kenspeckle ordered, moving forward. "Let me see him."

Valkyrie bounded away and allowed Kenspeckle to examine his patient.

"Do you remember your name?" he asked, shining a light into Ghastly's eyes.

"Yes, I do, Professor. My name is Ghastly Bespoke. I'm a tailor, my favourite colour is green, and I don't have any pets."

"Does this hurt?" Kenspeckle asked and poked him in the face with a finger.

"Ow. Yes."

"All right then." Kenspeckle stood back. "You're fine."

Without waiting for a response, he turned and strode out the door.

"His bedside manner hasn't improved," Ghastly murmured.

Skulduggery stepped in front of him. The two friends looked at each other.

"Tanith told me I've been gone a little over two years," said Ghastly.

"That's right."

"That's a long time."

"It is."

"Not as long as it *could* have been, but still, a long time. You're... you're not going to *hug* me, are you?"

Skulduggery considered it for a long moment. "Probably not," he concluded.

"It would just be weird," Ghastly explained.

"I understand."

"I'm OK with shaking your hand though."

"I'm not really comfortable with that."

Ghastly shrugged. "I get it, you like your space."

Valkyrie stared at them, unable to believe what she was witnessing, and then Ghastly's grin broke out and she realised

172

this was a guy thing. The two friends hugged and she smiled happily.

Fletcher leaned over. "When is someone going to tell him that his head is all scarred?" he whispered, but she ignored him.

Bespoke Tailor's squatted on the edge of the dirty street like a mangey dog, too old and too dumb to move in out of the rain. The Purple Menace pulled up outside and Skulduggery and Ghastly got out, then pulled the seats forward to allow Valkyrie and Fletcher to climb out after them. Fletcher was doing a terrible job of trying not to stare at Ghastly's scars, but his discomfort was amusing, so Valkyrie didn't try to make him any more at ease.

Tanith rode up and parked beside them. The rain dripped off her leathers as she swung her leg off the motorbike and removed her helmet, and Fletcher finally had something new to stare at. Valkyrie rolled her eyes.

Ghastly nodded to a passing neighbour and got a quiet "Welcome back" in return. He opened the door of his shop and led them in. It was musty inside, but neat. Half-finished clothes hung on mannequins, and the walls were lined with shelves that held fabrics both familiar and exotic.

"Did you dream?" Tanith asked, like it had been a question that had been bugging her on the way over.

"I did not," Ghastly said, going straight to the shelves, his hands running over the materials.

"Nothing at all? You just have a blank space in your head where the last two years should be?"

"The last memory I have is fighting the White Cleaver. Then I opened my eyes and I was kneeling in the chamber. As for dreams, I didn't have any that I can remember – but then I can *never* remember my dreams."

"I had a dream last night," Fletcher said, looking at Tanith. "I think you were in it."

"You didn't know me last night."

"And that is a tragedy."

"OK!" Tanith said, forcing a smile on her face. "I'm making myself a cup of tea. Anyone else want one?"

"I would *love* a cup of tea," Ghastly said, sounding like he really, truly meant it.

Fletcher gave her a sleazy little smile. "I'll have a whisky."

"You can have a cup of tea too," Tanith said brusquely and disappeared into the back room.

"Then I'll help you make it," said Fletcher, trailing after her.

Ghastly looked at Valkyrie. "I think you've outgrown that outfit."

"I think I have," she admitted.

"What do you think we should do for the new one? Black again or do you want to mix it up a little?"

She hesitated. "I really like the black."

"But with something else thrown in? I think we should throw in a little colour. Maybe something in the lining." Ghastly pulled down a roll of deep red material and held it to the light while he spoke to Skulduggery. "So Serpine's dead. What about the White Cleaver?"

"We don't know where he is," Skulduggery told him. "He abandoned Serpine just when he was needed the most. That kind of worked out well for us."

"And then Vengeous came back, but now *he's* dead, and now the Diablerie have resurfaced and they're going to bring the Faceless Ones back and we're *all* going to die."

"Yes."

Ghastly put the red material on the table and went hunting for more. "And this Batu person?"

"Solomon Wreath believes that Batu is just a name Jaron Gallow has been using, but I'm not so sure. Whoever Batu is, he released Vengeous, set him up as the mastermind and used him to do what needed to be done. Now that Vengeous is gone, he might be doing it again – setting *Gallow* up as the mastermind to throw us off the trail."

"Keep us distracted long enough to bring the Faceless Ones back," Ghastly said. "Well, that's a particularly insidious plan, I have to say. It means our true enemy could be anyone. Have you spoken with China about this?"

"She doesn't have any leads."

"Please tell me you're not trusting her these days."

Skulduggery hesitated and Ghastly sighed.

"The leader of the Diablerie, whether it's Gallow or Batu or someone else entirely, has been planning this for years. If there is anyone we know who could use that time to manipulate everyone into thinking she is on the side of the angels, it's China. Manipulating people is what she does."

"I know what I'm doing."

"When it comes to China Sorrows you *rarely* know what you're doing." Ghastly laid out a black fabric on the table, nodded to himself and looked up. "Valkyrie. Boots."

"I need new ones."

"You certainly do. Come this way."

They left Skulduggery and went into a smaller room where Ghastly's old-fashioned shoemaking equipment lay. Different types of leathers hung from the walls, and there were trays of nails and glues and needles and threads.

"Everything a cordwainer needs," he said when he saw Valkyrie examining her surroundings.

"I don't know what that means."

"Skulduggery's not the only one who knows odd words," he smiled. The scars, precisely spaced and covering his whole head, had once seemed to her ugly. But they weren't ugly any more. They were a symbol of what he had lived with, what he had lived through, and as such they had become something good, something noble.

His smile turned sad. "He's been dragging you into quite a bit of trouble, from what I hear."

She kept her voice neutral. "I've had this talk with Kenspeckle, so I'll tell you what I told him. Skulduggery wouldn't take me if I didn't want to go." She paused, let a moment go by. "Ghastly, why don't you like me?"

His eyes widened slightly. "What?"

"I know you think I'm too young, but there are younger kids than me doing magic. They're all over the place. And *you've* been doing magic since you were born."

He went quiet, then turned to the sink and filled a basin with water. "Could you take off your boots and socks, please?"

She did as he asked, and he laid the basin on the ground and motioned for her to step into it. She hiked up her trousers and plunged her bare feet into the cold water.

"The first time we met," Ghastly said, "I told you to forget about all this and go home. Remember?"

"Yes."

He waved his hand and the water in the basin started feeling thicker, heavier.

"I still believe that. You should be in school, Valkyrie; you should be living the life you were living before magic interrupted everything. You should go to college, get a job, fall in love, live happily ever after. If you don't, you're going to die."

"Everyone dies," she said, with an attempt at a casual shrug.

"But when you die, it's going to be something awful."

"You can try to scare me as much as you want, but it's not going to work."

"I'm not trying to scare you." With a gesture, the water parted. "You can step out now." She did so, and with another gesture, the water returned to the position it had held moments ago. Two perfect imprints of her feet remained in the basin. Ghastly put the basin on a small table and poured in a black powder, almost emptying the box it came in, then looked at her while she dried her feet with a towel and pulled on her socks.

"Did Skulduggery ever tell you about my mother?"

"About her being a champion boxer?"

"She wasn't just a boxer. She wasn't just a wife, or just a mother, or just an anything. She was an exceptional woman. She was a Sensitive, did he tell you that?"

Valkyrie started putting on her boots. "Like, a psychic? Like Finbar Wrong?"

"That's right. My mother's particular gift was as a Seer, but it's a gift she didn't want. She didn't cultivate it. She had no interest in learning what the future held for her, or for others. She preferred to find out when she got there. But sometimes she didn't have a choice. She'd see a vision, or dream a dream, or hear a voice from a conversation that hadn't yet taken place."

Valkyrie stood, glancing into the basin. The black powder was swirling around in the impressions her feet had made – swirling and congealing. "What does this have to do with me quitting?"

"She saw you," Ghastly said. "That was one of the few visions she told me about. She told me that Skulduggery would take a partner some time in the future, a girl with dark hair and dark eyes. I knew it was you when I met you, and I did my best to steer you away. You're a stubborn girl – anyone ever tell you that?"

"What did she see?"

"She saw you die."

Valkyrie stepped away from the basin. "Oh."

"If you're going to ask me for a time and a place, sorry. She was never that specific."

"How... how do I die?"

"In pain," he said. "Screaming."

She ran her tongue over her new tooth and said nothing.

Ghastly waved his hand over the basin and she heard the water slosh about as it returned to its normal state. He lifted out the black moulds of her two feet and put them on the table. "She said there was an enemy you had to fight. A creature of darkness. She said Skulduggery fought by your side for some of it, but... She *sensed* things more than saw them, you know? She felt terror, and death, and futility. She felt the world on the edge of destruction, and she sensed evil. Unimaginable evil."

Something caught in Valkyrie's throat and she forced it down. "Where did it come from, the creature?"

"I don't know."

"Well, what was it? Was it a vampire or a Faceless One or..."

"I don't know."

"So the only thing you *do* know is that I'm going to die? Well, I've seen time-travel movies. I know that the future isn't certain.

I know that *knowing* what happens can change what happens. That's what *I'm* going to do. I'm going to train harder, and when I meet this creature of darkness, I'll kick it to a messy pulp, and put a leash around its neck and make it my pet."

"I don't think this can be changed."

"Then you don't know me very well."

He looked at her for an age, then took a deep breath before letting it out in a long, resigned sigh.

"One other thing," she said. "In case you didn't notice, that was me making my decision on the whole *quitting* idea."

He nodded. "I won't bring it up again."

"Good. And, Ghastly, I really am glad you're back."

He smiled. "Thanks."

Skulduggery stepped in. "We have to go."

"But I'm waiting for my tea," Ghastly said, dismayed.

"We don't have time for tea. When we visited Aranmore Farm, I left my number with Paddy Hanratty in case he noticed any unusual activity on his land. Paddy just called. He said he saw a dark-haired man wandering around."

"You think it was Jaron Gallow?" Valkyrie asked. "Or Batu?"

"I do. Paddy overheard him on his phone, saying something about preparing the site, and then he left without telling Paddy what he was doing there."

"That's not good," Ghastly said, a little grumpily.

"What's wrong?" Valkyrie frowned.

Skulduggery looked at her. "It sounds like the Diablerie know precisely where the gate will open. If things were going our way, they'd have to spend a few hours roaming the farm to find the exact spot before trying to open it. Obviously, and in keeping with our lot in life, things are *not* going our way."

"So if they already know where the gate will open," Valkyrie said, "and if they somehow get their hands on Fletcher, they can get straight down to business."

"Indeed they can."

"What do we do?"

"The first thing we do is know what our enemy knows, so we find it ourselves. Or rather, Fletcher does."

They walked into the main part of the shop, where Tanith was sitting upside-down on the ceiling and looking annoyed. Fletcher was gazing up at her, lovestruck.

Skulduggery shook his head. "Oh, for God's sake..."

19

THE MAN WHO WOULD BE KING

he room was just another room in the conference centre. In the other rooms, business people were showing flow charts and diagrams to their clients, but there were no flow charts in this room. In this room, nine people sat around a long table and they were all looking at the bald man standing at the window.

Mr Bliss looked out over Dublin. "What you're talking about here is illegal," he said.

"We have no choice," a man with golden eyes responded.

"We can see where Guild is taking us, and we have no wish to follow him down that road. The Sanctuary needs a new leader."

"There are those who are more qualified than I."

A woman in grey shook her head. "But they want the job too much."

"Replacing Guild would provoke an international scramble for power."

"Not if his replacement had international respect. Bliss, if we overthrow Guild and you become the Grand Mage, it will strengthen our standing. The Councils around the world know you. Many of them fear you."

"I have no desire to lead."

The man with the golden eyes spoke again. "Maybe it's not your choice. Someone has to make a stand. Someone has to oppose these new laws Guild is intent on introducing. I am sorry, my friend, but you are the only one who can do this without starting a war."

Bliss was silent. "If we do this, we do it my way."

"Of course."

"And we wait until this current crisis is over."

"Agreed."

Bliss turned to them and nodded. "Very well."

20

ARANMORE FARM

Skulduggery drove Ghastly's van, with Valkyrie in the passenger seat. Ghastly, Tanith and Fletcher sat on the cushions in the rear. No matter how sharp the corner they turned or how deep the pothole they plunged into, Ghastly and Tanith remained perfectly still. Fletcher, on the other hand, was being thrown about like an old shoe in a washing machine, and he did not appreciate it.

They reached Aranmore and drove up to the farmhouse. By the looks of things it hadn't rained much here. Valkyrie was getting tired of the rain.

The van stopped and Skulduggery made sure his scarf and sunglasses were on securely. He pulled his hat down low and got out. Valkyrie scrambled out the other side as Paddy walked over to them, a shovel in his hand, face red from recent exertion.

"I called you because I said I would if I saw anything suspicious," he said, sounding annoyed. "Not because I wanted you to come back."

"We understand that," said Skulduggery, "but we had little choice."

"You don't get it. I'm not going to sell this land, to you, or that other fella, or *anyone*."

"We're not trying to buy your home."

"Good, because you won't."

Valkyrie stayed quiet. On the way over here they had discussed the best way to approach the old man. They needed him to leave before anything bad happened, but they had both agreed that he wasn't the type to be scared off. So they'd decided to tell him the truth.

"Do you follow any particular faith?" Skulduggery asked.

Paddy raised his eyebrows. "You're not trying to sell me a bible, are you?"

"No."

"Then you want to convert me? That's very flattering, but

look at me. Is it really worth your while?"

"We're not here to convert you," Skulduggery said, gentle amusement in his voice.

Paddy looked at them both. "Are you purposefully trying to baffle me?"

"Not at all. The bafflement is effortless."

Paddy sighed. "Yes. I follow a particular faith. I would never say that I'm *overly* religious, but—"

"Then you're willing to accept that there are aspects to this life that are beyond our current understanding?"

Paddy shrugged. "The older you get, the more you realise you don't actually know. So, yes, I accept that."

"And what about magic?"

"Bunny-from-a-top-hat magic?"

"No."

"You mean real magic? Do I believe real magic exists?"

"Do you?"

Paddy paused a moment. "Funny you should say that. My father, Pat Hanratty, he believed. At least, I think he did. From little things he said when I was growing up, I got that impression. Why do you ask?"

Skulduggery looked at Valkyrie, and Valkyrie clicked her fingers and summoned a flame.

Paddy's face cracked and Valkyrie realised he was smiling. "Well, that *is* impressive, I have to say. How do you do it?"

"Magic," Valkyrie said and pulled back her sleeve to show that it was no trick.

Paddy's smile faded a little. "I'm... I'm not sure I understand..."

"Your father was right," Skulduggery said. "Real magic exists. Real *sorcerers* exist. Paddy, there are bad people who want to change the world, and they need this land to do it."

Paddy shook his head slowly. "I don't know what you want..."

"This land is important," Valkyrie said, extinguishing the flame. "This is where it will all happen."

"Where *what* will happen?"

"A gateway will open," Skulduggery told him, "between this world and another, and the Faceless Ones will come through."

"Faceless...?

"They're the bad guys. We're the good guys."

"No offence," Paddy said, "but I think you're both a little insane."

Skulduggery took off his sunglasses, and his scarf, and his hat, and Paddy stared at him.

"No," the old man said. "Apparently, *I'm* the insane one."

Valkyrie watched him carefully. His face was pale and his eyes were wide, and she readied herself to rush forward if he passed out. But instead of passing out, Paddy pressed his lips together and nodded.

"All right. OK. Fair enough. You're a skeleton."

"I am."

"Right so. Just making sure. And you, are you magic too?"

"I am," Valkyrie said.

"Right. I might need to sit down."

"Before you do that," Skulduggery said, "I want to introduce you to some friends of ours."

The side door of the van opened and Ghastly and Tanith got out, followed by Fletcher.

Paddy stared at Ghastly. "What happened to you?"

"I was cursed before I was born," Ghastly told him.

"That'd do it all right. And you're all magic then? Even the boy with the ridiculous hair?"

"I'm Fletcher Renn," Fletcher scowled. "I'm the most important person in the world right now."

Paddy looked at Fletcher, then at Skulduggery and turned to Valkyrie. "Does magic automatically make you an insufferable pain, or am I just lucky to get two at the same time?"

"Just lucky," she grinned.

He shook his head in wonder. "My father would have loved

this. He would have really loved this. And my land is important, is it?"

"Very," Skulduggery said and turned to Fletcher. He told him what to do and Fletcher looked at him sceptically, but eventually did as he was instructed. He raised his hands and walked slowly forward with his eyes closed. Skulduggery followed.

Leaving Tanith with Ghastly, Valkyrie and Paddy walked along behind.

"Do you still need to sit down?" she asked.

"I think I'm OK, thank you."

She looked at the shovel in his hands. "Working hard?"

He nodded. "Digging. Do you have a spell for digging?"

"Uh, not that I know of..."

"That would have been handy. I wasted so much of my life digging holes with a shovel. I probably wasted so much of my life doing other things as well. Life would have been easier with magic. What's it like?"

For a moment Valkyrie was going to downplay everything, but the look in his eyes made her tell the truth. "It's amazing," she admitted.

"How do you know I can even do this?" she heard Fletcher ask.

"You can do this because it's something you can do," Skulduggery said. "You'll start to feel a tingling sensation when you're at a spot where the walls of reality are thinnest."

"Tingling?"

"Or tickling. Or burning."

"Burning?"

"Or you might get a toothache or a nosebleed or you might have a seizure – it's hard to say."

"I might have a seizure?"

"Don't worry, I'll stop you from swallowing your tongue."

Fletcher scowled.

"Can I ask you something?" Paddy said quietly. "When you meet the people you used to know, like other kids your age, what do you feel? Do you despise them?"

"Why would I despise them?"

"Someone who can run fast dismisses the people slower than he is. What if it's someone who can run *really* fast? Then the slower people become little more than an annoyance, and then an irritation. Superiority breeds contempt."

"I don't agree with that at all," Valkyrie said, shaking her head. "I can do some things other people can't, but those other people can do things I can't. It evens itself out."

Paddy smiled. "But those other people might be better than

you at schoolwork, or tennis, or fixing bicycles... whereas you have magic. I wouldn't call that a level playing field."

"Well, OK, I'd agree with that, but it still doesn't mean that mortals have to be despised."

"Mortals? That's what you call us?"

Valkyrie blushed. "It's not, like, an official term or anything. I mean, it is accurate because you're mortal, but so are we, so..."

He couldn't help but smile. "I think my point has been proven."

"What? No, it hasn't."

"What do magic people call themselves? Magicians?"

"Sorcerers," she said. "Or mages."

"So magic people view themselves as mages and everyone else as mortals. And that doesn't sound like a group of people elevating themselves to godhood to you?"

"Sorcerers don't believe that they're gods."

"Why shouldn't they? They have the power of gods, don't they? They have magic at their fingertips. Their affairs affect the world. If you fail in your current 'mission', what will happen?"

She hesitated. "The world will end."

Paddy laughed. "Wonderful! Beautiful! Do you see it? The importance of your work! A mortal fails at his job and what happens to him? He doesn't get his Christmas bonus? He gets demoted? Fired? And life continues around him. But if a mage fails, if you and your friends fail, everybody dies. Why shouldn't you think of yourselves as gods? You hold the fate of the world in your hands. If that's not godlike, I don't know what is."

"Can we change the subject?"

"To what?"

"Anything that doesn't make me sound like a crazy person?"

He laughed and they walked closer to Skulduggery as Fletcher announced that he was feeling something. They had crossed the yard, standing in the long grass. Fletcher's eyes were open and his fingers were splayed. His steps grew smaller as he honed in on the spot.

"It's a buzzing," he said, "in my fingers, like I get when I teleport. OK, now I can feel it all over." He turned slightly. "It's there. I know it is. Right there."

To Valkyrie, he was staring at empty space, but his voice was strong and his eyes were sure.

"What's so special about here?" Paddy asked. "It's just the same as anywhere else."

"You can't see it," Fletcher said scornfully, "but I can *feel* it. It's amazing. I can open it right now."

"No, you can't," Skulduggery said. "But well done for finding it."

"No, I can do more than that," Fletcher insisted. "I can go through."

"You can't and I wouldn't advise trying," Skulduggery said, and he'd barely uttered the last word when Fletcher disappeared.

Paddy jumped back. "Good God!"

Valkyrie spun to Skulduggery. "Could he have done it? Could he have gone through?"

"I... I don't know," Skulduggery said.

Valkyrie's hand flew to her mouth. "If he did go through, he's in there with the Faceless Ones. They'll tear him apart."

Skulduggery shook his head. "He didn't have the Isthmus Anchor. Without that, there's no way to open the gate, let alone go through. No, it's impossible."

"So where is he?" Paddy asked.

Valkyrie's phone rang and she put it to her ear.

"Hey, Val," Tanith said on the other end, "did you happen to lose something? Not too bright, vacant expression on his face, silly hair? Ring any bells?"

Valkyrie sighed in relief. "Skulduggery, he's back at the van."

"I'm going," Skulduggery said as he strode quickly past her, "to kill him."

*

They got back to Dublin and Fletcher still hadn't said one word. Skulduggery had spent close to five minutes berating him for what he had tried to do, and by the end of it, even Fletcher's hair had wilted into a sullen pile. It had been the most fun Valkyrie had had in ages.

Ghastly needed to return to Kenspeckle for a check-up and Tanith agreed to go with him. Now that the two of them were back in the game, Skulduggery was feeling better about keeping Fletcher at the labs. When he said this, Fletcher narrowed his eyes and spoke up for the first time in half an hour.

"This is feeling a lot like everyone is babysitting me."

"That's because they are," Valkyrie smiled.

They left them just as Fletcher was asking Tanith if she'd tuck him in tonight.

"What's our next move?" Valkyrie asked as they walked to the Purple Menace.

"We have to prepare for the worst," said Skulduggery. "If, despite our best efforts, they get the gate open and the Faceless Ones return, we're going to need the only weapon powerful enough to kill them."

She frowned. "Which is?"

"The Sceptre of the Ancients."

He got in behind the wheel, and she climbed in the passenger side and buckled her seatbelt. "Skulduggery, you *broke* the Sceptre."

"No, I broke the black crystal that *powered* it. In theory, all we need is another black crystal and we have a weapon capable of killing a god."

"Do you *know* where to get another black crystal?"

He started the car and they moved off. "Not exactly."

"Do other black crystals exist?"

"Almost certainly."

"How do we find one?"

"Research, my dear Valkyrie."

Her shoulders slumped. "I hate research. It's almost as bad as homework."

"When was the last time *you* did homework?"

"I *always* do my homework."

"Your reflection does your homework."

"But I still have to suffer through the *memory* of it. That's practically the same thing."

"I hear millions of schoolchildren around the world crying in sympathy for you."

"Oh, shut up."

"But don't worry, your research will be fun."

"How do you work that one out?"

"Your uncle was planning to write a book about the Sceptre before he died. Knowing Gordon, that means he made quite a lot of notes."

Valkyrie's mood lifted. "So all I have to do is read through his notes?"

"You read his notes, I'll do some research of my own in the library and we'll see who comes up with an answer first. Agreed?"

Valkyrie kept her grin to herself. "Oh, all right," she said, trying to sound irritable. Her uncle had been dead for two years, and he'd had a treasure trove of secrets locked away behind his study in his old house. Valkyrie loved going through the secret room and she welcomed any opportunity to do so.

Besides, she hadn't talked to her dead uncle in *weeks*.

21

OPPORTUNITY RINGS

he Sea Hag heard someone ringing her bell and rose to the surface of the lake. She poked her head out, making sure it wasn't the skeleton and the girl, back to inflict more pain.

She emerged from the lake and looked down at a man standing by the shore. "Who disturbs me?" she demanded.

"I do," the man said.

"What is your name?"

"I am Batu."

"That is not your name."

"It is the name I have chosen and so it is my name."

The Sea Hag sighed. "Why do you disturb me?"

The man, Batu, looked at her. "You have been wronged, my lady. Fifty years ago I gave you a corpse, allowed it to slip beneath your waters and now it has been stolen from you."

The Sea Hag snarled. "I am aware of what happened. What concern is it of yours?"

"I can offer you an opportunity," the man who called himself Batu said, "an opportunity to pay back the ones who have wronged you."

"How?"

"It would mean moving you from this lake to the sea, my lady. Would you be interested in such an opportunity?"

The Sea Hag stared at him. "You would move me back to the sea? You could do that?"

"The world has changed since you were first trapped here. There are water tanks big enough to hold you and vehicles powerful enough to transport you. I ask again, my lady – would you be interested?"

"Yes," said the Sea Hag, smiling for the first time in a hundred years. "Oh, yes."

22

CONVERSATIONS WITH A LATE UNCLE

The Purple Menace pulled into Gordon's estate, and Valkyrie took the door key from her pocket and slid it into the lock. The alarm beeped insistently until she entered the code.

Gordon's house, for it would always be *his* house and never hers, not even on the day she turned eighteen, was big and quiet and empty.

"I'll start in here," Skulduggery said, walking in behind her and heading for the living room. "If you want to start in the study, hopefully we'll find something by morning."

"Hopefully," Valkyrie said and climbed the stairs. She went into the study, closed the door behind her, then made straight for the large bookcase along the wall. She pulled back the false book, the bookcase swung open and she passed through into the small room beyond. For once, she didn't even glance at the objects and artefacts on the shelves around her. The Echo Stone in the cradle on the table started to glow and a slightly overweight man in shirtsleeves shimmered into view. He grinned.

"Hello there," he said. "I take it, by the serious look on your face, that this is business and you haven't just dropped by because you miss your dear dead uncle?"

Valkyrie raised an eyebrow. "Is that who you are now? You're Gordon? Not just a recording of his personality?"

"That's who I am," Gordon said proudly.

"And you're sure about this? You're not going to change your mind halfway through this conversation?"

"I have come to a decision. The flesh and blood Gordon may have imprinted me on to this Echo Stone, but I continue to learn, to experience, to evolve. I make my own memories now. I am as real a person as he was, and because we were the same person, I am now him, now that he's not. It all comes down to philosophy really. I think, therefore I am, I think."

"That's good to know," Valkyrie nodded. "To be honest with you, I see you as my real uncle too."

"Well, that's that then."

"Does this mean I can tell Skulduggery about you now?"

"Ah," he said. "Not yet. I... I'm not ready for other people to know what I have been... reduced to. But it won't be long now before you can share me, I promise."

"Well, good. I don't like keeping this secret."

"I understand and I appreciate it. So tell me, how are your parents?"

"They're good. It's their anniversary tomorrow so they're heading to Paris in the morning."

"Ah, Paris," Gordon said wistfully. "I've always felt a real affinity for the French, you know. One of my books was set in France, among the cathedrals and along the Champs-Élysées."

She nodded. "*Braineater*. It was one of your best. Gordon, have you ever heard of a man called Batu?"

"I don't think so, no."

"We think he's behind a series of murders, and he wants to use a Teleporter to open a gateway between this reality and whatever reality the Faceless Ones are stuck in."

"Is that possible?"

"Skulduggery seems to be taking it seriously, so I imagine it is."

"So what can I do to help?"

"If the Faceless Ones return, we're going to need the Sceptre to stop them."

"But didn't you tell me that Skulduggery broke it?"

"The *crystal* doesn't work any more, but if we got *another* crystal..."

"Ah. And you want to know if I found out anything about them in my research."

"Exactly."

"Well, you're in luck, because I found out a lot."

"Do you know where we could get one?"

"I do as a matter of fact."

"Really? Where?"

Gordon pointed down and Valkyrie frowned.

"In your shoes?"

"In the *caves*."

She blinked. "Seriously? There are black crystals in the caves beneath this house? Mind telling me why?"

"This house was built over the mouth of the caves hundreds of years ago, by a sorcerer named Anathem Mire."

"Skulduggery told me about him. He used to throw his

enemies into the caves and let the monsters at them."

"He was not, as you can imagine, a very nice man."

"Did he worship the Faceless Ones?"

"No, but he studied them. He studied the literature and the history of the Faceless Ones and the Ancients because he wanted power. He bought the land, built the house and made some tentative efforts to explore the caves. He wanted the secrets the caves hold, and they *do* hold a lot of secrets."

"Like what?"

"Why are the creatures down there unaffected by magic? Is it something in the air? In the rocks? Is it because of the mix of minerals? Is it something else? There is no explanation for it, Valkyrie. We simply do not know. According to his journals, Mire made seven expeditions into the caves. The first had a ten-man crew. Mire was the only one to return. In the second, fifteen sorcerers were lost. Again, Anathem Mire was the sole survivor. He realised that the larger the group, the fiercer the attacks. The creatures were drawn to the magic.

"Once he made this discovery, the expeditions became smaller and more successful. Mire continued to be the only one to emerge alive, but only because he was killing his colleagues to make sure they kept their mouths shut.

"On his sixth journey into the caves, he found a vein of

black crystals. He instructed one of his party to take a sample, but when the sorcerer laid one finger on an exposed crystal, he was consumed by what Mire described as 'black lightning' and turned to dust."

"Do you know where this vein was?"

"There's a map in the last of his journals, on one of the shelves in here. That's the journal that prompted me to buy the house in the first place actually, so I could explore the caves for myself. I never got as far as the black crystals, mind you. Because I had no magic, I was largely ignored by the creatures, but even so, there were a few close calls that convinced me to leave the adventuring to the adventurers."

"That guy who tried to take a crystal was killed. How are we supposed to get one?"

"That is where your Ancient heritage will come in useful. It was the Faceless Ones who mined the crystal in the first place, this is true, but the Ancients made themselves invisible to its senses and thus immune to its power."

"They weren't *immune*. They used the Sceptre to kill each other."

"Ah, but that was when the crystal was embedded in the Sceptre, when its destructive power could be directed at whomever and whatever the wielder desired. What we're talking about is the crystal in its original form. I think it reacted the way it did and killed that expedition member because, unlike you, the expedition member didn't have Ancient blood."

Valkyrie looked at him. "You think?"

"I'm relatively sure."

"Relatively?"

"Very relatively. Virtually positive."

"And you're willing to stake my life on that?"

Gordon smiled reassuringly, then the smile dropped and he shook his head. "God, no."

"But it's your opinion that I'll be OK, right?"

"Don't do it. It's a silly idea."

"But still, that's your theory?"

"A theory is the academic equivalent of a *guess*. How would I know? Don't do it."

"Where's the journal? Is that it on the shelf behind you?"

"No, it isn't."

"Does it have *The Journal of Anathem Mire* written along the side?"

Gordon hesitated. "No."

Valkyrie stepped towards it and Gordon barred her way. She took a deep breath, then put her hand through his face.

"Hey!" he exclaimed. "Stop that!"

She brought her hand back, the journal clasped in her fingers and Gordon scowled.

"That wasn't fair."

"Sorry."

"You just can't go around putting your hand through people's faces. It's rude for one thing. Deeply unsettling for another."

Valkyrie put the journal on the table, opened it and flicked through the yellowing pages. "Really am sorry."

"Something like that, such an obvious demonstration of what is substantial, and what isn't, what is real, and what isn't – it's enough to make you question yourself, you know?"

She took a folded piece of parchment from the book and opened it. The map of the cave system was incomplete, with vast areas of blank space between known trails and the supposed edge of the underground tunnels.

"A man is only as effective as the effect he has on his surroundings," Gordon was saying. "And if a man is not effective, if his very *being* is as insubstantial as thought, then what is this man? Is he a man? Or is he merely the *thought* of a man?"

Valkyrie traced her finger from the words *black crystals*,

captured in a circle, back along a trail and through all its intersections, back to the cave opening. By the scale Mire had provided, she judged it to be a little under two miles west.

"I suppose I couldn't fool myself forever," Gordon said, dejection in his voice. "I'm a fake. A fraud. A shadow of the real Gordon Edgley. I'm a mockery of a great, great man."

Valkyrie folded the map into the journal. "What's that you're saying?"

"Nothing," he grumbled.

"Thanks for this," she said, leaving the room. The bookshelf closed behind her and she hurried down the stairs and into the living room.

Skulduggery was standing on a chair, looking through the books on the top shelf.

"Got it," Valkyrie said.

His head tilted. "No. Impossible. You can't have found anything."

She grinned. "There are black crystals in the caves below us," she told him. "Apparently, I'm the only one able to touch them because of the whole Ancient thing. I even have a map. How impressed are you right now?"

There was a moment of silence. "You're such an unbelievable show-off."

"I learned it all from you."

Skulduggery got off the chair and took the journal from her. "I don't show off. I merely demonstrate my abilities at opportune times." He examined the map. "It looks like we're going into the caves."

"Now? Just the two of us?"

"Too many people will draw too much attention, and we simply don't have the time to waste. The Diablerie have been one step ahead of us all along. It's time that changed."

The key rotated in the lock and the floor of Gordon's cellar opened. Valkyrie clicked on her flashlight and followed Skulduggery down the stone steps that led to the caves.

Skulduggery read the air around them at regular intervals to make sure they weren't being tracked. Three times they had to turn off their flashlights and crouch in the darkness until the path was clear. Valkyrie kept a wary eye out for any dangling vines.

Narrow beams of sunlight, caught up above and cast down below, illuminated their surroundings. Mire's map proved to be precise, but the further they travelled the colder it got, and Valkyrie was glad that she'd taken one of Gordon's overcoats to wear over her sleeveless tunic.

They followed the tunnel as far as it went, then had to crawl through a gap in the wall. Valkyrie had images of the entire cave system crashing down on top of her. She didn't like tight spaces. They made her want to lash out, to flail for no reason. She didn't like them one little bit.

Skulduggery helped her out the other side and they consulted the map again.

"The crystals should be around this corner," he said. They looked at the corner in question. "Bear in mind," he continued, "that this is where things usually go spectacularly wrong."

"I've noticed."

They turned off their flashlights as they approached the corner. The only sound was their own footsteps.

"Do you want to go first?" Skulduggery whispered.

"Why would I want to do that?" Valkyrie whispered back.

"I just thought you might want to prove something to me."

"Like what?"

"I don't know, maybe that you're as brave as I am, or as capable, or maybe something to do with not needing a man to protect you."

She shrugged. "I'm OK with all that."

"Really?"

"Really. Poke your head around, see if there's a monster waiting for us."

Skulduggery muttered something, then peered around the corner. Valkyrie prepared herself to either hit something or run.

"Well," Skulduggery said. "This is unexpected."

23

ANATHEM MIRE

The tunnel opened into a huge cavern, the size of a football stadium. Shafts of light pierced the ceiling like stars in the night sky and fell upon the two-storey house that stood before them. Valkyrie stared at it, somewhat stunned.

"That looks familiar," she eventually remarked.

"It does," Skulduggery agreed.

"That looks a whole lot like Gordon's house."

"It does."

They stayed where they were and looked at the house. It

wasn't an *exact* twin. It was thinner, and the windows were too narrow, and the door wasn't in the proper place. The roof was a lot higher and the angles were wrong. It was like a memory of Gordon's house, filtered through a bad dream.

Valkyrie didn't like asking obvious questions. In fact, she hated it. There were times, however, when the obvious questions were the only ones available.

"How do you think it got here?" she asked.

"I don't know," Skulduggery answered. "Maybe it got lost."

They walked towards it. The house was dark. Some of the curtains were closed. Skulduggery didn't bother scouting around. He knocked on the front door and waited, and when no one came out, he pushed the door open.

"Hello?" he called. "Anyone home?"

There was no answer, so he took out his gun and stepped in. Valkyrie followed. It was somehow colder in here than it was in the caves and she shivered. If it wasn't for the flashlights, they would have been enveloped in pitch-black.

There were no power lines down here, no access to electricity, so when Valkyrie flicked the light switch, she wasn't expecting the diffusion of sickly green that rose in the dust-covered light bulbs.

"Interesting," Skulduggery murmured.

It was an unsettling feeling, to stand in a place familiar yet alien. The staircase that, in Gordon's house, was solid and wide, was here narrow and twisted. There were paintings on the walls, images of depravity and torture.

They moved into the living room and Skulduggery turned on a few lamps. That same sickly green changed the absolute darkness into an unhealthy murk. The colour was making Valkyrie nauseous.

There was an armchair and a sofa by the cold fireplace, and an ornate mirror above the mantelpiece. Valkyrie nudged Skulduggery and pointed. Someone was sitting in the armchair.

"Excuse me," Skulduggery said.

The figure didn't stir. All they could see was part of an arm, and the top of a head.

They moved slowly to the sofa, giving the armchair a wide berth. Valkyrie saw a shoe now. Then a knee. A man was sitting in the chair, his right hand on the armrest, his left in his lap. His suit was old-fashioned and stained with something dark around the chest. His moustache drooped over the corners of his mouth, down to either side of his chin. His hair was dark. He looked to be in his fifties. His eyes were open and gazing at nothing.

"Hi," Skulduggery said in greeting. His tone was warm and

friendly, but he hadn't put his gun away. "I am Skulduggery Pleasant and this is my partner, Valkyrie Cain. According to our map, there is a vein of black crystals in the rocks around this cavern. Have you seen any?"

The man in the armchair didn't look up.

"The reason I ask," Skulduggery continued, "is that we really need one and time is of the essence. If anyone would know where to find these crystals, I'd say it would be you, am I right?"

Skulduggery nodded, as if the man had answered.

"This is a nice house by the way. We know of a similar one, up on the surface. The *real* one actually. This is like a half-remembered copy, but that doesn't mean it's any less of a home. I'm sure you're wonderfully happy here, Anathem."

Valkyrie turned her head to Skulduggery. "What?"

"I'm assuming that's Mire," he told her. "He came down here, all those hundreds of years ago, intending to continue his exploration. Obviously, he was wounded, as evidenced by the blood on his clothes, by either a fellow explorer or one of the creatures who inhabit these caves, but he didn't want to die here. Who would? It's dark and cold and miserable. So, being a conjurer of some power, he conjured this house, so that he could pass away in more familiar surroundings."

"This house is made of magic?"

"Can't you feel it? There's a certain *tingle* to everything."

Valkyrie looked at the man. "He's been sitting there for the last few hundred years, slowly bleeding to death?"

"No, no. He's quite dead by now."

"Then why hasn't the house disappeared?"

"Because he hasn't left."

Skulduggery stepped forward.

Valkyrie frowned. "What are you doing?"

"Waking him up."

Skulduggery kicked, hard. The chair tipped over backwards, taking the body with it, but the body that hit the ground was decayed and mouldy, and it left an indistinct after-image of the moustached man, sitting on thin air. His eyes flickered, like he'd finally noticed something different, and slowly, he looked up.

"Trespassers," he hissed, face contorting, and his image blurred as he stood. "Interlopers!"

"Calm down," Skulduggery said.

Anathem Mire screeched and went for them, and Valkyrie jerked back and lashed out as he charged straight through her.

"He's a ghost," Skulduggery said. "He can't touch you."

Mire's form turned and came around. His face took shape. "This is *my* house," he snarled. "You are intruders!"

The sofa picked itself up and hurtled at them. Skulduggery

hauled Valkyrie out of its path.

"The sofa *can* touch you," he told her and pushed at the air, deflecting the table that rushed at them from behind.

Mire spread his arms wide. "I will bring this house down upon you," he said as the house started to shake.

Skulduggery ran to the large mirror over the fireplace and took it down, turned and swung it into Mire. The glass soaked him up and Skulduggery pressed the mirror against the wall.

Valkyrie had read about mirrors being the only thing able to capture souls and spirits. The fact that she didn't have to *ask* what had just happened made her glow a little inside.

"We're not looking for a fight," Skulduggery said, loud enough for Mire's ghost to hear. "We just want a single black crystal."

"The crystals are *mine!*" Mire shouted. "Release me, demon!"

"I'm not a demon, I'm a sorcerer. Like you. We didn't come here to hurt you."

"Trickery! Lies! You're another demon of the caves, another monster, sent here to torture me! To drive me mad!"

Skulduggery sighed and looked at Valkyrie. "Take a look around. If he's claiming ownership of his surroundings, maybe he's managed to get a hold of some crystals."

She nodded, and left Skulduggery to try and reason with the

ghost. She walked into the kitchen, turning on lamps as she went. A giant black stove stood under a chimney that didn't exist in Gordon's house. Valkyrie opened a cupboard, and an insect the length of her finger scuttled around the edge of the door and vanished up her sleeve. She jumped away, ripping the overcoat off and throwing it down, but the insect was on her bare arm, climbing to her shoulder. She swatted at it, but it hung on and darted inside her tunic. She tore the tunic open, reached in and grabbed it, feeling it squirming in her grip. Valkyrie flung it to the other side of the room and she flailed with revulsion.

Once she was done flailing, she picked up Gordon's coat, dusted it off and checked to make sure nothing else had sneaked in. She put it on, buttoned her tunic and smoothed down her hair. *That*, she told herself, *was revolting*.

She opened the rest of the cupboards much quicker, taking her hand away faster and faster each time. She had a horrible vision of a bat-like thing flapping out at her, so she stood to one side as she did it. There were no black crystals in the cupboards, no more insects and thankfully no bat-like things.

Valkyrie left the kitchen, glaring at the corner where she'd thrown the insect, and climbed the stairs. They creaked with every footstep. The bedrooms were in roughly the same places as Gordon's bedrooms, but the beds were all four-poster, and the headboards had apparently been carved by a degenerate. The bathroom looked uninviting and the light didn't work, so she didn't enter.

She stepped into the study. Instead of a desk and bookshelves and awards, there was a single rocking chair in the middle of the room. The window looked out across the cavern. It was not a breathtaking sight.

Valkyrie ran her hands over the wall that opened to the secret room. She knocked, listening to the sounds, but none of them sounded hollow. Disappointed, she left the study and carefully descended the staircase. When she got back to the living room, the ghost was out of the mirror and standing beside Skulduggery.

He had calmed down an awful lot.

"The crystals are not in this cavern," Mire was saying. His voice was unsteady. "I purposely detailed this part of the map incorrectly, to stop others from gaining from my work. But they are close."

"Can you take us to them?" Skulduggery asked.

"I dare not leave this house. Whatever dark power lives in these caves, it sustains me, even in this spirit form. But I cannot venture from here."

"Then will you tell us where the crystals are?"

"What is the point? You will be turned to ash as soon as you touch them."

"We have a way around that. Will you help us?"

Valkyrie stepped in and Mire heard her and turned.

"She lives," the ghost said, its face showing something akin to awe.

"I told you," Skulduggery said.

"I had almost forgotten what one looked like."

"*One?*"

"One of *them*. One of the *living*. These caves have been my home for so long. I have been *dead* for so long, alone down here. I stay away from the creatures of course. Some of them can hurt me, even in this form. These caves are cursed for sorcerers."

He moved closer to Valkyrie.

"You are splendid," he murmured.

She raised an eyebrow to Skulduggery and he quickly stepped between them. "Will you help us?" he asked again.

The ghost dragged its gaze away from Valkyrie and looked at Skulduggery. His head blurred with the movement. "Of course," he said, and the wall behind him shifted and grew a door. The door opened. "Beware. The crystals kill."

Mire stayed where he was as Valkyrie followed Skulduggery through to a tunnel with walls of rock. Embedded in those walls were thin veins of crystals, glowing with a black light.

Skulduggery looked at her. "And you're absolutely *sure* you won't be harmed?"

"Absolutely."

"How do you know?"

She reached out and touched the nearest crystal. "See?"

He stared at her. "That was an amazingly foolish thing to do."

"*Potentially* amazingly foolish," she corrected. "It was a theory of Gordon's I read about in his notes."

"He could have been wrong, you know."

"I have faith in his theories," she said with a shrug. "Give me the chisel."

He took the chisel from his jacket and handed it over. She lined it up against a crystal, then, using the butt of Skulduggery's gun, she hammered at it, barely making a scratch.

"Hold it in place," Skulduggery told her. He flexed his fingers and swung his hand, and a concentrated blast of air hit the chisel like a piledriver. A chunk of crystal flew free, a little bigger than the one that had been housed in the Sceptre. Valkyrie wrapped it in cloth. Skulduggery held out a small box and she placed it within, then he closed the box and put it in his jacket pocket. She gave him back his gun and chisel.

"Easy," she said.

"Never do anything like that again. You could have been turned to dust, and then I'd have to explain to your parents why they were burying their beloved daughter in a matchbox."

"Kenspeckle would never let you hear the end of it either."

Skulduggery looked at her as he led the way back to the door. "I've been meaning to ask you, with everything Kenspeckle has been saying – do *you* think I should treat you differently?"

"No," she said at once.

"Don't be so quick to answer."

"Nooo..." she said slowly.

"You are amusing to me, but the question remains. Maybe I should leave you in the car on occasion."

"But I never stay in the car," she reminded him.

"That's because I've never insisted before."

"It wouldn't make any difference."

"I can be very commanding when I want to be."

"Yeah, but not really though."

He sighed and they emerged into the living room. Mire's body was still on the ground near the overturned chair and his ghost was standing, looking at them.

"You're not dead," he said. "That is a surprise."

"Thank you for your co-operation," Skulduggery said. "Is

there anything we can do for you in exchange?"

"Waking me was enough."

"What will you do now?" Valkyrie asked.

Mire smiled. "I will be happy, I think. Yes, I think I will."

"I hope we meet again, Anathem," said Skulduggery. "You are an... interesting being."

Mire bowed and as he did so, he caught Valkyrie's eye. She gave him a polite nod in return and followed Skulduggery to the front door.

"China owns the Sceptre," he said as he stepped out of the house, "so she'll be the only one able to use it. Assuming it works when we replace the crystal."

"And if it doesn't?"

"If it doesn't, I'm sure I'll come up with something brilliant to—"

The front door slammed shut just as Valkyrie reached it and she whirled. Mire drifted to her, a smile that had been neglected for centuries struggling to form on the memory of his face.

"You are not leaving," he said. "The skeleton can return to the surface, but *you* are mine."

24

THE CHANGING HOUSE

She heard Skulduggery slam his fist against the door from the other side. "Valkyrie?" he called. "Open the door."

"I'm *not* yours," she said to Mire. "I have to leave now."

"You will never leave me," Mire responded.

She stalked by him, into the living room, reaching the first window just as the wall melted into it. The other windows followed, enveloped by the walls, sealing off her escape.

She turned angrily. "You *can't* keep me here!"

"But I can. You are living. You are breathing. This house

hasn't seen a living, breathing person for centuries."

"This house doesn't *exist*! *You* don't exist! You're a *ghost*!"

Valkyrie clicked her fingers, summoning fire.

"You cannot hurt me," the ghost said.

She went over to Mire's body and held the flame close. "If you do not let me out, I'll burn your corpse. I will."

"You will stay here with me?" the ghost asked. "You will keep me company? Tell me of the world above? You will be queen of this darkness?"

"*I'll burn you.*"

Mire smiled, and the body reached out and grabbed her wrist. Valkyrie cried out in shock, losing the flame. The body got to its feet and forced her back against the wall. She swung a punch, her fist colliding with the left side of the body's face, and the cheekbone collapsed into the head. She withdrew her hand in disgust. Bits of the face were stuck to her knuckles.

"I can feel your life," Mire said, ignoring her actions. "It fills *me* too. Together we will rule the cold and the empty places."

Valkyrie looked at the ghost and struggled to keep her voice even. "I don't want to," she said. "I'm still alive and I want to go back."

The ghost shook his head and the body did likewise. "The

light hurts you. The sun burns you. Once you are my queen, you won't have to worry about these things."

She tore herself away and ran through the ghost as his form scattered and regrouped. The body spun on its heel and lurched after her.

Valkyrie got to the hall and took the stairs two at a time. She glanced back as the body clutched the banister and started climbing, its feet clumsy on the shallow steps. When she reached the landing, the ghost was already there, watching her.

"There is nowhere for you to run," he said. "I am master of this house and I will make you safe. You are my guest."

She went to Gordon's study, but the door was locked. She kicked it, but it didn't even rattle in its frame. The ghost smiled at her.

Valkyrie clicked her fingers and hurled a fireball at Mire's body. The fireball struck its chest and the body stumbled. It beat at the flames and lost its balance, hitting the banister and falling through. Mire's ghost hissed and he was forced to divert his attention away from Valkyrie. The moment he did so, she slammed her shoulder against the door and this time it burst open. She fell in, then pushed at the air and the window smashed.

"You do not want to be my enemy," Mire warned.

Valkyrie lunged, but the window moved, sliding up the wall and across the ceiling until it was raining broken glass down on top of her. The wallpaper changed, becoming a thousand faces, all Mire's, glaring at her and echoing his words.

"My enemies suffer," the ghost and his thousand faces said. "My enemies bleed. They scream and beg and cry."

The window slid from the ceiling and then horizontally down one wall, offering glimpses of the rooms that lay beyond, as it moved to the floor and zipped towards Valkyrie. It stopped under her feet and she fell through, but managed to grab the edge. Her legs dangled. Mire's body was below her in the kitchen, reaching up to try and grab her boots.

She kicked away its hands and pulled herself up. The room was changing like crazy. Colours swept through the walls, which moved in and then out again, like the lungs of a great beast. The window shrank to the size of an eye. Carpets sprang up from between the floorboards and then withered and died. Anathem Mire was angry and losing control of his house.

The blank wall, the wall that led to the secret room in Gordon's house, grew a doorway and Valkyrie ran through it. The corridor was dark and much too long. She had visions of the exterior of this building, the whole thing mutating to accommodate the spasmodic needs of its master.

"You are my enemy!" Mire screamed after her. "You are not my queen! You are my enemy!"

She took a turn, not knowing where she was going, and stumbled into a well-lit room with a large table set for a banquet. Candles flickered and wine was already poured into goblets. There were no windows and no doors.

Part of the floor sagged and fell away to steps. The body climbed the staircase and Valkyrie backed away. The ghost came in as smoke and took shape before her.

"I tried being *nice*," he snarled. "I was *glad* to see you. I was *happy* you were here."

"You don't have to do this, Anathem."

"But you have *rejected* me. *Me!*"

The banquet melted on the table, turning to slop that dripped off the edges. The candles melted, but still burned. The carpet stretched over the staircase and the floor sealed itself.

Valkyrie needed a way out. She needed a door or a window, and she needed to get Mire angry enough to make one.

"I'll be your queen," she said suddenly.

The ghost's face contorted. "I am no fool."

"I'll stay here with you and be your queen. That's what you want, isn't it?"

"You make bargains," the ghost said as the body advanced, "because you are scared. You tell lies because you fear the death that is to be visited upon you."

Valkyrie splayed her hands and the air rippled. The body sprawled on the ground and then clambered back up.

"Your last moments will be memorable ones," the ghost said and floated sideways, disappearing into his ravaged body.

Unlike when she had first seen him, when spirit and body were aligned to look like a normal man, this new form had no such vanities. Here, its function was simple, the ghost possessing the body, steering it as a vessel of destruction. The head moved, looked up, saw her with eyes that were no longer there.

"It has been a long time," Mire said, his new voice a harsh thing of scrapes and sandpaper, "since I spilled the blood of a living being."

He moved suddenly and quickly, took Valkyrie off her feet and slammed her down on the table. She twisted and drove her knee into his side, but his nerve endings had long since deadened and withered away. She gripped his wrist and kicked, and when he released her to strike, she rolled off the table.

She barely had time to stand before the table melted

between them and he strode through. She clicked her fingers and threw a fireball. It exploded against his arm and she pushed at the air and he staggered.

The walls were melting, and the floor lurched, and the whole room began to slip slowly down through the house.

"I am Anathem Mire," he said. "I am master of reality."

"You're losing control."

"I am master of reality," he insisted angrily, "and you are a fool to oppose me."

"You're insane."

"Shut up!" he roared and knocked her back.

The carpet turned into a puddle that latched on to his feet and formed shoes, polished to a gleam. It rose up his body, covering his rags with a new suit of clothes, covering his dead skin with a new layer that looked fresh and alive.

"I am whole again," he said, once his new face had settled into position.

The room dropped suddenly, and for a second Valkyrie had nothing beneath her feet but air. She hit the ground again and tumbled. The room had collapsed into the living room, the geography of both squashing together. As each room tried to assert its own form and retain its own integrity, the walls rippled and a window was revealed.

Skulduggery appeared and fired his gun, the bullets shattering the glass and driving into Mire, who bellowed in rage. Valkyrie ran to the window and jumped through. Skulduggery caught her and they sprinted across the cavern.

She glanced back. The house shifted, all but two of the windows disappearing and the front door widening. The two windows formed a pair of gigantic eyes that glared at them, and the door grew teeth and shrieked its rage. Mire stood in the mouth, but dared not cross its boundary.

"*I'll find you!*" he screamed. "*I'll find you, girl!*"

They reached the tunnel and ran through, and even though Valkyrie knew he couldn't follow, she didn't slow down.

25

THE RAID

At a little after nine that evening, a large bread van pulled up at the back of the Hibernian Cinema. It attracted no attention. A car with tinted windows followed and parked beside it. Again, nobody noticed.

Tanith was leaning against the doorframe of a spare room at the front of the Medical Facility. Ghastly had brought some of his equipment there so he could work while Kenspeckle carried out whatever tests he had to carry out. Tanith watched Ghastly, sitting at a table, making Valkyrie's new clothes. He was telling Tanith about his mother.

The rear doors of the bread van opened and the men who jumped out did so silently and without fuss. They were dressed in grey and had scythes strapped to their backs.

"My mother was a boxer," Ghastly said, testing the stitching on a sleeve. "Her nose was broken four times, but according to my dad, she was still the prettiest woman in any room."

"I've heard some of the stories," Tanith said. "She sounded like a remarkable woman."

Ghastly smiled. "I fought alongside her at the Battle of Black Rock, and I saw some of Mevolent's best men just turn and *run*. She fought both Serpine and Vengeous and beat them both into retreat. 'Remarkable' doesn't even begin to describe her. She was magnificent, right up to the end."

"How did she die?"

"She made a mistake," he said. "She went up against Lord Vile."

An old man who moved more like a young man got out of the car. He had an air about him of someone who was accustomed to wielding authority. His eyes were cold. The man who got out after him had a weak chin and no such authority, but his eagerness was evident for any who wished to see.

The man with the cold eyes walked into the cinema and the eager man gestured to the men in grey. They moved like liquid, seeping into the building through windows and side doors and skylights, the eager man scurrying along behind.

High on a rooftop beside the cinema, a figure stood in the darkness and watched.

Ghastly put the coat to one side and went to work on the tunic. "There was a rule we had back then. You don't go up against Vile alone. You wait until your army is gathered behind you, you all attack together and you pray someone gets in a lucky shot."

"Vile was that dangerous?"

Ghastly shrugged. "Maybe, maybe not. It's hard to separate the fiend from the legend, you know? He had appeared from nowhere, became Mevolent's most fearsome General and then disappeared – all in the space of a few years. He had that armour, and that Necromancer power, and wherever he went he left a trail of destruction in his wake. My mother went up against him and he killed her, and he would have killed *me* but for—"

Clarabelle stepped in and Ghastly fell silent. "Have you seen the Professor?" she asked.

"Sorry," Tanith said. "Anything wrong?"

"There's a man in the cinema. He insists on speaking with Professor Grouse and he refuses to give his name. He is quite rude."

"Why don't you look for the Professor?" Ghastly suggested. "We'll have a talk with whoever it is, find out what he wants."

"That would be much appreciated," Clarabelle responded, suddenly smiling widely. She walked on, humming a little tune to herself.

Tanith and Ghastly set off towards the cinema, descending the steps into gloom. They passed through the door in the screen and emerged on to the stage. A man stood in the centre aisle between the rows of musty seats.

"Mr Bespoke," Thurid Guild said, his voice echoing slightly, "welcome back to the land of the living."

"Guild. What brings you here?"

"It's Grand Mage actually," Guild corrected. "But you've been a statue for two years – I'm sure I can forgive you one little slip."

"It wasn't a slip."

"What can we do for you?" Tanith asked, making her voice as cold and unwelcoming as possible.

"You can do nothing for me," Guild said. "I'm here to speak with the owner of this facility."

"What's this about?"

"Sanctuary business, I'm afraid."

Tanith looked around. The cinema was pitched in gloom and shadow. "You're here alone?"

"Why shouldn't I be? I am among friends, am I not?"

"That depends," Ghastly said. "Do you count Skulduggery Pleasant as a friend?"

Guild smiled tightly. "Pleasant is a traitor."

"That's what he said about you," Tanith pointed out.

"Skulduggery Pleasant is working with the Diablerie. Along with the girl, he aided in stealing the remains of the Grotesquery for unlawful purposes, and when confronted, he resisted arrest, assaulted Sanctuary personnel and evaded capture. He is an enemy of the Sanctuary and an enemy of all right-thinking people."

Kenspeckle emerged from the door in the screen to join Tanith and Ghastly. "What do you want, Grand Mage?"

"Ah, Professor. I require a mere moment of your time."

"My mere moments are precious. Say what you have to say."

Guild nodded graciously. "You are aware, I presume, of the threat posed by the Diablerie. You are aware of their plans involving the Grotesquery's remains and the last Teleporter, a boy called Fletcher Renn."

"I am."

"I have reason to believe that this boy is being kept on these premises. I would like you to turn him over to me, if you please."

"Grand Mage, I assure you I do not—"

Guild held up a hand. "Professor. I hold you in great regard. I admire your work and your principles. I implore you, do not do yourself the injustice of attempting to lie to me, when I know the boy is here. I would prefer it that you stay silent rather than fumble with a clumsy half-truth. Such things are beneath you."

Tanith glanced at Kenspeckle and saw the colour rise in his cheeks.

"Grand Mage," Kenspeckle said, "do not presume to know a person on the basis of a handful of meetings. This can instil irritation, and an immediate unwillingness to co-operate. Likewise, do not flatter in the hope of shaming that person into co-operation, and do not, under any circumstances, condescend. The fact of the matter is that while I do know of Fletcher Renn, I do not know of his whereabouts. I'm sorry, I cannot help you."

Guild shook his head. "You disappoint me, Professor."

A high-pitched alarm shrieked through the door in the screen, and Tanith and Ghastly spun.

"I'd stay here if I were you," Guild advised.

"What have you done?" Kenspeckle asked, but from the look in his eyes Tanith could tell he already knew the answer. Guild wasn't standing here to request that Fletcher Renn be handed over – he was standing here to distract them.

"My Cleavers have penetrated your Facility's defences," Guild responded, almost lazily. "They have orders to subdue, not to harm – but they will use force if they deem it necessary."

"You have no right!" Kenspeckle thundered.

"We came here for the boy and we're not leaving without him."

Ghastly was already running back to the door and Tanith was about to follow him when she saw the other people in the cinema. They walked through the gloom, down the aisles between the rows, moving quietly to join Guild at the foot of the stage.

Gruesome Krav. Murder Rose. Billy-Ray Sanguine. Jaron Gallow. Murder Rose was carrying Tanith's sword.

"You're part of it," Tanith breathed.

Guild smiled at her coldly. "Part of what, Miss Low?"

He realised that she was looking beyond him, and he turned, frowning. Gallow struck him and Guild fell to his hands and knees. Murder Rose giggled and kicked him, and he slumped sideways and lay still.

"Kill them," Gallow said.

Krav leaped on to the stage and charged, knocking Ghastly off his feet. Rose sprang at Tanith and Tanith flipped over her head, and Sanguine came at her. His straight razor missed her throat as she spun, her boot catching him in the gut.

Murder Rose whipped the sword and Tanith dodged. The red-lipped madwoman was smiling as she advanced. Tanith didn't have time to try anything fancy – this woman was far too good.

Ghastly had slipped out of Krav's hold and was firing punches into the grey man's side. Tanith was about to shout a warning that his punches would have no effect, but Ghastly quickly worked that one out by himself. Krav grabbed him again.

Tanith positioned herself with her back to Sanguine and the opportunity just proved too irresistible. Still struggling for breath, he lunged for her and she twisted, caught him and sent him stumbling into Murder Rose's path. The sword was knocked from Rose's hand and Tanith crashed into her.

Kenspeckle ran up behind Krav and placed his glowing hands on his back. Krav jerked in surprise and an instant later he screamed and whirled in sudden pain. Kenspeckle was knocked over and Ghastly pushed at the air, hurling Krav off the stage.

Sanguine snatched Tanith's sword from the ground and grinned, a blade now in each hand. Tanith shoved Murder Rose away from her and dodged as Sanguine swung, the steel little more than a bright blur between them. He was unused to wielding a weapon of that size, however. He swung too wide and she was on him before he could correct his mistake. Her hand closed over his as she kicked his knee, and she batted the razor away and then hammered her fist on to his forearm. His hand sprang open and she yanked her sword away from him.

"Enough," Gallow called and immediately Sanguine withdrew. Murder Rose glared at Tanith, but she strode back the way she had come without argument. Gruesome Krav stood, snarling, and followed. He stooped to pick up Thurid Guild as he went.

"No doubt the boy has teleported to safety," Gallow called to them from the gloom. "He probably did so the moment he sensed trouble, as we expected."

"You'll never catch him," said Ghastly.

"Nor do we have any wish to try. Instead, we want him delivered to us. Give us the boy and we will return the Grand Mage to you." He gestured to Thurid Guild's unconscious body, held casually in Krav's arms. "Somewhere nice and public, so you won't make a fuss. The Liffey Bridge, at noon tomorrow. If you're late, he's dead."

And then they were gone.

26

THE SCEPTRE

here was someone watching China's building.

He was parked down the street, far enough away to be discreet yet close enough to see the door. It was a cold night and he was wearing a thick coat. He was an Elemental, and every so often there would be a flickering light in the car as he heated himself up.

"One of the Diablerie?" Valkyrie asked. They were across the road and further down, standing at the corner. The evening wind caught the rain and slipped it over Valkyrie's collar. Water trickled down her back and she shivered.

Skulduggery didn't seem to notice the weather. He shook his head. She wished she had a hat like his, or even one of his scarves. "That's a Sanctuary agent," he said. "Guild will have them watching all known associates. He's trying to cut us off."

"Then they're probably watching Kenspeckle's place too," she said miserably. She *really* wanted to go somewhere warm and dry.

A car passed too close to the kerb and kicked up a large puddle. A year ago, her clothes would have protected her, but today the puddle water found its way through in a half-dozen places, and Valkyrie tightened up and barely managed not to squeal.

She glared at the car as it drove on, happy and oblivious, and turned to Skulduggery. "Just call China. Tell her to bring the Sceptre, and we'll meet her and put the new crystal in, and then I can go somewhere to change my clothes. I'm wet and I'm freezing."

"China's phone will be monitored."

"So how are we going to meet her?"

And then the Sanctuary agent started his car and pulled out sharply on to the road. They watched him speed away.

"That's worrying," Skulduggery mused.

"You think it's a trap?"

"Either that or there's an emergency somewhere in the city. Still," he said, injecting some brightness into his voice, "you don't look a gift horse in the mouth, unless of course it's made of wood. Let's go."

They hurried across the street, scanning their surroundings for any sign of an ambush. They reached the tenement building without incident and climbed the stairs. Valkyrie's feet squelched in her boots.

They got to the third floor, where the thin man opened the door when Skulduggery knocked and beckoned them in with a movement of his eyes. The library was practically empty as they walked through its labyrinth of bookcases.

China Sorrows was waiting for them. Her dress was red silk. On the table beside her was a case made of oak. A symbol, like a shark's tooth piercing a star, was etched into the wood.

"People are scared," she said, in a tone that made it clear she didn't approve. "You have every sorcerer in the country getting ready to either fight or run. It's bad for business."

Skulduggery nodded. "The end of the world usually is."

"I'm not going to dignify that with a response," China sighed, "no matter how caustic it may be. Do you have a crystal?"

"Yes, we do."

She passed her hand over the oak case and the symbol on the wood glowed for a moment. The case clicked and opened, revealing a golden rod, held in place by silver clasps. The clasps split apart slowly and China lifted the Sceptre of the Ancients from its box.

"You've already removed the old crystal," Skulduggery noted.

"I wanted to examine it. If I had known there was a chance that a single touch might have turned me to dust, I probably would have let someone else do it."

She handed the Sceptre to Valkyrie, who took the black crystal from her pocket. She slid it into the empty slot. It was a bigger crystal than the last one though, and it was taking some effort to fix it in place.

While Valkyrie worked, Skulduggery looked at China. "You realise what this means, don't you? We need your word that if the gateway opens, you'll be by our side."

"Considering the fact that, as the Sceptre's owner, I'm the only one able to actually *use* it, you had better hope that I am."

"I need a guarantee, China."

"I don't give guarantees. You're just going to have to trust me. And that's all you're going to get."

Valkyrie tried pushing the crystal in a different way and it slid into place. The Sceptre closed around it. The black crystal glowed.

"It's done," Valkyrie said, surprised that she'd managed it. China took it from her.

"Step away," she commanded. She pointed the Sceptre at the oak case and nothing happened. She stared at the weapon in confusion. "It doesn't work."

"Maybe the crystal isn't in right," Valkyrie suggested. "Maybe it's too big."

"I'm the last one who used the Sceptre," Skulduggery mused as he took it from China. "Maybe *I'm* its owner."

He pointed it at the case, but no lightning erupted.

Valkyrie sagged. "So it was a waste of time. And now we have nothing to use against the Faceless Ones."

"No," China said. "Look at it. The crystal's glowing. The Sceptre *has* power; it's just not identifying its proper owner."

Skulduggery held it out to Valkyrie. "Try it."

She frowned. "I don't own it. You used it after Serpine, you gave it to China. It's one of you two – it's got nothing to do with me."

"When I gave it to China, it was broken. You've just replaced its power source, and you were the first person to hold it since it was brought back to life."

Still not seeing the logic, Valkyrie took the Sceptre and held it up, pointing it at the oak case.

"How do you fire?" she asked.

"Will it to fire and it'll fire."

"Yeah, but is there a particular command you have to think, like '*fire*', or do you just have to *want* it to—"

Black lightning streaked from the crystal and the table turned to dust and the oak box fell heavily to the floor.

Valkyrie stared. "I missed the box."

"Yes, but on the bright side, you killed the table."

The crystal glowed again and lightning flashed, and a bookcase disappeared in a cloud of swirling dust. China shrieked in dismay and Valkyrie shrieked in surprise.

"I didn't mean to!" she shouted. "I just thought of it and—"

Skulduggery yanked China back as lightning hit the bookcase behind her.

Valkyrie whirled and thrust the Sceptre into Skulduggery's hands. "Get it away from me!"

"My books!" China cried.

"I can't use it! Skulduggery, I can't use it! I tried not thinking of the Sceptre firing, and that's the only thing I could think of! It kept popping into my head!"

"It's OK," Skulduggery said soothingly. "No one was hurt."

"My books!" China raged.

"China, I am really sorry..." Valkyrie began and then ran out of words.

China glared at her, then glared at Skulduggery. "Some of those books were one of a kind."

"I understand that."

"Priceless, Skulduggery. Beyond priceless. The secrets they held, the histories they contained..."

"I'll be happy to pay for any damage caused."

"You cannot pay for priceless books! That's why they call them priceless!"

"Then let me at least pay for the bookcase."

"The bookcase?" China screamed and then she whirled, hands over her face, and Valkyrie could hear her counting, slowly, to ten.

At ten, she turned and tried to smile, and after a few moments, it actually became convincing. "Valkyrie, it appears you are the Sceptre's owner. This is wonderful news. It means, among other things, that you need not leave the ultimate weapon in the hands of someone you don't trust."

"China," Skulduggery began, but she held up a hand to silence him.

"You can't use it of course," she continued. "Not now anyway. You have to keep it hidden."

Valkyrie frowned. "Why?"

"If the Diablerie find out that it is operational, they will target you. They'll try to take you alive, subdue you, keep you breathing so that the ownership of the Sceptre won't pass to the next person to pick it up."

"And there's another reason," Skulduggery said. "If they manage to get their hands on it, we have nothing with which to stop the Faceless Ones. It's a last resort weapon – it needs to be kept hidden until the gate opens."

"*If* the gate opens," Valkyrie corrected.

"Optimistic to the last," China said dryly.

"We could still do with your help," Skulduggery said to her.

"Nonsense," China responded. "You'll do fine without me. Besides, the portal opens on a farm. A *farm*, Skulduggery. Do I look like I have any shoes suitable for a farm?"

The thin man hurried over and whispered in her ear. She nodded and looked at them. "I think you should get back to the Hibernian. There have been developments."

27

BLINK

Mr Bliss met them as they strode towards the cinema. He told them what had happened, then told them that Remus Crux had left with the Cleavers in a preposterous attempt to catch the Diablerie as they made their getaway with Guild. The main problems with this course of action were that first, the enemy had too much of a head start, and second, nobody knew what kind of vehicle they were in, if they were even in a vehicle at all. But Bliss had let Crux go, simply because he wanted him gone.

They hurried down the aisle, as Ghastly and Tanith emerged

from the door in the screen, on to the stage. Valkyrie looked at them, checking for injuries, but Tanith caught her eye and winked. A small gesture, but reassuring, and Valkyrie's heart stopped beating so hard in her chest.

"Sorry," Ghastly said to Skulduggery. "We tried our best, but..."

"Your job wasn't to protect Guild," Skulduggery reminded him, "it was to protect Fletcher. Where is he?"

"Here," Fletcher said from right behind Valkyrie. She jumped and glared at him, then he vanished and reappeared on the stage beside Tanith. "You're not going to give me to those nutcases, are you? I mean, I know they have a hostage and all, but he's an old guy, he's practically dead already. I'm the important one, so I'm the one who has to stay safe, yeah?"

"We're not doing the trade," Tanith said.

"Actually," Bliss said, "we are."

Everyone stared at him. He stood there like a rock in a churning sea.

"That's insane," Ghastly said. "You're telling us to hand over the last Teleporter just because they *ask* us to? And in return for Guild, of all people?"

"If we do not, they will have no hesitation in killing the Grand Mage."

"Bliss," said Skulduggery, "if we give them Fletcher Renn, this world dies."

"And if we let them kill Thurid Guild," Bliss countered evenly, "the world collapses into chaos."

"I'd rather chaos over death," Ghastly said.

Bliss shook his head. "Ireland is the Cradle of Magic. Our people were the first Ancients. Our people fought the Faceless Ones on *these* shores. This land holds secrets, both magnificent and terrifying, that are coveted by Councils across the world. If we lose another Grand Mage a mere *two years* after we lost Meritorious, how long do you think our friends and neighbours will wait before stepping in?"

"You all know I'm not the biggest fan of the English Sanctuary," Tanith said, "but even they wouldn't do anything as stupid as try to take over."

"If they could claim that it was for our own good, they may decide it's worth the risk. This isn't about politics. It's about *power*. We have a duty to protect what is ours – not out of selfishness, but out of necessity. In the wrong hands, the magic of this land could change the face of the world."

Skulduggery took off his hat and brushed a speck of imagined lint from its brim. "And yet if we hand over Renn, and the Diablerie succeed in their scheme, the face of this world will be changed anyway."

"Which is why, Detective, it is going to be your job to make sure that doesn't happen. You have two tasks – to get Thurid Guild back alive and relatively unharmed, and to make sure the Diablerie do not get their hands on Fletcher Renn."

"So you're saying we should double-cross them."

"That is indeed what I am saying."

Skulduggery shrugged. "Well, I was going to do *that* anyway."

"Are we still fugitives?" Valkyrie asked.

"Unfortunately, yes," Bliss said. "In Guild's absence, I am in command, but while there is a spy in the Sanctuary it is far too dangerous to bring you back in. I will do my best to keep Remus Crux away from you, but I'm keeping him on as Prime Detective so that our spy will have something to keep himself occupied."

"Out," Kenspeckle said.

They looked at him as he stepped through the door in the screen.

"Out," he said again. "All of you. Get out. This is a science-magic facility, a place of knowledge and a place of healing. What it is *not* is a place of violence."

"Professor," Skulduggery started, but Kenspeckle held up a hand to silence him.

"You bring death and destruction to my door, Detective Pleasant. You always have. And while I am happy to patch you up, and patch up your friends, I am not willing to just stand by while you use this place as your headquarters.

"This afternoon, this establishment was raided by *Cleavers*. And if that wasn't bad enough, I now have fanatical worshippers of the Faceless Ones attacking people right where you're standing. I took an oath to heal people, but today I was forced to take my power and use it to hurt. Unforgivable. *Unforgivable!*"

Valkyrie shrank back, dreading the moment where he'd use her injuries as another weapon against Skulduggery. Kenspeckle glanced at her, then looked back at Skulduggery, but the moment came and went.

"I will heal your wounds," he said, "but I will not facilitate your battles. All of you, get out."

He turned and walked back through the door in the screen. A moment later the picture of the door faded and the heavy curtains started to close. The few remaining house lights came on.

Bliss was the first to leave. The others looked at Skulduggery, who put his hat back on. They shrugged into coats and Ghastly picked up two large bags, then they left the cinema.

The rain had stopped. Skulduggery unlocked the Purple Menace.

"Back to my place, I suppose," Ghastly said as he threw the bags into his van.

"OK," Fletcher said, taking hold of Valkyrie's arm, "we'll meet you there."

And they teleported.

It was like she blinked, and within that blink there was a rush of air and she felt light, and her belly lurched, and there was nothing around her or beneath her except for Fletcher's hand on her arm. His hand was the only thing that was real, and it felt good, and warm, and comforting.

And then they were standing on the roof of Ghastly's shop. A wave of dizziness swept through Valkyrie and she nearly fell to her knees. Fletcher was smiling at her.

"You OK?" he asked gently.

She punched him across the jaw and he went stumbling backwards.

"*Why'd you do that?*" he bellowed.

She glared at him, the dizziness passing. "*Shock* mostly," she said angrily. "You just can't teleport people without asking them! What if something had gone wrong? What if you'd only teleported half of me?"

"That'd never happen."

"Or you let go of my arm halfway through?"

"It can't be done."

"Or we reappeared in a wall or something?"

He hesitated. "OK, now that *was* a danger... But as long as I've been somewhere before, and I can picture it in my head, that's all I need. I thought you'd like it to be honest."

Her phone rang. It was Skulduggery. Valkyrie assured him she was OK and waiting for him at Ghastly's. She hung up.

"He said he's going to kill you," she told Fletcher, who shrugged.

"He's always saying that."

"But this time he means it."

"What does it matter? If he hands me over to those lunatics, I'm dead anyway, right?"

Valkyrie didn't say anything. Fletcher looked at the city around them.

"It's quite pretty up here," he continued. "All the streetlights. The rain makes everything kind of glitter, doesn't it? It's like this in London too. You can sometimes forget how dirty everything is." His eyes found her. "What'll happen to that Guild guy? Do you think they'll kill him?"

Valkyrie hesitated. "I don't know."

"Do you care?"

"What? Of course."

"You don't like him."

"I still don't want him *killed*."

Fletcher didn't say anything for a bit. "Does Tanith have a boyfriend?"

Valkyrie looked at him in disbelief, amazed by the radical change of topic. "You don't have a chance."

"You don't know that."

"Yes, I do."

"Give me three good reasons."

"I only need two. The first one is that she is way too old for you, and the second one is that you are really annoying."

"Hey, just because you're too young to appreciate my charms doesn't mean I don't have them. I'm a catch."

"Is that what your mummy says?" Valkyrie grinned.

"Not really. My mum's dead."

The grin faded. "Oh."

"What about *your* family? What do they think about all these magical adventure crime-solving things you do?"

"They don't know about any of it. At home I have this mirror, and all I have to do is touch it and my reflection steps out and does all the boring stuff like go to school and do homework and be nice to people."

"Your reflection comes to life?" Fletcher said, eyes wide.

"Yep."

"You're serious? That is so *cool*! So everyone thinks you're just this normal girl?"

"They think I'm a tad weird, but yes, basically."

"That is amazing. So there are two of you?"

"Kind of, yes."

He went quiet and after a few moments she began to wonder what he was thinking about.

"Cool," he said at last. "So could I get one of these mirrors? Maybe we could trade my reflection for this Guild guy. Unless the reflection would have the same abilities as me, which'd kind of defeat the purpose."

"No, they can't do magic, but it wouldn't work. Sorcerers can generally spot a reflection a mile off."

Fletcher shrugged. "Worth a shot. I tell you, it'll sure be nice when all this is over and I can get back to my life."

"What *was* your life? What did you do all day?"

"Whatever I wanted. I have this power and I didn't train for it, I wasn't told about it, it just happened. I'm a natural. And it means I can go anywhere and do anything. And that's what I do all day – whatever I want."

"You should get someone to train you."

"Who? Every other Teleporter is dead."

"As Skulduggery keeps telling me, magic is magic. The basic underlying principles are the same no matter what your power is."

Fletcher made a face. "Sounds a lot like school."

"It's generally more fun," she smiled. "You may be a natural at this, but you're never going to be as good as you can be if you don't train."

He vanished, then said from behind her, "I'm good enough already."

She sighed and turned, but he was already gone. "OK," she said, "this is mature."

He tapped her on the shoulder and she laughed and swiped for him, but he appeared in front of her, flashing that cocky grin.

They waited on the roof for another ten minutes, and Valkyrie did her best not to smile at his annoying remarks. Despite her best intentions, however, she found herself being amused by him. When the headlights of the Purple Menace and Ghastly's van approached, Fletcher extended his arm and she took it. Once again it was like she blinked, and was swept away, and then they were on the pavement. Valkyrie held on to him while the dizziness passed.

They parted as Skulduggery strode up. He towered over

Fletcher, who was looking quite nervous. Ghastly and Tanith hurried to join them.

"Never," Skulduggery said, "do that again."

Fletcher nodded.

"Someone's in the shop," Ghastly said quietly. They followed his gaze to the door, which stood open slightly. Inside was darkness.

Skulduggery took out his gun and glanced at Fletcher. "Forget what I just said and teleport somewhere. Valkyrie, go with him."

She took Fletcher's arm and motioned upwards. He nodded and they reappeared on the roof. The dizziness was fleeting this time and she moved quietly, leading the way to the skylight. They crouched and peered through the glass.

The light from the streetlamps pierced the gloom as the door opened fully. Valkyrie couldn't see them, but she imagined Skulduggery and the others swarming in, checking the corners, moving with silent purpose. A few seconds later, she heard voices – not raised in alarm, but in conversation.

Someone turned the light on.

Skulduggery was putting his gun away and Tanith was sheathing her sword. Ghastly walked back from the light switch to join them as they stood facing Solomon Wreath and two other Necromancers.

"It's safe," Valkyrie told Fletcher. "Let's go."

They stood and he held her hand. She blinked, then they were in the shop, heads turning at their sudden arrival. Wreath nodded her a greeting before resuming talking.

"What you see before you is the full extent of the Necromancer contingent. The opinion held by the majority is that we should leave you to fight your battles alone."

"But you don't agree with this?" Skulduggery asked.

"I think it is a foolish approach to take, and my colleagues agree with me."

His colleagues wore black. The woman had a cloak thrown back over her shoulders, the ends of which seemed to writhe in the shadows. The man had an old flintlock pistol in a holster on his leg. Neither of them looked remotely friendly.

"Three Necromancers isn't much of a contingent," Ghastly said, clearly unimpressed.

"Four actually," Wreath said and tapped his cane on the ground.

A figure walked in from the back room. Immediately, Skulduggery's gun was out, and Tanith's sword was flashing, and Ghastly had fire in his hands.

The White Cleaver took his place beside Wreath.

Skulduggery thumbed back the hammer of his gun. "Explain yourself, Wreath. This man has been on the Sanctuary's Wanted List for over two years."

Wreath smiled innocently. "I assure you, Skulduggery, my colleague was not responsible for his actions."

"He almost killed me!" Tanith snarled.

"Under orders from Nefarian Serpine," Wreath pointed out. "His will was most certainly not his own."

The White Cleaver just stood there, perfectly still. The scythe that had sliced through Tanith was strapped to his back.

"How did he end up with you?" Skulduggery asked.

Wreath shrugged. "It was *our* technique Serpine used to bring him back from the dead. Once we had realised what he had done, we managed to break the hold he had over the Cleaver, and the Cleaver came to us."

"So that was *you*, when he ignored Serpine's orders in the Sanctuary?"

"That was us. If only we could have severed Serpine's influence *earlier*, Miss Low would not have been injured, and Mr Bespoke would not have had to turn himself into a garden ornament."

Ghastly lunged and Skulduggery had to hold him back.

Tanith walked up to the White Cleaver, who looked down at her, his visor reflecting her face.

"Does he have Necromancer powers?" she asked, directing the question at Wreath, but not taking her eyes off the Cleaver.

"No. He is merely a Cleaver, albeit one of their best. He is also dead, self-repairing and somewhat unstoppable. He is the result of one of our techniques, and so, being a soldier, his natural instinct is to take *our* orders and stand at *our* side. In this case, our side is, happily, also *your* side."

Tanith turned and walked away. "He doesn't stand at *my* side."

"Mine neither," Ghastly growled.

"Nevertheless," Wreath said, "he is part of the Necromancer contingent you have requested. The three of us and the White Cleaver. Unless, of course, you think you can stop the Diablerie without us."

Skulduggery put his gun away. "If any of us survive this, Wreath, you and I are going to have a conversation."

28

SAYING GOODBYE

n Saturday morning, Valkyrie climbed through her bedroom window just as her reflection was waking up.

"You look dreadful," it remarked, sitting up and looking at her.

"Cheers," Valkyrie responded, throwing her coat into the wardrobe. She'd had two hours of sleep on Ghastly's couch and was feeling drained. She sat down and pulled off her boots.

"Your parents are leaving for Paris in half an hour," the

reflection said. "Are you here to say goodbye?"

"That's the plan."

"Do you want me to return to the mirror?"

Valkyrie undressed and kicked her black clothes into the corner, then wrapped herself in her dressing gown. "I won't be staying long," she said. "I'm going to have a shower, kiss my folks goodbye and then I'm gone again."

"So shall I stay here?"

"Hide under the bed, just in case Mum walks in." The reflection did as she was told, and Valkyrie watched as it tucked a bare foot undercover. "You OK down there?"

"I am," came the reply. "I have also found some of your missing underwear."

"Good news all round then. Don't make a sound."

Valkyrie padded to the bathroom, locked the door and turned on the shower. She stepped in and sighed as the hot water hit her. Her head drooped and her eyes closed, and within seconds her hair was plastered to her scalp. She could feel the dirt and the grime and the sweat being washed away, and it felt good. She ran her tongue over her teeth again, testing the new one. It still felt too big and Valkyrie was afraid of probing too hard in case she pushed it out of place.

She washed her hair. Her muscles were loosening. She was

starting to relax. She hadn't realised how tense she had been, but she figured she could really do with a massage right about now. China would probably know who to call about that.

Valkyrie tried to think about what she was going to say to her parents and butterflies swarmed in her belly. She'd had to say what could have potentially been a final goodbye to them too many times over the past two years, and it wasn't getting any easier.

Once she was finished, she stepped out of the shower and towelled herself dry. She heard footsteps pass the door.

"Morning, sweetie," her mother called.

"Morning!"

Valkyrie cleared the condensation from the mirror and looked at herself. Her face was unmarked. No cuts, no bruises. The shower had revived her and she wasn't looking so tired any more. She was confident there was absolutely nothing about her appearance that would cause her parents to worry. They'd be able to leave without even a hint of anxiety.

Provided, of course, that Valkyrie could say goodbye without acting like it was the last time she'd ever see them.

She took a deep breath, pulled on her robe and went back

to her room. She dressed in jeans, T-shirt and a zip-up top, then pulled on a pair of trainers. She tried a few practice smiles, and when she was sure they'd be convincing, she clumped down the stairs with a scowl on her face.

"Someone's grumpy," her dad said as she entered the kitchen.

"Why can't I go with you?" she whined. "Why do I have to stay with Beryl?"

"Because it's a romantic weekend," he told her. "It wouldn't be very romantic with you tagging along, now would it?"

Valkyrie collapsed into a chair. "Why do you need romance in your life? You're already married. Romance should be saved for people like me."

Her dad frowned. "You're not looking for romance, are you? You're only fourteen. You should be thinking about other things. Like dolls."

"When was the last time you saw me with a doll, Dad?"

"I know we got you one when you were a baby, but I'm pretty sure you laughed at it and beat it up."

"I was a cool baby."

Her mother walked in. "Des, where's your passport?"

"Do I need it?"

"We're getting on a plane. Yes, you need it. Where is it?"

"Uh, where is it usually?"

"You said you had it. Last night, I asked you, and you assured me you had it."

Valkyrie's dad nodded thoughtfully. "I do remember that. However, I may have been lying."

"Oh, for God's sake, Edgley..."

Her mother only ever called him by his last name when she was getting mad with him.

"It's around here somewhere," he laughed. "You just carry on with your packing and I'll have found it by the time we have to go."

"We're going in seven minutes."

He swallowed. "That's no problem."

Valkyrie's mother sighed and walked out. Valkyrie called after her. "Mum, what age were you when you had your first boyfriend?"

"My first proper boyfriend?"

"Yeah."

Her dad frowned. "Define 'proper'."

"Thirteen," she heard her mother say. "Des, find that passport."

"What do you mean by 'proper'?" he called, but she didn't answer. He turned to Valkyrie. "Things were different when your mother and I were kids. It was a more innocent time. We had to wait eighteen months to even hold hands. That was the law and we were happy."

"I think you're making that bit up, Dad."

"Boys are horrible," he said. "I should know, I was one."

Someone rang the doorbell. While her father looked for his passport and her mother finished the packing, Valkyrie went to open the front door.

"Hello, Stephanie," said Remus Crux.

She froze. He was wearing his usual slacks and blazer, but today he had finished off his outfit with a sickly little smile.

Her mouth went dry. She kept her voice low. "What are you doing here? You can't be here."

"I have a warrant for your arrest," said Crux sweetly. "What, you didn't think I'd be able to work out who you were and where you lived? If your quite obvious connection to the late Gordon Edgley wasn't enough of a giveaway, there were a dozen vampires chasing you through the streets of this lovely little town last summer. I am a detective, Miss Cain. Working things out is what I do, and this particular mystery wasn't exactly taxing."

"My parents are here. You can't do this."

"You have a choice. Either I arrest you now or you tell me

269

where the skeleton is, and where he is keeping the Grand Mage."

"The *Diablerie* have Guild. *Batu* has Guild."

"From what I've heard over the course of my investigations, there *is* no Batu. Valkyrie, no one is blaming you. You understand me, don't you? Skulduggery led you astray. It happens all the time. None of this is your fault. But now you have to do the right thing."

She glared at him. "You can't come to my house and threaten me."

"Are you going to tell me where he is?"

"No, I am not."

"In that case you are under arrest."

Valkyrie tried to close the door, but Crux caught it, held it open.

"Get away from here," she said, her rage cracking her voice. "There are rules. You can't demonstrate a power in front of civilians. My parents are civilians. If you take me away, you will be exposing all of us."

He pressed his face through the gap. "You're under arrest."

She glanced around when she heard her mother approach, wheeling her suitcase after her, and when Valkyrie looked back, Crux was gone.

"Who was that?" her mother asked.

"No one," Valkyrie answered quickly. "Wrong house."

Her mother nodded, then saw a passport on the table beside her. She shouted up the stairs. "Desmond, I found your passport. Time to go."

Valkyrie opened the door wide, like she was making room for her mother's suitcase. She stepped out of the house and looked around, making sure Crux couldn't be seen.

Her dad came down the stairs, picked up the passport and opened it. "This isn't mine," he said. "This belongs to an ugly man wearing a stupid expression."

Valkyrie's mother sighed. "Get in the car."

"This is *my* anniversary gift to *you*," he protested. "And that means *I'm* in charge."

"Get in the car."

"Yes, dear," he mumbled, picking up his bag and shuffling out the door. He stopped to give Valkyrie a hug and winked at her. "You behave, OK? And be nice to your cousins. God knows *someone* has to be."

He continued on and her mother came next, giving her a hug and a kiss.

"Beryl is expecting you for lunch," she said. "It's not going to be as bad as you think."

For a single moment, Valkyrie managed to push all thoughts of Crux out of her mind. She looked at her mother and wished she could warn her of what might be coming.

"Hope you have a great time," was all she could say, and she watched her parents throw their bags in the back of the car and reverse out of the driveway. Her dad was driving and her mum was waving. Valkyrie forced a smile on to her face and returned the wave until the car was out of sight.

Then she broke into a sprint.

It was a few seconds before she became aware of Crux behind her. She turned sideways, slipping between a fence post and a wall, to run across the grassy embankment that bordered a field of cauliflowers. She heard the fence rattle and glanced back in time to see him squeezing through.

Valkyrie left the embankment and ran across the field. Her feet were heavy, her trainers picking up great clumps of muck. It wasn't easy keeping her balance, but she used to do this all the time as a kid – her friends and her, racing each other home from school and taking all the short cuts imaginable. There was a certain kind of rhythm required to traverse the deep cauliflower drills – a rhythm that Crux didn't have. He had only crossed ten drills when a thick stalk snagged his foot and he sprawled into the dirt.

"You're under arrest!" he screeched.

By the time he had pushed himself up, Valkyrie was halfway across the field. Running like this, with her feet so heavy and having to lift her knees so high, was rapidly draining her energy. She turned and ran up one of the drills, heading for a break in the hedge. She looked back and saw Crux go sprawling once again.

She reached the edge of the field and ran straight for the gap. When she was eight, she had tried this jump and had ended up waist-deep in ditchwater, her skin slashed by thorns and briars. But that was a long time ago.

She pushed at the air behind her to add distance to her leap, and landed on the other side, her tired legs stumbling slightly.

This field was mercifully free of cauliflowers, and Valkyrie ran diagonally across it. By the time she hauled herself over the gate to the narrow road on the other side, she was exhausted. She looked back, saw Crux jump the ditch and then stagger to a halt, bending over with his hands on his knees. He looked like he was about to collapse.

She scraped her feet against the ground, shaking loose the remaining clumps of muck, and took off, heading away from town. She needed somewhere quiet and isolated to hide, and then she'd call Skulduggery and get him to pick her up. She really wanted to be there when he got his hands on Crux.

She reached the part in the road where it split into two, heard an engine and looked back. A black van had stopped by the gate, just as Remus Crux was climbing over it. Even from this distance, Valkyrie could see the state of him – covered in muck from head to toe. He was saying something, gasping out his words probably, to whoever was inside the van, and then the side door opened and a Cleaver got out.

"Oh hell," Valkyrie breathed.

Crux pointed and the Cleaver's grey helmet turned to look at her.

She ran.

She knew Cleavers were fast, but she had never been chased by one before. He was like those athletes she'd seen on the Olympics, the 100-metre sprinters, and he got faster and faster as he came. She'd never outrun him, and if she tried to fight him, she feared he might use the scythe strapped to his back.

A tractor with a rotovator attached rumbled out from a nearby field. Valkyrie ran to it, relief washing over her. Cleavers were the Sanctuary's police and army rolled into one, and she knew they would be more mindful of alarming civilians than Crux seemed to be.

The tractor stopped and the farmer got out. She knew him – he was a friend of her dad's. He stepped between the rotovator and the tractor and tightened the chains that connected them. She checked behind her, but the Cleaver had disappeared.

"Heya, Steph," the farmer said when he saw her, half smiling and half frowning at her filthy jeans and trainers. "What have you been up to?"

"Hi, Alan," she said, trying to catch her breath. "I'm just out for a run."

"Ah, I see. Right then." Satisfied that the chains were tight enough to stop the rotovator from swinging as he drove, he wiped his hands on his trousers. "It's just you're not exactly dressed for a jog, are you?"

"It was a spontaneous decision. Didn't really think it through."

"That's what I said about marrying Annie," he nodded. "Everything's OK, is it?"

"It seems to be," she said.

"Your folks away for the weekend?"

"They just left."

"And you're in trouble already?"

"What's new there?"

"You got me. You're sure everything's OK?"

"Apart from the fact that I'm staying with Beryl for the weekend," Valkyrie said, "yes, everything's fine. You headed home? Give me a lift as far as Main Street?"

"What about your run?"

"Running's overrated."

"Climb aboard," he said and the grin was just spreading across Valkyrie's face when she heard the black van behind her. She went cold as it stopped and Crux got out.

Alan looked at him, at the muck on his clothes and the anger in his eyes, and then stepped in front of Valkyrie.

"Can I help you?" he asked.

"You can get out of my way," Crux snarled.

"Your van can get past my tractor. The road's not that narrow."

"Your tractor's not in my way, simpleton, *you* are."

Valkyrie couldn't believe this was happening. This was against every rule she had been taught.

Alan looked at Valkyrie. "This guy the reason you decided on that run, Steph?"

"I don't know him," she lied. "Never seen him before."

"Would you do me a favour, Steph? Would you call the police?"

"I'm a detective," Crux snapped, stepping forward, and Alan hit him – slugged him right across the jaw.

"You stay away from the girl," Alan said evenly as Crux retreated, his eyes blazing.

Valkyrie grabbed Alan's arm, holding him back. "It's OK," she said quickly. "We should just go. Can we go? Please, I just want to go."

"If I were you," Alan said to Crux, "I'd get out of town now. I don't ever want to see you back here. Do you understand me?"

Crux glared at him. As Alan turned away, Crux snapped his hand against the air. Alan slammed into the side of the tractor and collapsed on the road. Valkyrie screamed and darted to him, but there was a flash of grey and her arm was twisted behind her. She fell to her knees even as the shackles closed around her wrist, and before she could react, both hands were cuffed.

The Cleaver hauled her to her feet.

"You can't do this!" she yelled as a second Cleaver knelt by Alan. He checked for a pulse and nodded to Crux.

"He'll regain consciousness in a few minutes," Crux said. "And hopefully, he'll have learned a little lesson."

"You attacked a civilian!"

"He attacked *me*. I have witnesses."

"You used magic on him," she seethed, "when his back was turned. You coward."

Crux sighed. "I was doing my duty. If a civilian gets hurt or, heaven forbid, killed during the pursuit of a fugitive, then the blame lies with the fugitive."

"Wait till Bliss hears about this."

Crux took hold of the shackles and twisted them savagely. Valkyrie yelled in pain.

Crux leaned in. "You may think Elder Bliss will come to your aid, but he is a *very* busy man, and sometimes my reports get mislaid on the way to his desk. There is every possibility that he won't even know you've been arrested."

"You're going to regret this," Valkyrie said. "I swear to God, you're going to regret this."

"I doubt that," Crux said as he marched her to the van and threw her in. "In fact, if your capture leads me to Skulduggery Pleasant, I might even get a promotion."

He slammed the door, shutting out the sunlight.

29

CELLMATES

"nfortunately," Crux said as he led Valkyrie to the holding cells, "we're a tad overcrowded at the moment. I suppose that's as a result of the Sanctuary finally having a Prime Detective who is good at his job."

"Have I met him?" Valkyrie asked and got an angry yank on her shackles in response.

"What that means," Crux continued, "is that you'll have to share a cell."

Valkyrie paled. "What? You can't do that."

"It's not ideal, but we do what we must," Crux said, failing to hide the glee in his voice.

She tried to pull away, but he dragged her viciously on.

"You can't do that!" she shouted, hoping that someone would hear. "Let me talk to Mr Bliss."

"Elder Bliss is busy with Sanctuary matters," Crux said. "We'll get this sorted out, I assure you. But for now, you're going to have to be a good girl and share your room."

He opened a cell door and shoved her inside. The door slammed behind her and the man on the narrow bed turned over and looked at her.

"Cain," Scapegrace snarled.

The slot in the door opened up. "Hands," Crux said.

"Get me out of here!" Valkyrie shouted.

"Put your hands through the slot, unless you want to stay manacled."

Scapegrace's right eye was swollen shut, his nose was bruised and his lip was cut. He moved slowly, like his whole body was sore.

Valkyrie thrust her hands through the slot and Crux removed the shackles. "The cell is, of course, bound," he informed her, "so please try to behave."

She bent low, so he could see her eyes through the slot.

"Detective Crux, you cannot do this."

He smiled at her before closing the slot. She turned as Scapegrace got to his feet.

"They broke my fingers," he said, holding up his bandaged left hand. "Those Cleavers broke my fingers and beat the tar out of me. Did you have a good laugh, did you? You and the skeleton? Were you grinning to each other as you sent me off to distract them?"

Valkyrie's mouth was dry. There was nowhere to run and nowhere to hide. She couldn't use her powers and she wasn't wearing her protective clothing. She was an ordinary girl, trapped inside a small room with a grown man who wanted to kill her.

"I'm going to beat you to death," said Scapegrace, nodding. "I wanted my first kill to be something artful. Something beautiful. But I suppose I could settle for something brutal. It would give me something to work up from."

"You'll never get out of jail," Valkyrie said, her words thick in her mouth. "If you kill me, you're going to spend the rest of your life in a cell like this one."

"No, I'll get out. Something will happen and I'll get out. I always do."

"You'll be a killer. Security's tighter for killers."

"And why is that? Because people are *afraid* of killers. People are going to be afraid of *me*."

He stepped forward and she stepped back, feeling the cold steel of the door through her clothes.

"What about Skulduggery?" she asked quickly.

"I don't see him in here," Scapegrace smiled.

"You don't want him as an enemy, Vaurien. You know you don't. Once he finds out that I've been arrested, he'll come for me. He'll appear at this door just like he did two days ago and he'll open it and see what you've done. Do you really want to be standing here when that happens?"

Scapegrace hesitated. "They'll put me in protective custody," he decided. "They don't much like your friend these days, in case you've forgotten. They'll put me in a special cell where he won't be able to find me."

"He'll find you. He'll hunt you down."

Scapegrace sneered. "Let him try."

Valkyrie knew the rules. Tanith had drilled them into her often enough. With no other choice, when the onset of violence was a virtual certainty and retreat was not an option, the rule was to strike first and without warning.

Scapegrace was a grown man. He was a little under two metres tall and of average strength for a man his size.

Valkyrie was a fourteen-year-old girl who was tall for her age, and she'd been working out with two of the best fight trainers around for two years. Physically, Scapegrace was still superior, but he was also injured. He was keeping his weight off his left leg and his body was twisted slightly. She suspected cracked ribs.

Strike first and without warning.

Valkyrie kicked Scapegrace's left leg and he howled. She tried shooting an elbow into his face, but his arms were up, flailing. She pushed him back to give herself room, and he looped his right fist against her jaw. Her head spun and she hit the door and nearly fell.

He came in with another punch, but she swerved away and it caught her on the shoulder. If she had been wearing her black coat, the blow would have been absorbed by the material. As it was, she went stumbling.

He reached for her again and she grabbed his bandaged hand and wrenched it. He shrieked and forgot all about his attack. She moved away from the door and, still leading him by his broken fingers, spun him in a tight circle around her. She brought his hand low and he dropped to his knees.

"Let go!" he pleaded, tears in his eyes. "I wasn't going to kill you, I swear! I was joking!"

She released his hand and he clutched it to his chest, and she grabbed his head and drove her knee into the hinge of his jaw. He fell over backwards and didn't get up.

The back of her legs hit the side of the bed and she collapsed into a sitting position. Her breathing was fast and shallow, and her eyes stayed glued to Scapegrace's unconscious form.

Her shoulder started to ache. His punch had caught her right on the side of the head, and her ear was burning. She thanked God he hadn't busted her in the mouth. She didn't think she could handle losing another tooth.

She wondered what she would do when he woke up. There was nothing in the cell that she could use to tie him up, and no one had come to investigate the sounds of struggle.

She had beaten him. She had beaten him without using magic. True, he was already injured, and she had caught him by surprise, but the fact remained – she had fought a grown man and she had beaten him.

She started to smile, and then the smile faded as she thought what would have happened if she *hadn't* beaten him. She'd probably be lying dead on the cell floor right now.

She got off the bed and unwrapped the bandage around Scapegrace's injured hand. His fingers were badly swollen, the skin blue and yellow and purple and black. He didn't even murmur as she tied one end of the bandage around those fingers, and the other end around the iron leg of the bed. At least now he wouldn't be able to jump her when he woke up.

She sat on the bed again, well away from him, her back against the wall. She tied her hair into a ponytail and wondered if Skulduggery had realised yet that something had gone wrong. She tried to think of what he would do.

First, he'd call her phone and get no answer. After a while he'd turn up at the house – or more likely send Tanith, someone a little more normal-looking. He'd definitely speak with the reflection, and hopefully work out what had happened. And then he'd come for her.

Valkyrie sat back and waited.

30

BERYL

Beryl Edgley was a busy woman.

She really didn't have the time to take in and feed abandoned waifs. But that being said, when Melissa Edgley had asked if she would take care of Stephanie while she jetted away to Paris for the weekend, Beryl had of course accepted the challenge graciously.

Her niece had always been a stubborn and wilful child, with a sharp tongue and an attitude that Beryl found quite distasteful. Although even *she* had to admit that over the past couple of years Stephanie had seemed to become a lot more subdued. Beryl liked to think that this new, quieter Stephanie was a result of her own hints and tips to Melissa and Desmond about raising well-behaved children. Beryl's twins, Carol and Crystal, were not *perfect* by any means, and they had both been losing far too much weight lately, but at least they didn't drink or smoke or hang around with loutish boys like so many of their friends.

The family, plus Stephanie, ate lunch at the kitchen table without speaking. Fergus's eyes were glued to the television and the twins were picking at their food without enthusiasm. In fact, only Stephanie seemed to be intent on eating what Beryl had placed before her. Which was surprising, given what had happened to her earlier that day.

The doorbell rang and Beryl went to answer it. There was a young woman standing on the doorstep, smiling. She had tousled blonde hair and was wearing a brown leather outfit that was far too tight. The poor girl was practically falling out of her top.

"You must be Beryl," she said in an English accent. "I've heard so much about you."

Beryl didn't trust new people. Ever since they had sold the gigantic boat that Fergus's brother had left them, she'd had a niggling suspicion that everyone wanted their money.

"And you are?" Beryl asked, standing with her back straight so she could look down her nose.

"Name's Tanith," the young lady replied. "I was wondering, is Stephanie about?"

"She's having lunch."

"Could I talk to her for just a moment?"

Beryl frowned. "She's having lunch I said. She's eating. She cannot come to the door while she is eating."

The young lady, Tanith, looked at Beryl for a few moments and then she smiled again.

"Maybe she can stop eating, come to the door, I'll be really quick saying what I have to say, and then she can go back to eating. That sound good to you, Beryl?"

"I would prefer it if you called me Mrs Edgley."

Tanith took a deep breath that threatened the integrity of her top. "Mrs Edgley, be a dear and get Stephanie for me, will you?"

"I don't like your tone."

"I don't like your shoes."

Beryl looked down, wondering what was wrong with her shoes, and Tanith moved in and around her. Before Beryl realised what was happening, she was walking into the kitchen.

"Bloody hell..." came Fergus's whispered voice.

"Stephanie," Tanith said, "could I have a word?"

Beryl stormed in after her, outraged, as Stephanie stood up from the table. The twins were looking at the young lady curiously, and Fergus was staring at her, his eyes wide and full of wonder.

"Stephanie, you are *not* leaving this room!"

"This is a private matter," Tanith said.

"And this is private *property*! Fergus, call the police!"

Fergus just kept staring at the intruder.

"If this has anything to do with what happened earlier today," Beryl said, "the police will certainly want to talk to you!"

Tanith frowned. "What happened earlier today?"

Stephanie opened her mouth to speak, but Beryl took control of the conversation. "Three hours ago, Alan Brennan came to my door and told me he had been attacked by a man who had been chasing Stephanie. Attacked! In Haggard!"

"Who was the man?"

"I don't know," Stephanie said. "I don't remember much of it. I think I must still be in shock. He probably thought I was somebody else. After he attacked Mr Brennan, he went away and I returned home."

"We found her hiding under the bed," Beryl said, and Carol and Crystal snorted.

"Have you seen Val?" Tanith asked Stephanie, ignoring Beryl completely. "Do you know what happened to her?"

"She was meant to come back," Stephanie shrugged. "But she never did."

"Who is this Val?" Beryl asked, confused. "What has she got to do with anything? There is a dangerous lunatic on the loose, claiming to be a policeman!"

Tanith's eyes narrowed. "He said he was a cop?"

"Mr Brennan said he told him he was a detective."

"Crux..."

"I beg your pardon?"

"I know this man," Tanith nodded. "And you're right, he *is* a lunatic. Have you called the police?"

Fergus spoke up at last. "They, uh, they said they'd call by this afternoon..."

"Tell them not to bother. This man has a history of psychiatric problems. He just forgot to take his pills this morning, that's all. I'm his doctor."

"What kind of doctor dresses in brown leather?" Beryl asked suspiciously.

The young lady flashed her a quick smile. "The kind that

looks good in it," she said. "Thank you for your time. You all have a good day now. Goodbye, Stephanie."

"Goodbye," Stephanie said and sat down to finish off her lunch.

Beryl followed Tanith to the front door, her mind overloading with questions, but Tanith just kept walking and didn't look back. She got to the road and a dreadful purple car pulled up and she got in. Beryl tried to catch a better look at the driver, but all she could see was a man in a hat, and then they were gone.

Beryl frowned. The man in the hat seemed awfully familiar...

31

OLD FRIENDS

Crux burst into her apartment and China turned, appraising him coolly.

"We have the girl," Crux said triumphantly. "I tracked her down and arrested her. Put her in the cell myself."

"She's fourteen," China said. "That was very brave of you."

"You can save your snide comments. The Diablerie have the Grand Mage."

"It's the talk of the town, but apparently, you'd still prefer to go after Skulduggery than the real enemy."

"He *is* the real enemy. I worked it out and it's all so obvious. It fits."

"What fits, Remus?"

He stood with his hands on his hips. "Skulduggery Pleasant *is* Batu."

"Oh my God..." China stared at him. "You *are* actually thicker than you look."

Crux stepped in close. "Where is he? Where are they keeping the Grand Mage?"

"I tried to help you, Remus. I told you where Skulduggery was making his headquarters and you went in, you stormed the place, and what happened? You missed Skulduggery, you missed Valkyrie, and you got the Grand Mage kidnapped. I've done what I can – it's not my fault you're not very good at your job."

"I'm good enough, China. I was good enough to work out your dark little secret, wasn't I?"

"You didn't work anything out. A dying man told you because you were the only one around at the time."

"Where is the skeleton?"

"I don't know."

"Then where will he *be*?"

"Oh, now that one I *do* know. Once he learns that you've

arrested Valkyrie, you're not going to have to look for him. He'll come to you."

"I'm not scared of Skulduggery Pleasant."

"Yes, you are, Remus. Everyone is."

"You have failed to co-operate with a Sanctuary investigation, and furthermore, you are an obstruction to said investigation. I'm placing you under arrest."

Crux produced the handcuffs with a flourish. China sighed and allowed her hands to be shackled behind her back.

"Once again, you're concentrating on the wrong people. First it was Skulduggery and now it's me, when the people you should be after are the Diablerie. Why are you doing this, Remus? Are you afraid of challenging them? Is that why you're going after everybody *but* them?"

"You will lead me to the enemy. You're working with Pleasant—"

"If Skulduggery *was* Batu then he wouldn't have brought in Fletcher Renn in the first place, would he? He'd have locked him up until he needed him."

"Your attempts at logic are as pathetic as your attempts at seduction."

China laughed. "You have my word, Remus – I have *never* tried to seduce you."

His face reddened. "You've made a huge mistake in underestimating me, China. You chose to believe that I am not a man of my word. I told you what would happen. I made it quite clear. But you *haven't* helped me, and so I must go public with your secret."

"I don't know where he is," she insisted.

"It's too late." Crux took her by the arm and escorted her to the door.

"Remus, listen to me. No matter what you think you know of what happened, no matter what you were told, it isn't the whole story."

"You can tell your friend that when he finds you," Crux replied. "I'm sure he'll be in the mood to listen."

"You don't know what this could *do*," she snarled.

He smiled back at her. "I have an idea."

Crux opened the door and there was a man standing outside.

"Hello, China," Jaron Gallow said.

He walked in and Crux quickly backed into the apartment, taking China with him. She wrenched her arm from his grasp.

"You're part of it," Crux said to her, as Gallow gently closed the door. "You're all part of it. You're all working *together*."

"You're absolutely right, Detective," Gallow said, a small

smile on his lips. "Everyone is in on it. It's a conspiracy the likes of which you have never seen. China, Skulduggery Pleasant, even the Grand Mage. We *were* going to invite you to join us at Aranmore Farm for the final act, but we took a vote and nobody wanted to ride with you. Please don't take it personally."

Crux snapped his hand against the air, but Gallow moved out of the way, hooked his foot under the coffee table and sent it into Crux's chest. Crux staggered and went for his gun, but Gallow twisted it from his hand.

"Not much of a fighter, are you?" Gallow asked, and threw the detective across the room.

Crux tumbled and spun. He was panicking. Gallow was blocking his escape route and he must have known he didn't stand a chance against him, because he turned and ran for the window. He leaped, crashing through the glass and falling from sight.

Gallow strolled over, eyebrow arched in quiet amazement. He leaned on the sill, looking out, and smiled.

"He's alive," he said. "He's not crawling away particularly fast, but he's alive. It looks like his leg is broken. Possibly an arm. Can you hear him screaming? Unusually high-pitched."

"Why are you here, Jaron?" China asked.

He turned to her. "We can't be stopped, I hope you realise

that. In an hour we'll have Fletcher Renn, and then we'll be at the farm, and the gate will open, and we'll win. Just like we were always meant to."

"You're inviting back an angry race of gods who hate us. I hope *you* realise *that*."

"Have faith, China. Maybe they will rule, maybe they will scorch, maybe they will obliterate, or maybe they will just simply *be*. It is not our place to question them. A long time ago you told me that. You told me this world belongs to them. We've overseen it for millennia and now it's time to give it back. You taught me well."

"You *were* an excellent student," she admitted. "But if you're trying to get me to return to the fold, I'm going to have to disappoint you."

"Is that what you told Baron Vengeous when he asked you?"

"Something along those lines, yes."

"But he was alone, and unaware that Batu was orchestrating everything. Things are different now. This is a chance for you to come back to the Diablerie. Batu is a good leader. He has his plan. But he's not you. He could never be you."

"You want me to take over, just when Batu's plan is coming to fruition?" She smiled. "Why, Jaron, how delightfully treacherous of you."

"The Diablerie is yours, China, it always has been. Your family has been devoted to the Dark Gods for a thousand years. It's in your veins. It's in your blood. It's in your heart. This isn't something you can just shake off."

"My brother managed it."

"Mr Bliss is... unique."

"And Batu?"

"Will die by your command."

China strolled to the middle of the room, thinking about it. Finally, she stopped and looked at him. "The offer is, admittedly, somewhat tempting, but the fact of the matter is inescapable. I am a traitor to a race of sadistic gods who loathe humanity. Why would I want them to return?"

Gallow sighed. "That is unfortunate. I really didn't want to have to kill you."

"And I really didn't want to have to be killed. I don't suppose you've developed a sense of fair play since last we met?"

"You mean would I free you from those shackles? I'm afraid not." He picked Crux's gun up off the floor. "I'll make it quick though. I promise."

China stamped her foot. "How gracious of you." She took a step back and stamped her foot again.

He frowned. "No one's going to hear that, China."

She moved again, stamping her foot a third time. Gallow looked down at the carpet and his eyes narrowed when he recognised the three symbols she had just stamped on. She stepped out of her gorgeous shoes and stood in the middle of the triangle. She smiled as the floor gave way beneath her.

China dropped through the trapdoor, landing awkwardly in the second-floor corridor. The ceiling closed up above her just as Gallow was about to follow her down. She rolled to her knees and got up and ran for the stairs.

There'd be someone out the front waiting for Gallow to emerge. It would either be someone in a car – Gruesome Krav or Murder Rose – or someone capable of their own kind of travel, like Sanguine. She didn't want to find out which.

She got to the first floor. Gallow's footsteps were heavy on the stairs above her. She ran the length of the corridor, the floor sticky beneath her bare feet. She had built a lot of escape routes into this building and she ran for the nearest one.

Once again, events beyond her control had dragged her into the middle of things. China was *not* impressed.

32

THE TRADE

The Liffey Bridge is a bridge with three names.

It is a pedestrian bridge a little over 40 metres long, spanning the River Liffey from Ormond Quay to Aston Quay. Steps on either side lead up on to the walkway, and there are three lamps – one at the centre and two on either side – supported overhead by ironwork that curves out from the railings.

Its *given* name is the Wellington Bridge, its *true* name the Liffey Bridge, but it is by its taken name that it is most commonly known.

As a young girl, Tanith had been taken over to Dublin by her parents. The first time she crossed this bridge there were turnstiles, and the cost of travelling was one penny and one halfpenny. The turnstiles were done away with a few years later, around 1919 or so, but by then everyone knew the bridge as the Penny Ha'penny Bridge, which was eventually shortened to, simply, the Ha'Penny Bridge.

And it was at the Ha'penny Bridge, the bridge with three names, that they were expected to hand Fletcher Renn over to the enemy, giving them exactly what they needed to end the world.

"This is a really bad idea," Tanith said.

"I agree completely," Fletcher Renn murmured from beside her.

They had cordoned off the bridge on both sides, put up signs that alerted passers-by to delicate maintenance work. There was a red and white striped tent at either end to shield workers from wind and rain. There wasn't much of a wind today, and while the dark clouds rolled threateningly, no rain had yet fallen.

Tanith and Fletcher stood in the tent on the north side of the Liffey. There was a rush of sound as Ghastly joined them, and then the flap fell again and muted the noise from the traffic at their backs.

"No one sneaking up behind us," Ghastly informed them. He shook his head as he pulled down the well-tailored hood of his coat, revealing his scars.

They looked to the middle of the bridge, where Skulduggery was taking a cloaking sphere from his coat. He twisted both hemispheres in opposite directions and a bubble of haze erupted outwards, enveloping him, the bridge and the tents. He put the sphere down at his feet.

"What was *that*?" Fletcher asked, stunned.

"It makes us invisible to everyone outside the bubble," Ghastly said. "They won't be able to see or hear anything that goes on."

"So if I die screaming in agony, I won't disturb anyone? Oh, that's comforting."

Skulduggery walked back into the tent.

"Any word from Valkyrie?" Ghastly asked.

"Still none," Skulduggery said darkly. "When we have Guild, we'll make him release her, and then let me in a room alone with Crux for five long and painful minutes. Until then, we concentrate on the job."

"So what's the plan?" Fletcher asked. "How does this trade thing work?"

"In theory," Ghastly said, "the two of you will start walking

302

across the bridge at the same time, passing in the middle and walking on to the opposite side. In practice, however, that's not how it's going to work at all."

"Here's how it *really* works," Tanith told him. "Both sides start out playing fair. Then one side double-crosses the other. Then the other side springs *their* double-cross. Then the first side reacts accordingly."

Fletcher nodded. "So it's all about how many double-crosses you have?"

"Exactly, and the side with the most double-crosses wins."

"How many double-crosses do we have?"

Ghastly looked at Skulduggery.

"Two," Skulduggery said.

"That's... that's not an awful lot."

"Sometimes simplicity is best."

"Is this one of those times?"

"Probably not," Ghastly admitted.

"We're restricted in what we can do," Tanith said. "This is a public place, in broad daylight. We can't have a hundred Cleavers ready to spring into action."

"Do you have a hundred Cleavers?"

"Well, no."

"This is an unofficial operation," Skulduggery said. "There

is a spy in the Sanctuary, and until we find out who it is, we can't trust any of them."

"But if *we* are restricted in what we can do," Ghastly said, "then so are they."

"Right," Fletcher said. "All right. OK. And they value this whole 'never in public' rule as much as you do, yeah?"

Ghastly hesitated. "Sure," he said, completely failing to sound convincing.

"They're here," said Tanith quietly.

They all peeked out. At the other end of the bridge a black van had pulled into the side of the road, eliciting angry horn-blaring from the cars in the lane behind. Gruesome Krav stepped out and suddenly the blaring stopped. The cars behind indicated politely and pulled into the other lane.

Murder Rose got out next, followed by Sanguine and then Gallow, pulling Thurid Guild with him. Guild's hands were shackled and his face was bruised. The sordid little group were attracting a lot of attention, but they quickly disappeared into the striped tent.

"What are our double-crosses?" Fletcher asked.

"If you're expecting them," Skulduggery said, "you'll give them away."

Fletcher was growing paler by the second. "I'm really not sure about this."

"They don't want to hurt you," said Tanith.

"No, they just want to use me to destroy the world, and seeing as how I'm *in* the world, that would still be a bad thing for me. I know you all think that I'm really confident and nothing can faze me—"

"None of us think that," Ghastly said.

"My point is, I'm not going to walk over there and risk being caught. And I'm not even sure why you'd *want* me to."

"Mr Bliss wants Guild back," Skulduggery said, "and his argument is valid. Guild's death could have catastrophic consequences."

"*Could have*," Fletcher pointed out. "But if they get me to bring back the Faceless Ones, that *will* have catastrophic consequences! The first one's a possibility, the second is a certainty! Why am I the only one to be logical about this?"

Skulduggery looked at him. "When you have lived as long as we have, you see things in the long term and you plan accordingly."

Sanguine emerged from the other tent and strolled happily across the bridge.

"It's starting," Tanith said. "Fletcher, I'm really sorry about this, but you're going to have to trust us."

"Oh, bloody hell..."

Sanguine was a few steps away.

"You'd better not let them take me," Fletcher whispered.

"Knock knock," came Sanguine's slow, lazy drawl. He walked in, smiling, hands up and empty. "How ya'll doin' today? You don't mind me sayin', there are some serious faces lookin' back at me. A more sensitive fella than me might believe not everyone's excited about this. Come on, people, it's a trade! It's meant to be fun!"

"You talk an awful lot," Tanith said, "and you say precious little."

"Sword-lady," Sanguine smiled. "I have missed you, y'know that? Many a night I have lain awake, thinkin' of all the different ways I could kill you. My favourite scenario, it's a silly little thing, but it's where I cut your throat and your head rolls back, and your eyes are wide open and really, y'know, pleading, and I grab your hair and just..." He stopped and laughed. "Listen to me, gettin' all sentimental when there's business to be done. I been sent over here to orchestrate this whole affair, so... So I suppose let's get to orchestratin'."

"Send Guild over," said Skulduggery.

"Now that ain't how it's gonna be played, an' you know it. Rules of the game are fairly simple, but I'll go slow on account of the dumb-lookin' one – and I'll let you decide among yourselves which one of you I'm referrin' to."

Moving slowly, he took a pair of handcuffs from his pocket. "I'm gonna latch these here shackles on to Fletcher-boy's wrists," he continued, "just to make sure he don't do nothin' dumb like teleport away. Then he's gonna walk across to my friends there, as they send your boss man over here to you. It's fairly simple, all things considered. Even a child could understand it." He looked around. "Speakin' of children, where's the girl? I'm kinda missin' the scowl."

Skulduggery ignored the question. "You're staying this side of the bridge until the trade is complete."

Sanguine shook his head. "I got my orders. I gotta get back."

"We're not running the risk of you grabbing Fletcher and disappearing with him."

"It's a bridge, Bones. I travel through the ground, I travel through walls, I travel wherever I can fit – how am I supposed to fit beneath that little walkway?"

"All the same, you're staying here."

"All the same, no I ain't." Tanith's sword slid from her coat and pressed against his neck. Sanguine hesitated for just a moment. "You know what? I've just changed my mind. I'll stand over there and won't say a word."

Ghastly moved up behind him, twisting his arm into a lock that, if he moved, would result in excruciating pain and torn ligaments.

"I can't see why you don't just put me in shackles," Sanguine grunted.

"Because you said last year that shackles don't affect you," Tanith told him.

"I said that?"

"Yes, you did."

"I was lyin'. Shackles render me powerless. I swear."

"Try not to talk so much," Ghastly warned. "It annoys me."

"Tanith," Skulduggery said and stepped out of the tent. Tanith joined him and together they walked slowly across the bridge. Gallow and Murder Rose came to meet them.

The Liffey was dark and dirty beneath them.

"Skulduggery," Gallow said when they reached the middle. "Have you come to beg perhaps? To cry? Maybe you'd like to switch sides? It's too late, but it would be highly amusing to watch you try."

"Where's your master, Gallow?"

Gallow smiled. "I have no *master*. The Diablerie is a family of like-minded—"

"Batu is your master," Skulduggery interrupted. "He's the one giving you your orders, handing out your assignments, patting you on the head whenever you need it. So where is he? He's watching, isn't he?"

"He's around," Gallow smiled. Murder Rose whispered in his ear. "Oh yes, a very good point, Rose. Where is our Texan associate?"

"He's staying with us for the moment, until the trade is complete."

"A wise move, I suppose. You wouldn't want us cheating you, after all. Send the boy out, with the shackles on."

Gallow turned and walked back to the tent, Murder Rose behind him.

Tanith and Skulduggery returned to their tent.

"Are you ready?" Skulduggery asked Fletcher.

Fletcher looked at Tanith and she saw that he wasn't bothering to hide it any more – he was afraid. His eyes flickered back to Skulduggery and he held his hands out while Skulduggery cuffed him. "You have a plan, right?"

"I do."

"Can you tell me what it is?"

"We save the world, we all go home."

"That's a good plan."

"I have my moments."

Raindrops started to tap lightly on the tarpaulin cover.

"I'm not going to let anything happen to you," Skulduggery said.

"Do you think Valkyrie is all right?"

"Crux probably has her in one of the holding cells. To be honest, there's a fair chance that she's safer than any of us right now."

"OK. OK."

"They're not going to hurt you," Tanith said. "They need you."

Fletcher nodded. "After this, what say you and me go for a coffee or something? You'd really like me if you got to know me. I've known me for years and I love me."

She smiled. "Maybe."

"Really?"

"No."

He returned the smile with a shaky one of his own, and then he stepped into the bubble and vanished from sight. Tanith put her hand through, watching how it became instantly invisible, and then she took a step forward and now she could see him leaving the tent. Skulduggery was beside her, and Ghastly dragged Sanguine up so he could see what was going on.

Fletcher stepped on to the bridge. Across the way, the other tent opened and Thurid Guild emerged. They walked towards each other in the rain.

Skulduggery looked at Sanguine. "What are they planning?"

"What're who plannin'?"

Ghastly tightened his grip and Sanguine spoke quickly. "They ain't plannin' nothin'! This is a straight trade!"

"Ghastly, break his arm."

"Ghastly, do *not* break my arm!"

"Do it."

"There's a bomb!"

Skulduggery leaned in. "Where?"

"Guild's jacket," Sanguine said through gritted teeth. "He doesn't even know it's there. Gallow has the detonator. It's a small bomb, but enough to kill everyone here. Me included. So if you could do me a favour and stop him from getting' close, that'd be just swell."

Tanith looked back at the bridge. Fletcher and Guild had met in the middle and were passing each other without saying a word. Then Skulduggery was beside her, holding his gun out through the tent flap, pointed at Guild.

"What are you doing?" Tanith asked, alarmed.

"Stopping him from getting close," Skulduggery said and fired.

The bullet hit Guild's leg and he went down, screaming. Fletcher jumped back.

Horrified, Tanith grabbed Skulduggery's arm. "Are you *insane*?"

"Do not move!" Skulduggery shouted to Fletcher. "Stay beside him!" He shook Tanith's hand off. "Gallow won't detonate the bomb if Fletcher's going to be caught in the blast."

There was movement at the far tent, Gruesome Krav emerging with Murder Rose, but before they could run at Fletcher, Skulduggery clicked his fingers and sent a fireball into the air. It cleared the cloaking bubble and flared before dying out. It drew some curious looks from passers-by, and Tanith saw three figures in black – two men and one woman – converging on the enemy's tent from the other side of the bridge.

The Necromancers.

There was a burst of blackness in the far tent and Gallow came hurtling out. He hit Murder Rose and they both went down. The Necromancers strode on to the bridge after him, shadows curling around them.

Gallow recovered quickly and pulled a gun from his jacket

and fired. The nearest Necromancer used the shadows of her cloak to absorb the bullets, then spun, her cloak whirling and lengthening, slashing towards Gallow who had to dive to avoid being cut in two.

Murder Rose ran at Solomon Wreath, who gathered darkness in his cane and whipped it. Shadows flew like spears, hit Rose's leg and went right through. She shrieked and fell.

Tanith saw the third Necromancer firing the flintlock pistol at Krav, firing it without the need to reload. The bullets hit and Krav dropped to one knee, frantically trying to pull away the darkness that spread across his chest.

"Guess it's time," Sanguine said and Tanith looked around. He'd been holding something in his hand the entire time and no one had checked, and now it was dropping to the ground...

It flashed white and Tanith stumbled back, blinded. She could hear the others cursing around her, and Sanguine laughed, for he didn't have any eyes to blind.

But then neither did Skulduggery.

Sanguine's laugh was cut off in a strangled *gurk* and Tanith heard a body crashing down. There was the thump of an impact and then she heard a pained wheezing. Someone charged by her, out of the tent, and there were gunshots and shouts.

She blinked hard, images fading in, hazy and indistinct, but rapidly taking solid form. She saw a figure in brown, Sanguine, curled up on the ground, but Ghastly was a mere shape to her.

"Skulduggery?" he called.

"He's gone after them," Tanith told him. His features were too blurred to make out, but she was starting to see his ridged scars.

"Typical," she heard him mutter. "Can you see anything?"

"Sure," she lied, and grabbed her sword and lunged out, on to the bridge. Through the rain and the haze, she could just make out waves of darkness on the far side where the Necromancers were doing their thing.

Skulduggery was ahead of her – tall and thin and unmistakable – and his arm moved and a figure that could only have been Krav went flying back.

Her foot hit a step and she stumbled, but her vision was clearing fast. Ahead of her, Fletcher's blurred form was kneeling at Guild's side. Even with her eyes the way they were, she could see that Guild himself was pale and losing blood.

She ran to them, hearing Ghastly behind her. The Diablerie were being fought to a standstill and the good guys were about to secure both Fletcher and Guild. The battle was over. They'd won.

And then the final part of Batu's plan made itself known.

Something surged up from the river and loomed over the railings, splashing them with water. The Sea Hag dipped, her bony hands closing around Fletcher's waist. Without even a snarl, she lifted him into the air. Guild tried to snatch him back, but it was no use. Tanith glimpsed Fletcher's terrified face as he disappeared over the side, and she heard a heavy splash and knew he was gone.

Gallow shouted an order and ran back through the far tent. He jumped into the jeep, Murder Rose right behind him, and the jeep screeched away, shunting cars out of its path. Skulduggery went for Krav, but it was too late. Krav pulled himself over the railings and dropped into the Liffey.

Now, Tanith realised, the battle was over.

The Necromancers looked at Skulduggery, and Solomon Wreath turned and walked away, his coat billowing in the wind and rain.

Ghastly came up beside Tanith.

"Sanguine's gone," he said, but she'd already guessed that. Guild lay unconscious, his blood mixing with the rainwater. They watched Skulduggery as he stood there, his suit soaked and his fists clenched. His glistening skull was lowered, held in a way Tanith was unused to. It was something like defeat. And then he straightened.

"OK," he said. "Looks like we have a fight on our hands."

33

JAILBREAK

Valkyrie brushed the dried mud off the bottom of her jeans. Dust rose as muck fell and she brushed it off the bed.

Scapegrace moaned, and she sat forward. He didn't make another sound for a minute or so, and then he moaned again, and moved slightly. She watched him return to consciousness and prepared to spring into action.

He raised his head, looked at the bandage that tied his broken fingers to the bedpost and made a sound like a particularly dim and miserable cat. He looked at the cell door, then swivelled his head and saw Valkyrie.

"Oh, no," he mewled.

"If you move—" she began to threaten, but he interrupted her.

"I'm not going to move," he said. "I'm just going to lie here. I'm not going to do anything."

"Because if you *do* move..."

"I'm not going to!" he insisted. "If I didn't have a broken hand, then yes, I probably would move, and I'd probably try and kill you."

"No talking. Talking is not allowed."

He glared at her. "You know, every time I see you, you're more and more like him."

"Like who?"

"The detective. You think you're so smart and superior."

"I'm going to take that as a compliment."

"You shouldn't. I've heard stories about him, you know. About the things he's done. He's not this great and good hero you think he is."

"You don't know what I think of him."

Scapegrace laughed. "I can see it in your eyes. Everyone can. It's cute actually, the way you follow him around, believing every word he says."

Valkyrie shifted her weight slightly and the bed creaked and moved, and the bandage tugged on his fingers. Scapegrace howled.

"Sorry," she said unconvincingly.

"You did that on purpose!" he raged.

The slot in the door opened up and a pair of eyes peered in.

"What's going on in there?" a voice demanded. Valkyrie bounded to her feet, jarring the bed and making Scapegrace howl again.

"You can't keep me here!" she called.

"Who is that? Are there... are there two people in there?"

She recognised his voice now – the cell guard they had encountered the previous day.

"Weeper?" she said.

His eyes found her and they widened in shock. "Valkyrie Cain?"

"Remus Crux put me in here, with a man who wants to kill me. You can't keep me here. Please."

Beneath her, Scapegrace snorted contemptuously. She nudged the bed with her foot and heard him mewl in pain.

"Why did he make you share a cell?" Weeper asked.

"We've got four empty ones. Are you OK? Have you been injured?"

"Please get me out of here."

"I can't transfer prisoners without orders from my superiors."

"But this isn't even a transfer! This is just moving from one cell to another! Please, Weeper. If you leave me in here another minute, he'll kill me."

She looked down at Scapegrace and glared, and he sighed.

"She's right," he said reluctantly. "I'll kill her."

On the other side of the door, Weeper was shaking his head. "I'm sorry, there is a procedure to follow. Just wait there, I'll get this sorted out in ten minutes."

"Don't go!" Valkyrie cried. She had moved her hands behind her back, and was hoping Weeper wouldn't have noticed that they had been at her sides. "Please, move me to an empty cell and then check with your bosses. I'm defenceless in here. Please, Weeper."

She made her eyes as wide as possible and Weeper sighed.

"Fine," he said gruffly. "Put your hands through the bottom slot so I can cuff you."

"I'm already cuffed. Crux didn't bother removing my shackles when he threw me in here."

"That is strictly against protocol," Weeper muttered disapprovingly, and she saw him open the cell directly across from hers.

"OK then," he said. "You are to move directly into the empty cell. You do not engage me in conversation or stall in any way. Clear?"

"Clear."

"And Scapegrace, you stay on the ground or I'll have the Cleavers here so fast..."

"I'm not moving," Scapegrace said.

"All right then. I'm opening the door."

The door swung open and Valkyrie breathed with relief. "Thank you," she said.

"Move to the empty cell."

She stepped into the corridor. "Thank you so much."

"The cell. In. Now."

"I'm really sorry about this," she said as she brought her hands up and pushed lightly at the air. The space between them rippled and Weeper stumbled backwards into the empty cell, tripping over his own legs. Before he could recover, Valkyrie slammed the door.

Immediately, his eyes appeared at the open slot. "Oh, no. This *can't* happen again."

"I'm so, so sorry."

Scapegrace got to his feet, carefully untying the bandage from his fingers. "How stupid are you?" he laughed. "Locked in your own cell, twice in two days! They give out medals for morons now, do they?"

He was grinning as he moved to leave, but Valkyrie stood in front of him, clicking her fingers and conjuring fire into her hand.

"And where do you think you're going?" she growled.

He blinked at her. "We're escaping."

"We?"

"Yes, we. We're breaking out."

"You're not going anywhere."

"But I helped you!"

"You lay on the ground and whined."

"In a helpful manner," he insisted. "You're going to need my help to get out of here. You think you're going to be able to just stroll out? You're going to need back-up, an extra pair of eyes, even a distraction – and I think I've proven what a good distraction I can be."

She wanted to slam the door in his face, but he was right. If she was discovered, they could split up and the Cleavers would automatically go after the adult first.

"Give me one good reason why I should even run the *risk* of helping you escape. Your grand ambition in life is to *kill* people."

"Yes, but..." Scapegrace faltered, then looked down at his shoes and his bottom lip quivered. "But as you keep pointing out," he continued, "I'm not very good at it, now am I?"

"I... suppose not."

Valkyrie sighed and let the flames go out in her hand.

"Fine," she said. "Come on and stay quiet."

She hurried to the desk and opened and closed drawers, searching for her phone. She found it, noted the five missed calls on the screen. She dialled Skulduggery while Scapegrace, a smile on his face, fished out loose money from an open drawer. She tapped the drawer closed with her foot, catching his fingers. He yelped and leaped back, grabbed his right hand with his left by pure instinct, and yelped again as both sets of injured fingers came into contact.

"Valkyrie," Skulduggery's voice said on the phone. He sounded relieved but urgent. "Where are you?"

Scapegrace hopped and screamed in silence beside her, and she did her best to ignore him.

"I'm in the Sanctuary," she said. "Did the trade happen?"

He hesitated. "Yes. They have Fletcher, we have Guild, but

he's unconscious. We're still fugitives until he wakes up. You're going to have to get yourself out. Can you do that?"

"Course I can. I'll use the secret passage."

"Don't. Guild will have deactivated it after last time. You're going to have to leave through the main door. If you're not out in ten minutes, I'm coming in after you."

"Someone's coming, I have to go."

Valkyrie jammed her phone into her jeans and motioned to Scapegrace to hide. They flattened themselves against the wall and she peeked out. A sorcerer passed in the corridor ahead, never even glancing at the holding area. She waited until his footsteps had faded away.

They didn't have much time. Every second spent undetected was a second stolen.

Then the lights went out.

Valkyrie whirled, bracing herself for the attack. The space around her was silent. She held out a hand, doing her best to read the air, and the only movement she felt was Scapegrace behind her.

"What's happening?" he whispered.

"How should I know?"

"You didn't do this? Or the skeleton? Or your friends?"

"This isn't us. Maybe there's a power cut."

"In the Sanctuary? Sanctuaries don't *have* power cuts. This is an attack. Maybe it's *my* friends, breaking me out."

"You don't have any friends."

"Which would make it unlikely, but not impossible."

She clicked her fingers, taking the spark into her palm and feeding it magic, letting the flame grow bigger and brighter. The light flickered off the walls.

She could hear someone shouting, and even though the shout was urgent, there was no danger in it. If Scapegrace was right, if this was an attack, then maybe it hadn't begun yet. And maybe she could use this to her advantage.

They picked up their pace, jogging through the dark. Occasionally, they'd see another flame ahead of them or behind them, and they'd divert course to stay away. Valkyrie was struggling to keep her sense of direction, following a map in her mind that she hoped was accurate.

Something moved ahead of her and she jerked back, stifling a scream. It was a Cleaver, crossing their path and immediately disappearing into the gloom. Either he hadn't seen her face or else he just didn't consider her a priority. Valkyrie wondered if they could see in the dark.

There were voices in the next corridor, so they turned right in an attempt to circumvent any crowds. So far, Scapegrace hadn't been a whole lot of help, and she was starting to think of the best way to abandon him.

She heard a familiar voice and stopped. Scapegrace ran into her, squashing his hands between them. He spun around and fell to his knees in muted agony.

"Quiet," she whispered and extinguished her flame. Mr Bliss approached, talking with a slender woman holding a torch. Valkyrie recognised the Administrator's soothing tones.

"With the respect due to your position," the Administrator was saying, "security matters are handled by the Cleavers, not the Elders. Besides which, with the Grand Mage injured, you need to be kept safe."

"By the time someone gets around to telling me what has happened," Bliss responded, "it may be too late to do anything about it."

Valkyrie straightened up. Bliss would help her get out and the Administrator would do whatever she was told. This would also be the perfect opportunity to send Scapegrace back to his cell.

"Sir," the Administrator said sharply and they stopped walking. The beam of her torch had picked out something on the wall. Valkyrie could see a carved symbol. The Administrator edged forward curiously. "I've seen this before," she said. "I just can't remember where."

"Stay away from it," Bliss ordered. "Symbols are my sister's forte, not mine, but even so..."

"Sir?"

"It's a warning sigil, a silent alarm. If we pass, it will alert whoever is waiting in the corridor ahead."

Valkyrie frowned. If there were enemies lurking nearby, ready to spring an ambush, then she hadn't seen them.

The Administrator stepped back. "We should go the other way and send the Cleavers."

Bliss knelt by the symbol. "Shine the light here."

"Sir, this isn't safe."

"Shine the light."

Slowly, Bliss reached for the symbol and it started to glow. He shook his head.

"I was wrong. This isn't a warning sigil."

"No," the Administrator agreed, "it's not."

She stepped back as a dozen symbols lit up, catching Bliss in a circle of blue light.

He tried to stand, but energy crackled and streams of light seared through his body, connecting the symbols to each other, with him at their centre. The Administrator, no longer needing her torch to light up her surroundings, flicked it off.

Valkyrie stared. The *Administrator* was the traitor – the one who had told Sanguine how to open the Grotesquery's cage, the one who had told him how to find Baron Vengeous's prison cell a year earlier. The Administrator, brought in by Guild, but working for the Diablerie.

Bliss grunted and fell to his knees. His strong shoulders sagged, and his head lolled forward.

"You're not an easy man to kill," the Administrator said. "Batu worked for a long time researching this. Another few minutes and then it'll be over. He assured me it would be quite painful."

Valkyrie turned to Scapegrace to try and formulate a rescue plan, and she caught sight of him just as he fled around the far corner. Seething, she looked back. Even if she somehow performed the miraculous feat of overpowering the Administrator, she didn't know how to deactivate the trap. That meant she needed the Administrator conscious, which added another layer of the impossible.

She couldn't think of anything clever to do, so she crawled, sticking to the shadows as much as possible. When there was no more room to sneak, she took a breath and launched herself forward. She pushed at the air and the Administrator whirled, her own hands open and flat. The spaces between them rippled and surged, the disturbance warping the Administrator's smile.

Then the Administrator waved and Valkyrie was yanked off her feet. She slammed into a wall, and the Administrator raised her arm and Valkyrie slid upwards, to the ceiling.

"You're a beginner," the Administrator told her kindly. "You couldn't expect to defeat me. But it was a noble effort."

The air around her was heavy, too heavy to shift. Valkyrie strained to move her arms, but she was pinned tight. She turned her head to take a breath, but there was nothing to take.

"Sorry," the Administrator said, "I can't allow you to breathe. You have to die, just as Mr Bliss has to die. It's all part of Batu's plan, you see."

Valkyrie gasped uselessly. She tried clicking her fingers, but with a gesture from the Administrator, the rest of the oxygen whistled away from her, and no flame would grow.

Her lungs, however, were burning fiercer than any fire.

She heard something beyond the blood pumping in her ears. Someone was screaming and the scream was getting closer. Her eyes flickered to the left as Scapegrace pelted out of the darkness, hit the wall and hurtled off again in another direction. Two Cleavers raced after him, and came to a sudden yet graceful stop when they saw Bliss in a circle of blue, Valkyrie pinned against the ceiling, and the Administrator standing between them, with a look of shock on her pretty face.

They unsheathed their scythes.

The Administrator released her hold and Valkyrie fell to the floor, gasping. The Administrator stepped back.

"Don't. Just... Listen to me. Just... don't..."

The Cleavers darted forward and the Administrator turned, tried to run, but Valkyrie stuck out her foot and she tripped. The Administrator toppled into the circle of blue and all those streams of energy branched off from Bliss and struck her. She screamed and her body twisted. There was a loud *pop*, a smell of ozone and the blue light vanished.

Darkness again, but for the hazy blue images that swam in Valkyrie's vision. A torch was turned on. The Administrator was on the ground, unmoving, and one of the Cleavers was checking Bliss.

The second Cleaver was standing over Valkyrie. She began to crawl away and the Cleaver moved to stop her.

"Leave her," Bliss whispered.

The Cleaver stopped and Valkyrie scrambled to her feet and ran.

She ran blindly through the dark until she saw moving lights ahead. She ducked into a room. She heard Crux in the lead, and waited for them to pass before stepping out and continuing on. She reached the Foyer, where someone had set up emergency lights, and she kept her head down as she joined the line of people leaving. She took the stairs out of the Sanctuary and passed through the disused Waxworks Museum. The sorcerers around her were talking about an attack and exchanging theories, and at the first opportunity, Valkyrie detached herself from the group.

She left the Waxworks Museum, stepped out under a grey sky spilling rain and jogged to the street. The Purple Menace pulled up sharply and she got in.

"Where are the others?" was the first thing she asked.

"Already on their way to Aranmore."

"Let's go."

Skulduggery put the black bag containing the Sceptre in her lap and with a squeal of tyres, her prison break was complete.

34

THE BATTLE OF ARANMORE

hey drove the rest of the way in silence, with only Skulduggery's skill stopping them from skidding off the road. By the time they reached Aranmore, it had stopped raining, and the Purple Menace took the turn and sped up the meandering driveway, long grasses growing on either side. There was a plume of smoke just over the hill and Ghastly's van came into view. It was on its side, burning fiercely. The doors were open.

There was an explosion up ahead and they saw Tanith

flipping away from it. She landed and ran for the corner of the farmhouse. She reached it just as a hail of bullets tore up the ground at her feet.

"They have machine guns," Valkyrie said quietly.

"And hand grenades."

The Purple Menace braked and Skulduggery kicked the door open. Valkyrie gripped the black bag.

"Stay low," he said and they ran.

She caught a glimpse of the Diablerie in the yard on the other side of the farmhouse. She saw Fletcher, his hands cuffed in front of him, staggering after Gallow. Murder Rose saw her, raised her gun and fired. Valkyrie stumbled, but kept running until she reached the cottage and got behind cover.

Skulduggery pulled his revolver from his jacket. "Ghastly?" he called to Tanith.

"He's somewhere around," she said, ducking back as more bullets slammed into the corner beside her.

The door to the farmhouse was yanked open and Paddy charged out, shotgun in hand and yelling a battle cry. Skulduggery pushed at the air, nudging the shotgun upwards just as Paddy fired, and then gestured and the gun flew into his grip.

Paddy realised who he had just tried to shoot and winced. "Sorry! Sorry!"

"What are you still doing here?" Skulduggery demanded. "I called to tell you to leave."

"To be honest, I don't really give a damn what you told me to do. Give me back my gun."

"Paddy, this isn't safe."

"You don't think I have a right to be here? This is my home. It has been for forty-two years. I'm not abandoning it just because a bunch of wizards are waving their wands about and firing a few bullets."

"This is dangerous," Valkyrie said.

"I am perfectly capable of taking care of myself, young lady. I have plenty of cartridges for my shotgun and this is a new pair of trousers. I'm ready."

"If you're volunteering," Skulduggery said, handing him back his shotgun, "stay here with Valkyrie."

"You can count on me, Mr Skeleton."

The ground erupted behind them and two figures flew from the spray of dirt – Ghastly, with his arm wrapped around the throat of Billy-Ray Sanguine. They hit the ground and tumbled, Ghastly losing his hold. Sanguine gasped, suddenly able to breathe again, and he unfolded his straight razor and came at Ghastly with a snarl.

Ghastly dodged, then jabbed, and Sanguine's head jerked back. Ghastly's fist crashed into Sanguine's ribs, lifting him off his feet. Stunned, Sanguine could only swing the razor wildly as Ghastly moved in and caught him with a perfect right hook.

Sanguine's legs gave out from under him and he dropped.

"Into the farmhouse," Skulduggery ordered.

Tanith went first, then Paddy. Skulduggery ushered Valkyrie in before him. Ghastly came last, shutting the door. They stayed low as bullets flew and glass rained down upon them.

Skulduggery crawled to the window that looked out on the yard and returned fire. The sheds and the farm machinery provided excellent cover for Murder Rose as she danced and spun, reloading her machine gun and laughing all the while.

"Where are the Necromancers?" he shouted to Ghastly.

"Wreath was supposed to be approaching from the west, to come up from behind. I don't know what's keeping them."

"Never trust a Necromancer," Tanith growled.

Valkyrie risked a glance. At the far side of the yard she saw Gruesome Krav drop the Grotesquery's torso inside a chalk circle that Jaron Gallow was drawing on the ground. Fletcher tried to run, but Krav hauled him back, throwing him down beside the torso. Gallow was drawing something else now – symbols, all around the circle.

Before Valkyrie could ask anyone what was happening, the symbols began to glow and red smoke rose from them, mixed with the black smoke that rose from the circle, collecting into a cloud that swirled around the circle's perimeter, roaring like a hurricane.

"Damn," Skulduggery said and switched targets from Rose to Gallow. But it was like the bullets hit the smoke and were caught up in it as it rose high into the air in a spiralling column.

Valkyrie glimpsed Fletcher, on his knees, the shackles on the ground beside him. Gallow was standing close, both hands gripping the boy's shoulders. The shackles were off, but if Fletcher tried to teleport away, he'd take Gallow with him – and she knew Gallow would waste no time in punishing him for his disobedience.

Gallow made Fletcher put his hands on the Grotesquery. He was doing it. He was going to open the gateway. The smoke swirled and he was hidden from view.

Valkyrie looked over at Murder Rose as the madwoman laughed and lobbed something at the farmhouse.

Valkyrie whirled. There was an explosion behind her and

she was thrown off her feet amid a shower of splinters and rubble and glass. She fell painfully, ears ringing, dust in her mouth and pain in her shoulder.

"Valkyrie!" Skulduggery shouted.

"I'm OK!" she called back, her voice dull. She looked around for the bag with the Sceptre, saw it in the corner.

Bullets peppered the wall above her and Ghastly dragged her from the danger zone.

"Hold still," he said, and he gripped something at her back and pulled. She hollered and jerked away from him. He was holding a shard of glass, the tip dripping with her blood. "Anywhere else hurt?"

"I'm fine," she lied.

"I've got a new set of clothes for you. Nothing will get through them. They're in a bag in the van. Think you can make it?"

She nodded and he pulled her up. She did her best not to wince. There was a fresh burst of gunfire and an ugly painting on the wall was reduced to tattered paper in a broken frame. Ghastly yanked open the door.

"Go," he said. Valkyrie bolted from the farmhouse. She ran for the burning van and dropped, skidding along the ground until she was behind it.

She pushed at the air to clear the smoke and saw the bag on the back seat. She reached in, stretching for the bag strap, and yanked it out. The smoke curled and washed over her and she closed her eyes against the stinging. She crawled backwards, coughing, until she felt grass under her. Her eyes watered when she opened them.

She used her toes to pry off her trainers as she threw away her tattered jacket, then zipped the sleeveless tunic over her T-shirt. Her jeans were filthy, splattered with mud. She discarded them on the grass and pulled on the black trousers, barely registering how well they fitted, how they were instantly perfect. Her new boots felt as if she'd been wearing them for years.

Valkyrie searched through the pockets of her old clothes, transferred whatever she found in there and then pulled on the coat. It was shorter than her last one, stopping mid-thigh. All these new clothes were black except for the coat sleeves, which were of a red so dark it looked like dried blood.

She tied her hair back and heard something like a whisper behind her. She turned in time to see a fist swinging her way. She dodged back, almost tripping over her discarded clothes. Her assailant kept coming, a thing of papery skin and stitches, dragging its heavy feet. Valkyrie clicked her fingers and sent a fireball into its chest. The fire burned through and ignited the gases within, but there was another one behind it, and another one behind that. Valkyrie ran to the farmhouse, giving herself some room before she looked back.

An army of Hollow Men, marching with that slow, awkward trudge, moved across the fields towards her.

She ran into the cottage, slamming the door behind her. There was a lull in the gunfire, but she ducked low anyway.

"Hollow Men," she said, and immediately Tanith leaped to the door, pressing her hand against the wood.

"Withstand," she said, and a sheen spread outwards from her palm.

"How many?" Skulduggery asked.

"I don't know. Two or three hundred."

"Oh, hell," said Ghastly.

"I don't know how the Diablerie got them here," Skulduggery said, "but we've fought Hollow Men before and they haven't posed a problem. They're only a threat if you let them surround you."

"There's 300 of them," Tanith pointed out. "Surrounding us isn't going to be an issue."

"They're throwing everything they have at us because they

need to keep us occupied. We *have* to stop Fletcher from opening that—"

He was interrupted by another hail of gunfire that sent everyone to the ground.

The Hollow Men hammered on the door, but the sheen that Tanith had applied to it held it firm and solid. There was nothing she could do with the windows, however, and it wasn't long before the Hollow Men smashed through the remaining glass. The glass tore holes in their arms, and green gas billowed out as they deflated – but there were more of them coming up behind.

Murder Rose was striding across the yard and back again, her machine gun spitting bullets. Skulduggery put his revolver away.

"I'm out," he said. "Looks like it's over the top for us."

"I hate going over the top," Ghastly muttered.

Paddy leaped up, still firing back, thanks to his endless supply of shotgun cartridges, but Skulduggery waited until the next time Rose had to reload.

"Move," he said, then leaped through the window, Ghastly and Tanith right behind him.

Valkyrie watched through the window as Skulduggery ran straight for the column of red and black smoke, leaving Ghastly and Tanith to deal with the others. Ghastly pushed at the air. Rose staggered and Tanith slammed into her. The machine gun went flying and Rose's knives were suddenly in her hands.

Krav went for Ghastly, Hollow Men swarmed the yard, and Paddy pulled Valkyrie out of sight.

"If we stay quiet," he whispered, "they might forget about us."

"I'm not just going to *watch*," she said angrily as she shook off his hand. She stayed low until she was clear of the window, and hurried to the black bag.

Paddy came after her with a defiant look on his face. "Your skeleton friend made it very clear, Valkyrie. You are only to leave this house if all else fails."

"I never do what he tells me. He knows that."

"Skulduggery said you were their last hope," Paddy tried. "Surely you owe it to everyone who is fighting right now to stay here, to wait until you are needed. If you go out now, if something happens to you, what use are you *then*?"

Valkyrie had her hand in the bag and her fingers curled around the Sceptre.

"I know you want to help," Paddy continued. "I know it is breaking your heart to watch this, but if you do *not* follow the plan, it will all be for nothing."

Valkyrie clenched her jaw, and looked at Paddy and his shoulders hunched in sympathy.

"I'm sorry."

She knew he was right. For the first time ever, they had a plan. The least she could do was stick to it.

From outside, she heard sounds of battle.

"What can you do?" Paddy asked. "Why are you their last hope? Do you have a special power no one else has?"

Valkyrie shook her head. "No. But I have a *weapon* no one else has." She took the Sceptre of the Ancients from the bag. "This is the only thing in existence that can kill a god, and I'm the only one who can use it."

Paddy's eyebrows shot up. "That's a lot of responsibility."

"That's what *I* was thinking," Valkyrie said softly. "There's a prediction about me, you know. I die and the world ends."

"The prediction is about today?"

"It fits, doesn't it? If I get killed, and there's no one around for the Sceptre to pass on to, then it's all over. So today is the day I die."

"And your parents don't know about any of this, do they?"

"No."

"If they did though, they would be so proud. I never had

342

children, but if I had, I'd have wanted them to turn out just like you."

He stepped over to an old photograph on the bedside table, and picked up a gold ring that lay behind it.

"This was my mother's," he said. "I always planned to someday give it to the woman I would marry. Such a shame. My remaining years will pass in the blink of an old man's eye, and I'll leave behind no legacy. No one will care."

Valkyrie busied herself putting the Sceptre back in the bag and zipping it closed. She didn't know how to respond to that.

He approached, holding out the gold ring. "Would you wear this?"

"I... Paddy, I couldn't..."

"I never got around to marrying."

"There's still time."

"You're a kind girl and a terrible liar. Of course, the fact that magic exists, means that miracles *can* happen – so would you do me a favour? Keep this for me until I need it."

"Are you sure you wouldn't prefer to hold it yourself?"

"It would mean a lot, to know that I'm passing it to someone who is worthy of it."

Valkyrie hesitated, then took the ring and slipped it on her right index finger.

"It looks good on you," Paddy said with a smile.

She found herself grinning back at him. "I'll keep it safe," she promised. "For however long we have left."

There were footsteps on the roof, moving quickly. They went to the window as a dozen or more Cleavers dropped from the farmhouse roof into the yard, their scythes already out, and before the Hollow Men could even turn, those scythes were slicing.

"Are they on our side?" Paddy asked, confused.

"Oh, yeah," Valkyrie smiled.

Valkyrie saw Ghastly throwing fire. Hollow Men wheeled, their internal gases bursting into flame. She saw China, dressed head to foot in black, tapping the symbols on her forearms and sending a wave of blue energy slamming into Krav as he charged at her.

Skulduggery was at the column of smoke, trying to push his way through. She glimpsed Fletcher, his hands on the Grotesquery, and even from this distance she saw the pain on his face. He tried to move, but Gallow kept him on his knees, and then Fletcher arched his back, and over the roar of the smoke, she heard him scream.

Ten metres away from him a yellow light appeared in thin air. It got brighter, and bigger. It was growing fast. In ten seconds it was the size of a human head. Valkyrie could see inside it now. At the centre the light was calm, and a little less bright, but the edges were like angry licks of flame, dragging the gateway ever wider.

The Necromancers had arrived at the yard, and by the looks of them, they had fought the whole way there. Solomon Wreath shouted orders and the female Necromancer swirled her cloak, its edges tearing through the Hollow Men around her. The male Necromancer fired his flintlock pistol, each dark bullet perforating multiple Hollow Men at a time.

Wreath used his cane like he was conducting music, sending waves of darkness crashing down upon his enemies.

Valkyrie watched the gateway get bigger and bigger, and their chances for survival get smaller and smaller.

Tanith was facing off against Murder Rose, but she had a look on her face Valkyrie had rarely seen – fear. Murder Rose was better than Tanith and Tanith knew it.

Blades flashed and Tanith gave ground. Rose's long knives parried and blocked Tanith's increasingly desperate sword swipes, and Rose was smiling. She was toying with Tanith, enjoying the fact that she could end this at any time.

And then, she decided to end it.

35

THE THINGS OF
IMPOSSIBILITY

anith tried to flip backwards but Murder Rose
lunged, one of her knives slicing into Tanith's
shoulder.

Valkyrie jumped to her feet and shouted Tanith's name.

Tanith slashed wildly as she backed off. Rose moved
sideways and in, stabbing through her right leg.

Tanith fell to one knee, but caught Rose's wrist just as the
madwoman went for her throat. Rose casually pressed the tip
of her other knife against the back of Tanith's hand, and in

one smooth motion she pushed it all the way in.

Tanith screamed and Rose kicked her on to her back, then moved in for the kill.

Valkyrie saw something blur, something white, and Murder Rose had to duck to avoid the White Cleaver's scythe.

The Cleaver spun low and Rose flipped, then closed in with unnatural speed. The White Cleaver dodged the swipe of one knife and blocked the other. He kicked at her leg. She stumbled and the scythe blade whipped by her, barely missing her throat.

Rose went to defend herself against a low strike that the Cleaver abruptly shifted. The scythe's handle cracked into Rose's jaw and she fell.

Valkyrie was about to run out to help Tanith when the wall in front of her exploded. She fell back, coughing. She heard Paddy beside her and looked through the dust and debris as Gruesome Krav, cursing vehemently, did his best to stand.

Mr Bliss stepped through the giant hole he had made in the wall.

"My sister?" he snarled, waiting for Krav to straighten up. "You tried to kill my *sister?*"

Krav swung a punch. Bliss closed his hand around the fist

and squeezed, and Krav roared as all the bones in his hand were crushed.

Bliss punched him and Krav hit the opposite wall, cracking it. "My sister is the only family I have *left.*"

He slammed into Krav and they went through the opposite wall and took the fight outside.

Ghastly came through the first hole, supporting Tanith with her arm around his neck. She was bleeding badly, but still gripping her sword. Valkyrie hurried to them as he sat her on a chair by the table.

"I can still fight," Tanith muttered.

"Look after her," Ghastly barked, and ran back out.

"Tanith," Valkyrie said, hunkering down to look at her. "Tanith, can you hear me?"

"She beat me, Val..."

"She got lucky." Valkyrie looked at Paddy. "Do you have any bandages or medical supplies?"

He nodded and moved off. "I keep a first-aid kit somewhere around here."

He started rummaging around in drawers, and Valkyrie went to help him search. It was when she glanced back to make sure Tanith hadn't passed out that she saw the wall starting to crack. She barely had time to shout a warning before Billy-Ray Sanguine leaped through. He grabbed Tanith's hair and slammed her head down on to the table.

Paddy swung the shotgun around, but Sanguine threw Tanith into him. Valkyrie clicked her fingers, but failed to summon a spark. Sanguine sank into the ground. She heard him step from the wall beside her and she kicked out without looking. Her boot hit him in the leg – he grunted and she tried to follow up with a right cross, but he blocked it and punched her, straight in the sternum. Valkyrie flew backwards, falling over a chair and sprawling to the ground.

The shotgun blasted and blasted again, and she looked up to see Paddy staring at a bare wall, eyes wide with astonishment. Sanguine rose up through the floor behind him and shoved him into the wall, hard.

"Everyone bein' so eager to die," Sanguine said, "almost takes the fun outta killin' them."

He went for Valkyrie and she jumped to the table and rolled over it. He laughed, diving at her, but she snatched up Tanith's sword and turned, bringing it around in a wide arc. The blade opened up Sanguine's belly and he stopped, mouth open, looking down at himself while she backed away.

"What have you done?" he asked, bewildered.

Blood ran from the cut, quickly soaking his shirt and

deepening the colour of his suit.

"*What the hell have you done?*" he screeched and the fury in his voice hit her harder than his fists ever had.

The ground swallowed him.

Paddy groaned on the floor, but appeared to be OK. Valkyrie helped Tanith back into the chair, and put the sword on the table beside her, then went to the window.

Something flew out of the gate and it caught in her mind and a shockwave hit the farmhouse and she was thrown back.

Her thoughts went quiet.

The broken glass beneath her hands. The breeze, stirred to wind outside. The world, dull and deadened.

Another shockwave hit the farmhouse.

And another.

Her mouth was dry and her head was pounding. Slowly, she crawled over rubble, to the hole in the wall.

Outside, there were others, on the ground. Lying down. Lots of paper people. Some people in black. Swirling red and black smoke. A skeleton. There was a skeleton, stumbling towards her.

She heard a voice that said, "Valkyrie."

The skeleton's hands were gloved. She felt the fingers, thin and tight on her arm, and that word again – "Valkyrie".

More words now – "Look at me, Valkyrie, look—" coming from the skeleton's mouth. From Skulduggery's mouth.

"Skulduggery," she murmured.

"—need you to focus. Did you look at them? The things that came out of the gateway, did you look at them?"

Her own voice was distant. "Glimpsed," she said.

She was pulled to her feet. She could hear more now. She could see others, trying to stand. China. Ghastly. She saw the Necromancers, attacking the last of the Hollow Men as they struggled to their clumsy feet.

She saw a boy, Fletcher Renn, crawling out of the column of smoke. A man, who looked like the shockwave had thrown him from the circle, saw Fletcher and reached for him.

Fletcher disappeared, instantly reappearing a short distance away. The man, Gallow, lunged, and once again Fletcher vanished and reappeared nearby. Gallow was furious, and Fletcher closed his eyes and concentrated, and this time, when he teleported, he didn't come back.

Now that Fletcher wasn't keeping it open, the bright yellow ring that hung in mid-air started to shrink. Valkyrie watched it until it disappeared.

"Valkyrie," Skulduggery barked. "I need you to snap out of

it, you understand me? Valkyrie Cain, I need you with me."

She looked at him, and her thoughts sharpened, and she nodded. "Yes."

"You're with me?"

They sharpened and became clear. "Yes. Yes, I'm with you. The gate's closed."

"Some of them got out. I counted three. We need the Sceptre *now*."

She nodded, and she was just about to get it when Krav came staggering around the corner. He ignored them completely and staggered on, Bliss striding after him.

"Leave me alone!" Krav shouted. He was bruised and bleeding, and the tattoo on his inner arm was pulsing with a red glow.

The pressure popped in her ears and Valkyrie winced. Goosebumps rippled across her flesh and she felt her heart slamming against her chest. She was scared. She was suddenly and incredibly terrified.

Skulduggery grabbed her and pulled her down. "Don't look at it," she heard him say.

For a moment, there was nothing.

She saw it out of the corner of her eye. Passing behind the trees, five times as tall, a towering, changing beast, a trick of the light, an abstract thing of unbelievable angles. She looked away, but she could still see it, in her mind. It had burned its way through. It was an idea, or the hint of an idea, or the memory of something she'd never known, or the shadow of all of these things, their inverted reflection, on a still lake at night.

It couldn't be real. It had no substance. It had no weight. It had mass, but behind the mass there was no depth. How could it be real? It made no sense. It couldn't be real and it made no sense.

She tried to look again at this being of fractured angles and broken reason, but her head wouldn't turn. It was impossibility made manifest, the formless given form, and it stalked across the landscape accompanied not by thunderous footfall, but by the whisper of a thousand dead languages and the muted cry of carrion birds.

There was a rush, and she heard Krav scream. The pressure popped again in her ears and she blinked. Her eyes gradually focused.

The creature of madness was gone. Gruesome Krav was standing with his shoulders slumped and his head down. He was perfectly still, though his hair whipped in the wind. Whipped and fell.

His hair fell gently out, strand by strand, and his head tilted upwards in time for Valkyrie to see his face melting. The nose and the ears were the first to go, sinking back into the skin. The lips congealed, sealing the mouth, and the eyes turned to liquid and dripped from the sockets down either cheek, like tears. The eyelids closed and ran into each other. The Faceless Ones had taken their first vessel.

Bliss ran at it, but Krav, or the Faceless One that had once been Krav, just held out its hand.

Bliss's run faltered. He doubled over, and Valkyrie could see the look of pain on his face, and something else too. Surprise. A man like Bliss wasn't used to feeling pain.

The Faceless One raised its arm, and Bliss was lifted off the ground.

The Faceless One curled its hand, and Bliss's body twisted into bits of pulverised bone and shredded flesh.

Her stomach lurching violently, Valkyrie watched him die.

Skulduggery grabbed her and pushed her back into the farmhouse. "Sceptre," he called, as he ran towards the Faceless One.

36

ENEMIES

Valkyrie hurried back into the farmhouse. Paddy turned to her and she looked at him blankly.

Mr Bliss was dead.

Bile rose in her throat and she lunged to the corner, throwing up.

"They're here, aren't they?" Paddy asked.

She retched and spat and wiped her mouth. "Three of them," she said.

He nodded. "I'll get you your magic stick."

He hurried to the bag. Valkyrie's knees were weak. Her face was cold.

"If I die," she said, "but we win, will you find my parents and tell them I'm sorry I put them through this, and that I love them?"

"You have nothing to worry about," Paddy said as he walked over, holding out the Sceptre. His eyes flickered to something behind her and she frowned, turned, saw nothing, and she turned back as Paddy swung the Sceptre into her face.

Valkyrie hit the wall and staggered. Paddy swung the Sceptre again and she managed to raise her arm to block it, but his fist came at her and her head snapped back and she fell.

She heard Tanith curse and looked up, lights dancing in front of her eyes. Tanith reached out to grab her sword, but Paddy smashed the Sceptre on to her hand. Tanith screamed and Paddy got behind her, wrapped his arm around her throat and hauled her off the chair. She tried to struggle, but she was much too weak, and after a few seconds, Paddy let her collapse.

Valkyrie's consciousness rattled against darkness and light, and the side of her face was wet. She clicked her fingers, but nothing happened.

"I'd forgotten what it was like," Paddy said, almost to himself. He put the Sceptre on the table. "The struggle, I mean. Usually, it's quiet. It would have been quiet for *you*, but you wear those enchanted clothes. My blade wouldn't have pierced them." He had a knife in his hand. "It'll pierce your throat though. Or your eyes."

Valkyrie licked her lips and tasted blood.

"You killed the Teleporters," she said, pushing herself up off the ground.

"I did."

"You're Batu."

He pulled up his sleeve as he walked over to her, showing her the mark on the inside of his forearm. "I am."

Valkyrie stayed where she was, waited for him to get close, and then she flexed her fingers and splayed her hand, but she couldn't feel the air, couldn't feel where it connected, and Paddy, *Batu*, ran the blade along her hand and she cried out.

"Stupid girl," he said, slashing at her neck. She stepped back and tripped, fell and rolled. She clicked her fingers and nothing happened. Batu rushed her and she barely managed to duck under him.

"You're one of them," she said, staying just out of reach.

"One of who? The Diablerie?" Batu darted forward and she jumped back. He smiled and they circled each other. "I'm not some mindless *drone*, Valkyrie. Everything you see around you? All this death and madness and mayhem? The end of the world that's about to happen? That's all *my* work.

"When I was a young man, Trope Kessel told me all about the gateway, and I knew I had my chance. I brought the Diablerie back from *nothing*, and they were only too eager to accept me as their leader. For I had *vision*, and I could get information no one else could.

"Sorcerers would tell me their biggest secrets – do you know why? Because I'm a mere *mortal*. Because they are far too arrogant to think that a *mortal* could pose a threat to *gods* like them.

"I was in their homes *dozens* of times before I killed them, drinking their tea and chatting and feeding their cats while they were away. The sheer domestic mundanity of it was *appalling*.

"Even you and the skeleton were fooled. I didn't know precisely *where* the gate would open until you brought the boy in to find it for me. Thank you for that, by the way."

A wave of dizziness swept over her and Valkyrie stumbled. The knife jabbed, but her coat protected her. Batu was smiling as he closed in.

She kept away. "Why? Why are you doing this?"

"Magic," he said. "My father was a sorcerer. So was my brother. But not me. I just didn't have that *spark*, you know? But now, finally, it's *my* turn."

She shook her head. "You're either born with it or you're not. You can't be *given* magic."

"There are ways around everything."

Valkyrie saw the glint in his eyes and she suddenly understood. "You're going to offer yourself as a vessel."

"Oh, you *are* clever."

"You're going to let a Faceless One *take you over*."

"And then I'll be brimming with magic that ordinary sorcerers would never even *dream* about. They're not gods, Valkyrie. They're as pathetic as the people you left behind in your old life. But me? I'll be a *true* god."

"But it won't be *you*. Your personality will be wiped clean. Even your body will be changed. You're not ever going to know what it's like to *use* magic."

"I'll know," said Batu softly. "There will be some part of me that stays, some part of me that joins with the Faceless One. I know it. I'm strong, you see? I was born without magic. I've *had* to be strong. My will is iron. I'm not going to be simply erased – not like the others."

Valkyrie frowned. "You're offering up the rest of the Diablerie as vessels too."

"I didn't want the Dark Gods wasting their time by seeking out suitable candidates. I just decided to make it easy for them."

He came in again. Ignoring the pain from the cut, she smashed her elbow into his face, then grabbed his wrist with both hands and twisted.

Batu rammed his shoulder into her. They crashed back against the wall and he got his hip against her and flipped her to the floor. He was an old man, but he was strong, and fast. Refusing to let go of the hand with the knife, she kicked at his leg and it buckled. She spun on her back and jammed her boot into his other leg. He collapsed on top of her and she raised her knee to meet his face.

The knife clattered to the ground and she rolled out from under him, kicking the weapon out of his reach. He spat teeth and blood and she moved to kick.

But he was faster than she'd anticipated. He hooked her kick to the outside and over his shoulder, and he rose and grabbed her jacket and she was lifted off the ground. He carried her backwards and slammed her on to the table. Valkyrie grabbed the Sceptre with her left hand and he grabbed her wrist, keeping it away from him. Black lightning turned a part of the ceiling to dust.

She turned the Sceptre towards him, but his hand moved from her wrist to the Sceptre itself, and once again, he diverted her aim. A section of wall crumbled.

Batu pressed against her, forcing the black crystal around. It glowed and spat lightning, hitting the corner of the table. The table collapsed and they fell, but their positions didn't change. Batu was still on top, and the Sceptre was now pointed directly at Valkyrie.

His face was frozen in a mask of hatred and determination. "End it," he muttered through clenched and bloody teeth. "Save yourself the pain of watching the world die."

She hit him in the ribs with her free hand and he grunted. She hit him again, but his grip didn't weaken. She tried pushing at the air, but nothing happened, and then she felt the gold ring on her finger.

The ring was bound. It had to be.

She curled the tip of her thumb against it. It was tight, but it moved, down her finger, and then she flicked it off and immediately felt the air against her palm.

She clicked her fingers and summoned a flame that burned fiercely into Batu's side. He screamed and thrashed and dived off her, trying to smother the flames on his shirt. He scrambled up and fled, out through the hole in the wall.

Valkyrie turned over and got up. She had a massive headache and there was blood running down her face, but she seemed to be otherwise OK. She went to Tanith and moved her on to her side, into the recovery position they'd been taught at school, and once she'd done that, she realised that she wasn't holding the Sceptre any more.

She looked back, scanning the ground desperately, but it wasn't there. Batu had taken it. Cursing, she ran through the hole after him, catching a glimpse as he disappeared into the trees.

Valkyrie tore after him.

37

FALLING INTO PLACE

Batu led that wretch of a girl through the trees and then changed direction, keeping low. She had broken his nose and some of his teeth, and his left side was badly burned, but he couldn't afford trivialities like revenge. Not now. He hid and watched her pass, then dug a shallow hole and dropped the Sceptre in it. He covered it with earth and leaves and doubled back.

When he reached the yard and saw the massacre, he laughed.

A dozen Cleavers were already dead. They littered the ground, an ill-made carpet of broken bodies and blood. The Faceless One, its clothes burned and torn and hanging in shreds, its face blank and smooth and terrifying, walked slowly through them.

A trio of Cleavers lifted into the air, and their bodies folded back on themselves and caved inwards. Their remains dropped, forgotten about. More Cleavers, their grey uniforms splattered with the blood of their colleagues, attacked with unceasing determination, but the blades of their scythes merely bounced off the skin of their enemy.

Batu turned as Murder Rose ran up to him and gripped his arm. "What have you done?" she raged. "You told us these marks would protect us! You said they'd shield us!"

"They are not shields," Batu said, his voice calm despite the exhilaration he was feeling. "They are invitations."

Rose stared at him, and then turned and sprinted away. Batu watched her disappear into the trees.

A torrent of impossibilities flowed after her, making the trees creak and sway. He heard her scream, and then there was silence.

There was one more god out there, and Batu went to find it.

38

FROM ALL SIDES

Valkyrie stopped and cursed. She'd lost him. There was no point going deeper into this wood – if Batu *was* ahead of her, which she doubted, he knew his surroundings a lot better than she did.

No, going deeper didn't make any sense. Not for Batu. He'd want to see his great plan coming together, and that meant being where the action was.

There was a sudden sound behind her and she turned as Remus Crux lurched out from behind a tree.

"You scared the hell out of me," she snapped.

He held his left arm close to his body like it was hurt, and he was limping badly. He was sweating and seemed to be in a lot of pain. There was dried blood on his face.

"Are you OK? Remus? Did you see anyone run by here? An old man?"

"You're under arrest," he snarled as he dug his right hand into his pocket. Valkyrie lunged, catching his wrist just as he pulled out a small gun.

"Resisting arrest!" he cried as their struggle took them back against the tree.

She whacked her elbow into his injured arm and he yelled, and she twisted the gun from his grip and pushed herself off him. She threw the gun deep into the trees and he snapped his palm. A wall of air slammed into her and she hurtled backwards. Her shoulders hit the ground and she tucked her chin to her chest as she flipped over gracelessly.

Crux was dragging his leg towards her, summoning a flame into his hand. "Assault on a Sanctuary official!" he screeched.

Valkyrie launched herself at him, smacking down his right hand as she punched him across the jaw and he went staggering back.

"You could have broken my neck!" she shouted, and lashed a kick into his bad leg. Crux screamed and dropped to the ground, and Valkyrie stepped back, clutching her fist. She hoped she hadn't broken it. Tanith was always telling her to use her elbows, not her knuckles. She really should have listened.

She looked down at him as he writhed and screamed and sobbed. He wasn't going anywhere soon. She turned and ran back the way she had come.

She saw someone ahead, sitting against a tree trunk. Fletcher Renn. His shoulders were slumped forward and his head was down. His shirt was soaked in blood. His hair was matted.

He heard her and looked up slowly, as if every moment brought with it a new kind of pain.

"I helped them," he said.

"I know. But now we need you to help *us*. Have you seen Paddy?"

He shook his head. "Haven't seen anyone. I didn't even fight them. They threatened me, they cut me, and that's all it took. I always thought I'd be the hero, you know?" His laugh was brittle.

Valkyrie looked down at him. "I don't mean to sound cruel," she said, "but we don't have time for this."

"You want to get out of here? I'm gathering my strength to

teleport somewhere, *anywhere*. Home, maybe. For some reason, I really want to go back to London right now."

"You can't leave. Paddy – you know that old man? He's Batu. He's the one behind all of this, and he has the Sceptre. He's probably already hidden it, or dropped it in a ditch or something. Fletcher, if I can't find it, we'll have to lure the Faceless Ones back through the gateway. We're going to need you to open it."

Fletcher stared at her, frowning. "Are you nuts? Opening it the first time wiped me out. I mean, if I *could* use my power, don't you think I *would* have by now? Do you think I'm staying here because I'm *brave*? The moment I'm strong enough, I'm gone."

"You can't leave us. This is our chance to save everyone. This is the only chance we're going to get."

"It's not my fight."

"It's *everyone's* fight."

"When the other sorcerers hear about this, they'll all come running to help, from all over the world. They'll stop them. Not me. I'm just a kid." He looked at her. "You should come with me."

"I can't. If you won't help us, finding the Sceptre is our only chance."

"You'll be killed."

"Apparently, that's been coming for a while now," she said, getting to her feet.

She gave him a chance. She stood there long enough for him to change his mind, but he didn't. He just sat there.

She ran on, emerging from the treeline in time to see Skulduggery battling the Faceless One. He pushed at the air, but it was no use – the air just rippled and folded around the Faceless One harmlessly.

The female Necromancer attacked from behind, swirling her cloak of shadows. The Faceless One extended its hand and her body turned inside out.

It kept walking, and Skulduggery backed off, and it raised its arm to him.

Then it saw her, and it stopped. Its body turned towards her.

"Valkyrie!" Skulduggery shouted. "Run!"

39

CRISIS OF FAITH

It was coming for him.

Jaron Gallow could feel it above him, feel it drawing closer. The mark, the one that Batu had made them all burn into their arms, it was a beacon. No matter where he hid or how fast he ran, the Faceless One would find him.

This wasn't how it was supposed to be.

He tore off his belt as he ran, wrapped it around his bicep and pulled it tight. Already he could feel his circulation being cut off. By the time he reached the yard beside the farmhouse, his left hand was numb.

He dropped to his knees and grabbed a Cleaver's fallen scythe. He laid his forearm flat on the ground and pressed the curved blade to just below his elbow. He was breathing fast and sweating, and he couldn't afford the luxury of doubt.

There was a rush of air and his ears popped. It had found him.

He closed his eyes and bellowed, forcing the scythe down on his forearm. The blade cut through flesh and bone in one smooth movement, and his bellow turned to a scream.

He collapsed, clutching the bloody stump to his body, and when he opened his eyes, he saw his severed arm lying next to him, and the Faceless One was gone.

40

KILLING GODS

China found Crux sitting on the ground between the woods and the meadow. His head was lowered and his arms were crossed over his body. He was hurt, she could see that as she walked towards him. There was no one else around. There was no one to see.

"Hello, Remus," China said.

He looked up. His pupils were dilated and he was muttering to himself.

"What happened to you?" she asked gently.

"You're all in on it," he mumbled.

Her blue eyes narrowed. "Did you see them, Remus? Did you see those things? Those flying things? Did you look at them?"

He tutted and shook his head and held himself tighter. His mind was broken. He must have looked up as the third Faceless One passed by in search of its vessel.

Which would make this *so* much easier.

China hunkered down, laying a comforting arm across his shoulders. "Did you tell anyone my secret, Remus? Anyone at all?"

"Secret?" he whispered.

"I won't be mad," she smiled. "I promise I won't. Who did you tell? About Skulduggery?"

"Skulduggery..." Crux said, trying to remember.

"Did you tell anyone?"

He turned his head to think, and his jacket opened, and she glimpsed gold.

"What have you got there?" she asked softly, reaching in slowly. His hands closed around it and she saw it was the Sceptre.

"Mine."

"Yes, it is yours, Remus. It's so pretty. Can I see?"

"It's mine. I found it. Saw a man dig a hole. Saw him dig. And then she came."

"Who came?"

"The girl. She hurt me."

"She's a mean girl. Can I see that? I'll give it right back, I promise."

Reluctantly, Crux released his hold, and China took the Sceptre from him, and smiled again.

"We're friends, aren't we? Did you tell anyone about my secret? I'm not going to be mad."

He shook his head. "No. No. Told no one."

"Good boy." She took a long, thin blade from the sheath on her boot. "You're confused, aren't you? I'm going to make the confusion go away. I promise."

"Give it back now."

"I'm afraid not."

He snarled and turned suddenly. The rock in his hand cracked against her head. China fell back and Crux tried getting up on his broken leg.

"You're in on it!" he screeched. "You're all in on it!"

He made it up and stood over her, the rock ready to smash down, but something hit him and he was flung off his feet.

China sat up, dazed, and Valkyrie ran up to her.

"Give me the Sceptre!" the girl shouted. There was a Faceless One right behind her and it was *running*.

China threw the Sceptre and Valkyrie caught it and turned. The Faceless One stopped running and studied her with its blank face. It raised its hand to her slowly.

China could see the panic on Valkyrie's face, like she expected her body to explode or implode or, at the very least, *twist*. Then she raised the Sceptre and fired.

The crystal glowed and the black lightning crackled and shot out, hitting the Faceless One in the chest. It staggered, and even though it had no mouth, it shrieked, an inhuman scream of pain and rage. The black lightning curled around its body and Valkyrie hit it again. The skin dried and cracked. China saw the god try to abandon its vessel, but it was too late, and the body erupted into a cloud of dust.

China got to her feet as the wind took the dust away. Valkyrie realised she was still holding the Sceptre straight out, and she tried to lower her arms, but they didn't seem to want to go down.

Skulduggery ran over. "What happened? Are you all right? What was that scream?"

"That was the sound of a god dying," China said.

"Paddy!" Valkyrie blurted. "Paddy is Batu!"

China didn't know who this *Paddy* was, but Skulduggery tilted his head and his fist clenched.

"That's how he got close enough to kill the Teleporters," he said. "I doubt he even came to Peregrine's mind when we asked him who he'd been talking to."

China could see that Valkyrie was barely listening. She pointed at the spot where the Faceless One had been standing.

"It just looked at me," she said. "It could have turned me inside out, but it didn't. Why didn't it?"

"It must recognise you," China said. "It must recognise the Ancient blood in your veins, marking you out as something different."

China wiped the blood from her forehead and glanced at Crux, but he was gone. Her jaw clenched in anger, but she said nothing.

"Now we can stop them," Valkyrie said. "We have the Sceptre, we can stop them. All I have to do is point and shoot."

"That's right," Skulduggery said.

"OK then, so where's the next one?"

China heard something in the trees behind her and turned.

41

BLACK LIGHTNING

There was a sound like a stampede behind them and the Faceless One that had taken over the body of Murder Rose crashed through the trees. It batted China away and slammed into Skulduggery. Valkyrie fell back and dropped the Sceptre. The Faceless One reached for her just as an arm encircled her waist.

Fletcher Renn said, "Hold on," in her ear and then they teleported.

A blink.

Then they were on the far side of the farmhouse, beside

the burning van. Fletcher let go and she whirled.

"You came back!"

"Naturally."

"Skulduggery!" she exclaimed. "We can't leave them!"

"Wasn't planning on it." He moved against her and she hung on to him.

In an instant, they were back in the field. China was still down and the Faceless One saw them, picked up Skulduggery and hurled him at them. Valkyrie dived and Skulduggery slammed into Fletcher.

The Faceless One strode to her.

She saw the Sceptre and opened her hand, felt the air and used it to tug at the weapon. It rolled slightly. The Faceless One was almost upon her.

She held out both hands, clutching at the air and dragging it back, and the Sceptre flew at her. She jumped to her feet, but the Faceless One snatched the Sceptre from her grasp.

Valkyrie tried to take it back, but the Faceless One shook her hand off with such force that she was sent sprawling. It took the Sceptre into a two-handed grip, and she saw the anger in its stance, and the violence, like it was remembering what this weapon was, and what it could do, and what it *had* done, an eternity before. The golden rod began to crumple, began to break, and she saw the black crystal, glowing fiercely beneath the fingers that were tightening around it. It shattered, and lightning spilled out, and then the Faceless One was crumbling to dust.

The Sceptre fell, mangled and beyond use, and the fragments of crystal, which were dull and robbed of power, fell with it.

Valkyrie got up, hurrying over to Skulduggery and Fletcher. "Are you OK?"

"I'm fine," Skulduggery said gruffly, but she ran by him and helped Fletcher to his feet.

"I'm OK," Fletcher groaned. "One more to go, huh? Not doing too badly."

"Actually," she said, "we kind of are. The Sceptre's been destroyed." She looked around at Skulduggery. "What do we do?"

Skulduggery straightened his tie and buttoned his torn jacket. "The first thing we do," he said, "is get over the fact that my wellbeing is obviously of less importance to you than Fletcher's here."

"I'm already over that," she told him.

"Oh, good."

"What's the second thing?"

"The second thing is for Fletcher to reopen that gateway. Do you think you can do that?"

Fletcher nodded. "Yes. I mean, I think so. I hope so."

Skulduggery stooped to help up China. "That fills me with such confidence."

"What's to stop more Faceless Ones from coming through once it's open?" Valkyrie asked as they all hurried back to the meadow.

"Absolutely nothing," Skulduggery said. "What we're going to do is make a really big wish that they don't notice."

"Seriously? Skulduggery, seriously?"

"Seriously. The fact is, we stand a decent chance. The Faceless Ones that *did* get through were drawn here because of the markings the Diablerie wore. Now that there are no markings left, there is nothing to make them look over."

"That's a plan that could fall apart in so many ways."

"The fun ones are like that."

"But how do we get the last Faceless One to go back through?"

"We're going to let it chase us."

"Us?"

"Well, I say 'us'. I mean you."

"Terrific," Valkyrie muttered.

42

THE MOMENT

he hair on the back of Batu's neck stood up. *The Faceless One was above him. He could feel it. His god was gazing upon him at that very moment.*

Batu turned, spread his arms, and raised his eyes to his god, and as it rushed to fill him, he screamed with terror and exultation.

And then Batu was gone.

43

THE GATEWAY

Skulduggery Pleasant and Valkyrie Cain found the Faceless One that had once been Batu on the other side of the wood. Ghastly was suspended in the air before it, his back arched, his mouth open, trying to scream. Veins were popping out all over his body, as if the Faceless One was bringing each one to the surface with the intention of ripping them all out.

"Hey!" Valkyrie shouted.

It looked over at them, didn't move for three or four seconds, then cast Ghastly aside and started to run towards them.

"OK," Skulduggery said, "the moment it—"

The Faceless One waved its arm and Skulduggery was wrenched off his feet and sent flying through the air.

Valkyrie cursed and spun, sprinting into the trees. The idea had been for Skulduggery to distract it if it got too close too fast, but now there was no one between them. This was already going badly.

She darted between trees and jumped over fallen branches. She glanced back, saw trees uprooting and branches disintegrating, clearing a path for the Faceless One to run straight through.

She saw it wave its arm and she was thrown forward. She hit the ground and got a mouthful of dirt as she rolled.

Something white blurred in her peripheral vision, and the White Cleaver jumped to intercept. He raked his scythe across the Faceless One's torso, then spun to go for the neck. Any other enemy would have fallen, such was the speed and precision of the move, but the blade didn't even penetrate the skin. The Faceless One slammed its fist against the Cleaver's chest and he hurtled back, quickly disappearing from view.

The Faceless One strode towards Valkyrie. She spat out dirt and wiped her mouth, watching it come. She timed its steps and then splayed her hands. The air rippled, striking not the Faceless

One, but the loose ground just in front of it. Its foot touched down and its weight shifted on to it just as the ground shot backwards, and the Faceless One fell.

Valkyrie burst from the treeline, and to her left she saw Skulduggery running parallel. They raced to the top of the meadow, to where Fletcher was once again kneeling with his hands on the Grotesquery. The yellow gateway was opening.

China was doing her thing with the symbols around the circle. Red and black smoke began to rise. "Where is it?" she shouted.

"Behind me," Valkyrie said breathlessly. A shadow fell and Skulduggery dived into her as the Faceless One landed where she had just been.

She saw Solomon Wreath, riding a wave of darkness that spilled from his cane. He jumped to the ground beside them and pulled her up, and used the cane to drive a hundred needles of dark into the Faceless One's chest.

"Drive it back!" China shouted from the swirling column of smoke. "Get it close enough to the gateway so it'll be sucked in!"

The gravitational pull from the yellow portal was immense. Even from where she stood, Valkyrie could feel herself slipping towards it. She forced herself back as Skulduggery joined Wreath in his efforts.

She pushed at the air to dislodge the ground beneath the Faceless One's feet, but she wasn't rewarded. Its movements were solid as it battled, and its steps were impossible to predict.

"Gateway's as open as it's going to get!" Fletcher shouted.

Wreath suddenly started screaming. His right leg buckled and twisted and blood spurted, and Skulduggery snapped his hand against the air, throwing the Necromancer out of the fight before he was killed. Wreath landed and clutched at his leg, but now Skulduggery was the only one left.

The Faceless One grabbed him, its fingers sliding between his ribs and gripping, and Skulduggery screamed as he was lifted off the ground.

"Valkyrie!" Wreath shouted from behind. She turned and he threw his cane at her feet. "Use it!"

"I don't know how!"

"Just use the damn thing!"

She grabbed it, felt the dark power contained within. Shadows leaked from the cane and wrapped around her wrist. She knew instinctively that if Wreath hadn't given it voluntarily, those shadows would tighten and turn her bones to dust.

She turned the cane in her hand, feeling the drag, as though it was moving through water, and then she whipped it straight out and a shadow sliced against the back of the Faceless One's leg. The shadow didn't break its skin, but it *did* get its attention. The Faceless One turned to her.

Valkyrie rotated the cane by her side, like she was gathering candyfloss around a stick, then flicked it at the Faceless One. Instead of candyfloss, shadows flew, hit the Faceless One and tried to wrap around it. It threw Skulduggery down and brushed the shadows away with one angry gesture.

She ran up to it, swinging the cane. The Faceless One caught it and snapped it. An explosion of darkness hurled Valkyrie backwards and sent the Faceless One staggering.

Valkyrie thudded into Ghastly's arms and he grunted, and let her down. She saw the Faceless One, standing just outside the gateway, struggling to escape its gravitational pull.

It was almost in. It was almost through.

"Hit it!" she shouted. "*Somebody hit it!*"

Ghastly stepped forward and China left the column of smoke, but tentacles burst from the Faceless One's chest, slammed into them and tossed them back. The tentacles, made of entrails and organs, wrapped around trees and burrowed through the ground in a last-ditch effort, an effort which was destroying its host body, to save the god within.

Then Skulduggery stood, looked at the Faceless One and stepped forward, sinking into the stance. He snapped his hands against the air and the air rippled. The Faceless One hurtled back, disappearing into the portal, its flailing tentacles yanked in after it, taking branches and clumps of earth along with it. Immediately, Skulduggery whirled.

"*The Grotesquery!*" he shouted. "*Now!*"

Within the column of smoke, Fletcher slid his hands underneath the Grotesquery's torso and heaved, and the torso rolled out of the circle. Skulduggery gestured and the air caught the torso and brought it into his hands. He grunted and stepped back and launched it into the gateway.

Now that the link was gone, the gateway started to rapidly close.

And then a tentacle slid out and wrapped around Skulduggery's ankle.

It tugged and he fell. He clutched at the ground as he was dragged quickly back.

"*Skulduggery!*" Valkyrie screamed, sprinting towards him.

He looked up and reached out to her, but it was too late. He disappeared through the gateway.

"*Keep it open!*" Valkyrie screamed to Fletcher.

"I can't!"

She was three steps away when the portal collapsed.

"Open it!" she yelled.

But Fletcher was standing, and through the swirling smoke she could see his stunned face. He shook his head.

"No! Fletcher, no! You've got to open it!"

"I don't have the Grotesquery," he said. "I can't."

China was standing, and Valkyrie ran to her, grabbed her. "Do something!"

China didn't even look at her. Her blue eyes, so pretty, so pale, were on the empty space where she'd last seen Skulduggery. Valkyrie shoved her away, turned to Ghastly.

"Come on!" she roared.

"He's gone," Ghastly said, his voice dull.

"He can't be!"

Valkyrie turned, turned again, looking for someone who knew what to do, someone who'd have a plan. She saw no one. No one knew what to do.

And then she was on her knees. There were tears running down her face and it was like a part of her had been cut out, somewhere in her belly, and her thoughts were frozen in her mind.

It was quiet. The smoke had stopped swirling, and it drifted away in the afternoon breeze. It was still, and it was peaceful, and around them were the dead bodies of friends and colleagues and enemies, and the air stank of ozone and magic.

44

THE TASK

aris had been nice apparently.

Her parents had come home, and her dad had hugged her reflection and then gone to read the newspaper. Her mother had told the reflection all about their weekend as she unpacked. Long walks and fine food and romantic evenings. She'd asked how the reflection had got on staying with Beryl and Fergus, and the reflection had lied with accustomed ease, and said it had been fine.

Valkyrie absorbed these memories and didn't bother

examining them. She hadn't even spoken to her parents since they'd got back – not personally. She was afraid they'd see her and instantly know something terrible had happened. She couldn't deal with that right now. She doubted she'd have even been able to come up with a lie.

She stood in the graveyard and waited. It was raining again. It was always raining. She was getting sick of the rain.

She didn't hear him approach, but she knew he was behind her.

"Thank you for coming," Solomon Wreath said. "Have you spoken with Guild?"

Valkyrie turned.

"He called me into the Sanctuary last week. He said that I'm no longer a fugitive."

"That must be nice."

"Did you know that he's telling everyone that the victory is all down to him and Mr Bliss? I'm sorry Bliss is dead and all, but he's saying Skulduggery did *nothing*."

"I had heard that, but the people who matter know the truth."

"*Everyone* should know the truth," she muttered.

"How is your friend? The one who was hurt?"

"She's healing. Nothing can keep Tanith down." Valkyrie

looked at the headstones around her, then back at him. "Sorry I broke your cane."

Wreath shrugged. "When the power was released, it flowed back into me, where it bubbled and boiled until I channelled it into something new." He showed her a cane, identical to the last one.

"How original of you."

He smiled. "I was very impressed with how you handled it by the way. You seem to have an instinctive grasp of Necromancy."

"Just blind luck to be honest."

"Nonsense. It made me wonder actually, if Elemental magic was the road you should be taking."

"You're saying I should be a Necromancer?"

"Why not?"

"Because I'm an Elemental."

"You're young. You can change your mind a hundred times before you settle on the discipline that's right for you. Is Necromancy as elegant as Elemental magic? Perhaps not. Are Necromancers held in as high regard as Elementals? *Definitely* not. But as a student, you would have instant power at your fingertips, and I think you're going to need as much power as you can get."

"Why do you think that?"

"Well, you want to get Skulduggery Pleasant back, don't you?"

Valkyrie's eyes narrowed. "Skulduggery's gone."

"Not necessarily."

"The gateway is closed."

"Actually, I don't think it is."

She shook her head. "If you've got something to say, just say it. I'm tired, and I want to go home."

"What made it possible for Fletcher Renn to open the gate?"

"The Grotesquery was an Isthmus Anchor, and there's a..." She sighed. "There's this invisible, magical, wonderful *thread* that runs from an Isthmus Anchor to whatever it links to, which keeps the gate from closing for good. Fletcher used it to force the gateway open."

"Exactly. So all you need is another Anchor."

"The Grotesquery is gone. Skulduggery lobbed it through the portal because he didn't want anybody opening it ever again. There are no more bits of Faceless Ones lying around."

"It doesn't have to be an object that links to the *Faceless Ones*," Wreath told her. "It just has to link to something in that reality."

"Like what?"

"Like Skulduggery."

"Mr Wreath..."

He smiled. "There is a part of Skulduggery still here, in *this* reality. In this *country* in fact. And you know what it is."

"I'm sorry, I have no idea what you're—"

"Skulduggery Pleasant's *head*, Miss Cain."

Something fluttered in her belly. "He lost that. He told me. He won the head he's wearing now in a poker game."

"All true. But if you were to retrieve this missing head and give it to Mr Renn, he would find that the link between the skeleton and his *real* skull is keeping the gateway from closing over."

"And... and he could open it? Fletcher could open the gateway?"

"And save Skulduggery, yes."

"Where is it? Where's his head?"

"I'm afraid I have no idea. That part is up to you."

"Why are you helping me?"

"You don't think I'm doing it because I'm a nice person?"

"You have something to gain."

"You are an astute young lady. I *am* hoping to gain something as a matter of fact."

"What?"

"You. In order to conduct this search, in order to do the things you will need to do, you're going to need more power than you currently wield. I'm hoping you choose Necromancy."

He stepped back and tapped his cane on the ground. The shadows moved in, curled around him, and she saw him smile before his face darkened.

"I'll be in touch," he said and the shadows scattered and he was gone.